Rescuing Lotty Pickle

C. J. Wellumson

To Roberta...always.

You can't go back and change the beginning...but
you can start now and change the ending.

— C.S .Lewis

Contents

Author's Note

This debut novel celebrates a snapshot of my life and times, taking us back to a decade not so long ago, when the world looked quite different from our own. Inspired by one memorable summer on the farm, the story takes place in a time when America's negative and sometimes dangerous attitudes toward race were beginning to change.

Turn back the clock and join Nate and Lotty for an exciting adventure. Enjoy!

C. J. Wellumson

Chapter One

Summer, 1958

"I can't stay here much longer," Nate Martin whispered to himself, soft enough his grandpa wouldn't hear him over the scratching's of his shop broom across the old wooden floor. "Wish there was some way to get back home faster. I'm really stuck." His thoughts often focused on ending his summer visit at his grandparents' small farm. It had started well, and there'd been some good moments too, but, soon to be fourteen, his summer long visit away from home had turned tedious and lonely.

While brooming small wood pieces and sawdust onto the wide grain shovel, Nate allowed himself to smile at the memory of something his grandpa liked to say about doing carpentry work.

"Good enough for who it's for," Grandpa would sometimes offer with a grin. Or, "We're not building a piano."

So true. Nate was just cleaning this old shop floor. Nothing fancy there. Good enough for them. His smile faded. Didn't have to be as spotless as Grandma's kitchen. "Good enough for us," he whispered again.

After putting away the broom and shovel, he left the shop and his grandpa, who was bent over the speedboat they were building, then he sat on the bench outside the door and stared across the yard at the gravel road.

He wanted to get home with some extra free time before school started. Small chance of that. Wiping sweat onto his white T-shirt's sleeve, he thought of his buddies. *Gotta be cooler up in Minnesota than this cooking Arkansas heat.* Heavy footsteps thumped just behind him, and he flinched.

"Nate, you look like all the fun's just run out of yourself," Grandpa said. "Why don't you walk into town, take a break, and hey, make your grandma happy, too. Get yourself a haircut. Go on, now. Here's some money. I don't need extra help with the boat just now."

Nate took the folding money Grandpa held out, and smiled. "Yes, sir," he said, fighting the urge to pump his fist in the air.

Grinning, he ran into the house to wash up. The rest of the day was his. No adults could interfere. Grandma wouldn't be back from teaching summer classes until late afternoon, and Grandpa would spend hours working on their boat-building project. Nate scrubbed his dusty hands in the kitchen sink, then dashed out the side door. Time for some adventure.

Starting the two-mile walk along the gravel road, Nate searched for a good stone to kick, one with rounded corners, the sort that almost always landed where his scuffed-up tennis shoe sent it. "There she goes," he yelled, sending the stone flying, his spirits rising with it. At last, freedom from his grandparents' little world and his chores. The perfect chance to explore on his own, the alleys and imagined hidden places of tiny Hartsville.

Once he reached the outer edge of their cornfield, he stopped to look it over. The corn had grown as tall as he was, some stalks even taller. He grinned at them and kept walking. During his summer here in the Ozark Mountains of northwest Arkansas, he'd watched that corn grow, raised nine baby piglets, learned to drive the tractor, and was helping build a wooden boat. His buddies wouldn't believe all he'd done, but today he could only think about getting back home. His whole summer spent here was just too long.

Following the road around the corner of the field, he started whistling. When he reached a point out of sight of the farmhouse, an out of place shape deep inside the shiny green stalks caught his eye. Slowing to a stop at the edge of the road, he peered through the rows. Something bright red just then moved. Colorful clothing and the faint outline of a person had his attention.

"Hey, you!" he called. "What are you doing in there?"

The shape froze, and the rustling stalks went silent.

Nate worked his way deeper into the cornfield, moving leaves and ears aside until he reached a young girl sitting on the ground between two rows. She appeared to be about his age or maybe a little older.

"You supposed to be in here?" he asked.

She kept her dark head lowered, saying nothing.

The smoothed down ground around her reminded Nate of places where deer would sleep near his cousin's lake cabin. Flattened foliage with a slept-on look, like an unmade bed. "Did you sleep here?" he asked.

Like a turtle escaping into its shell, she shrank into her own body, as if trying to make herself small. She kept her hands and arms high, protecting her head and face.

Maybe he should back up and create a more comfort-able space between them. He did so, then sat cross-legged on the ground like her. His towering over her had to be intimidating. "I wish you'd say something." He waited, then said, "Better not run." He'd chase her if need be.

She remained crouched low and silent.

Nate stared at the bug bites on her brown arms and hands. The most recent reddish ones were not yet scratched or bleeding. A few had opened with blood drops beading, and others had scabbed over. Fighting an urge to scratch at his own skin, he shivered a little, then gave in and scratched.

"Who are you?" he asked. "You in trouble?

Again, no answer.

"I live just past the corner, around the next bend that-a-way, at my grandparents' farm...just for the summer." He pointed, but she didn't look. "Can I help you?"

As her silence stretched on, Nate pressed his palms to the ground, fingers splayed. He held his arms straight and tight to his sides and lifted his body to swing his fanny and legs back again, farther away from her.

She spread two fingers and peeked between them.

Smiling, he said, "Hi," rather than the *peek-a-boo* he was tempted to offer.

She hid again behind her closed hand.

He eyed her wrinkled clothes and matted hair. A large cloth bag like those the older grannies sometimes carried sat nearby. It had wood handles stained dark from sweating hands and un-scrubbed years. Bulges from whatever she kept inside tried to poke through the heavy cloth.

"I hope there's a blanket in there," Nate said, pointing at the bag.

She took another quick peek, then closed her fingers.

"Do you think I'd hurt you? C'mon, no reason for that."

He lowered his head and cupped his chin in both hands, then sat, just studying her.

She remained quiet.

"What can I do for you?"

She moved her hands from her face, opened her eyes, looked into his, then whispered, "You're white."

Nate jerked upright, choking a bit on words that wouldn't form. He whispered back, "Of course I am. So what? And what's that supposed to mean?"

Again, she kept silent.

Nate's explorations back home had led him to find a few strange items, most of which he'd left where they lay. Some, he'd brought home, and one remained hidden in a secret spot his parents would never find. What should he do with this surprise? He couldn't just walk away.

"What's your name?" he asked. "I'm Nate. C'mon, what're you doing here? I'm not your enemy, you know."

Her direct stare never wavered from his eyes. When she suddenly stood and took a quick, short step toward him, he leaned back, tensing and ready to react.

Bending over him, she said at high volume, "You ask my name? It's Orphan. Just call me that...Orphan." She paused, still leaning over him, then relaxed and sat as before, her head buried in her hands, but keeping eyes on him.

Was she about to cry? Nate opened his mouth, but words again wouldn't come. What if Grandpa had heard her loud voice? What would he do about this?

The far-off, faint humming of an electric power saw floated above the corn rows. Nate's shoulders loosened. No chance his grandpa heard her if he was still working. "What's your real name? I'm Nate." His face heated. "Oh, I told you that before, so...tell me yours, will you? Please." He waited. "C'mon, and what are you doing here?"

"I told you," she said, staring through narrowed eyes.

He returned her stare. It was important to look strong. "Okay, take it easy and try to believe me. I'm not here to hurt you. I just wanted to know your name, is all. No big deal, for cryin' out loud." He smiled. He'd just used, for the first time, one of his dad's favorite sayings.

She stood again and stepped a little too close. Nate got ready to spring straight up if need be. He glanced at her narrowed eyes, flared nose, and a hand clenched into a fist, then braced for a punch.

Instead, she moved back a step and said, "I'm Lotty, and yes, I am an orphan. Nowadays, I mean, and I'm not going back there, never, to those people, so you just don't dare do nothin'."

Nate let out a breath. "Fine, then. Great. Lotty, you say? For sure, you're not going anywhere you don't want to, so sit down, now, and listen up."

She moved back another step but continued standing.

"C'mon, sit with me," he said. "Listen, I'm heading into town. Can I bring you anything? Food, maybe?"

In jerky motions, she looked toward the road, at her bag, then the road again, back to Nate, and again at the bag.

Nate frowned. She was jumpy as a rabbit and taller than he was. What would he need to do to stop her if she ran? Then, there was her color. He'd never talked to a negro person alone, in a cornfield or anywhere else. But why should they be scared of each other?

"Don't be afraid, and don't go running," he said. "I mean it. I'll try to help you. Looks like you could use some."

She twitched about like a trapped squirrel that had scampered into someone's crowded living room.

"Where are you trying to go?"

Again, only her tiring silence answered.

She must be on the run with no special place to head to. "Okay, Lotty," he said, "listen up. I'm going into town for a haircut. You wait here. Just don't run off, because I'll come looking for you, me and my grandpa. He knows every stick, stone, and rabbit trail around this whole county, and he'll bring the dog, too. I mean it, we will catch you, now we know you're here and all. Best you be listening. Later, you can come home to our house, and I'll hide you there for tonight, maybe in the barn loft. You'll be safe. I promise."

"Don't you dare tell them about me," she muttered in a weak voice, scratching both arms. "They'll send me back." She raised her voice and said again, "And I ain't never goin' back."

"Take it easy. I won't tell anyone," he said, lifting his hands. "No kiddin'. I know a few places to hide you." He leaned closer. "Here's what we do, and listen careful. You walk to the edge of this cornfield and turn right at the road." He pointed, and this time, she looked. "Keep walking all the way, straight to the end of these rows, and where they stop, turn sharp to your right. Then, follow the rows all the way to where they stop again. You'll see a dried-up creek bed. Around here, they call them a branch. Okay?"

She nodded.

Nate breathed a little easier. "Look to your right at the branch. There's a hillside, and you'll see a root cellar door. It's let into the ground, tilted back a little just like the slant of the hill. Open it, then quick go in. There's a chair inside, and a small glass window in the door will give you some light. Wait there and don't be afraid."

She put one hand on her bag and gave him a hint of a quick smile.

It was working. He nodded and smiled back. "I'll sneak you down some of Grandma's good supper if I can, and I won't tell them. Not sure what Grandpa would do. He gets...uh, well...cranky sometimes, but Grandma would be okay to help you, I'd bet anything."

They both stood, Lotty bent a little crooked to one side from the weight of her bag.

"Have you walked far with that heavy thing?" Nate asked.

"Plenty. Promise me again you won't tell," she said.

He put his hand over his heart, smiled, and gave her a little bow. When he straightened, he frowned at the sky. "See those big clouds forming?" He pointed. "It's going to rain bad tonight, Lotty. You've never seen such rain. The clouds come down right to the tops of the electric poles around here. We're up high, ya know. Then, the thunder shakes the whole world, and lightning's so close it makes your hairs stand up from the electricity. You gotta get your-self safe inside for this one, and I'm not kidding."

When she nodded, he waved and started working his way back to the road.

Once he reached it, he stopped and looked back toward the farm. What had he gotten himself into? His neck tight-ened. Maybe he should tell Grandpa.

Chapter Two

Nate walked toward town for a few minutes, looking back twice, but Lotty hadn't appeared from the cornfield. She must be hiding still. Maybe waiting until he was out of sight. Would he find her when he got back?

From around the bend behind him, a loud motor roared, and heavy tires crunched the gravel. Gaining on him fast, he spun around. A giant road grader's huge front wheels rolled straight toward him. Nate bent his knees, ready to dive into the ditch at the road's edge, but the machine slowed to a stop, the front tires barely a foot away.

His heartbeat throbbed in his throat. If he extended an arm halfway, he could touch one of the huge tires. "Plenty close enough," he called out.

Nate pushed hair back and tipped his head to peer up at the driver, who looked like a sitting giant behind a tall, glass wall.

The man leaned out the window and yelled over the engine's roar, "Going into town?"

Nate nodded and waved.

"Then, hop on up here," the driver said.

"This can't be happening," Nate paused. He had to do it.

"C'mon up," the man said. "Be careful but c'mon. I gotta keep going." He made hand motions, instructing Nate to walk around front and get to the right side.

Nate looked to the roadside and kept ready to jump out of the way if those huge front tires somehow lunged forward. They were almost his height, and either tire could flatten him like a tiny mouse caught in a spring-loaded trap.

The driver reached over and opened the right-side door. Nate watched his footing as he climbed the narrow steel ladder, then stepped in and sat on the wide seat.

"You're Henry and Marvella's grandkid," the driver said before Nate could greet him.

"How'd you know that?" Nate asked over the noise of the powerful engine close behind the seat.

The driver laughed. "Everyone in this little berg knows everything about everybody. Call me Stony. You're Nate, maybe. Did I get that right? Heard about you. I live west of you about a mile and a half. Bet you've seen my fancy green fence."

"Right," was all Nate could manage. This guy must be a friend of Grandpa's. Nate relaxed, smiled, and sat back to study the view through the glass that circled the entire cab. Stretching around in the seat, he looked back to see if Lotty was visible from this high perch. She wasn't. Nate let out a breath. *I bet she's waiting for us to go.*

"Looking for something?" Stony asked.

"Ah...no sir, not really. Just trying out the view from up here. No one around here today. Just me."

Stony lowered his voice. "So you say." He looked straight at Nate with tightened eyes and a partial smile.

Tensing, Nate turned away. The man must have seen her.

As they started moving, the roar of the engine and scraping of the wide blade smoothing the gravel drove all thoughts of Lotty from Nate's mind. How'd he get so lucky? He'd done nothing to earn something this special, other than being someone's grandkid. He squared his shoulders, feeling important in a way he never had before. This small-town hospitality was far better than the big city coolness he was used to. A gift, really, like a grandmother's welcoming hugs or the surprise of her making his favorite dessert for no special reason.

Even his school field trip to the local fire station hadn't been this exciting. Those guys were nice, too, but the whole thing was planned, and he'd needed written permission from parents to go. Today's adventure just happened. No doubt, it never would have up north in the large city.

Nate turned from the view to study Stony moving levers and steering this giant machine. Wanting to say something, anything, he blurted out, "Grandpa told me it's an election year."

"Okay, that's right, young man." Stony chuckled. "Why'd you mention it?"

"Well...um, because you're grading the gravel roads around here. Grandpa says that's the only time it ever gets done." Nate frowned. Had he gone too far?

"Oh boy, that's good. No kidding. But he's right. Those county bigshots gotta do something to keep the locals happy, and of course the tax dollars flowing in."

Nate laughed a little with Stony but wasn't sure why.

Stony reminded Nate of his dad's friend Ed. They both had bright red sunburns on their necks and were good-natured, and their arm muscles bulged under colorful tattoos. Ed's had a big ship's anchor with the letters *USN* beneath. Stony's read *Less Work For Mom* on his bicep.

Nate scanned the dozen or more levers, some rising from the floor and others poking straight out from behind the painted metal dashboard. Each lever had a shiny black knob on the end that he wanted to try. They drew his fingers like a bowl of shiny candies.

"How many levers does it take to run this thing?" he asked.

"All of them," Stony said, looking over and laughing.

Nate joined in. For the rest of the ride, he kept quiet and let Stony work. The big man kept turning the wheel and adjusting the huge blade below that leveled and shaped the gravel. Nate didn't want to be the reason for any mistakes.

Stony talked to himself as he worked, mumbling things like, "Dang it. Aw, nuts. There now...there we go. Okay... that's good. Right there. Oh, yeah, nice, nice. Just look at that." He smiled, bounced a little, and moved around constantly on the wide seat.

When the town came in sight, Stony slowed to a stop. "Gotta turn around here and do the other side. I'll make a nice crown in the middle—you'll see it—so off you go, son."

"Thanks for this, Mr. Stony," Nate said. "Really, it was great. See you around." He climbed down the ladder and backed far out of the way, giving Stony plenty of room. They both waved, Nate already thinking of the great story he'd tell his friends back home. Some maybe wouldn't believe it, but that didn't matter. Maybe Lotty would, if she was there waiting. He shook his head. Why'd he think of her?

Nate turned and hustled to the hotel, the biggest of

Hartsville's three buildings, though just as tattered-looking as the others. He glanced up at the second floor, which Grandpa had said held four sleeping rooms for rent, then entered the lobby. Walking up to the clerk, who was also the barber, he said, "I need a haircut."

The man stepped from behind the long desk and led him into the barbershop. No stack of comic books lay on the table for kids, like back home. With no wait time, he wouldn't've had long enough to read one, anyway.

After the cut, Nate ran a hand over the back of his head. It should last and still look okay until he returned home. He paid the barber and walked across the road to the drugstore.

Over by the counter, he saw it, sitting proud on its own perch. The only telephone in this part of the world.

"Welcome, kid," the clerk said.

"If you need to call somewhere, you have to come in here, right?" Nate asked, pointing at the phone. "If news came from far away, are you the guy who'd take the information and make sure it gets delivered? Like when my mom called here once to get word to my grandpa about someone dying?"

"That's me, or my missus if I'm not working." The clerk straightened some bottles on the counter. "No one makes those expensive long-distance calls unless they have to, and if you get one, you can almost bet it's bad news."

Nate nodded. "Sounds like my house when we get one."

"Usually, it's her answering because most folks wait until after supper," the clerk said. "It's the cheapest time to call. Rates cheaper then, ya know, and that's when she's almost always on duty here."

Nate smiled. "Glad you guys are here. Makes me happy to know that phone's nearby. Kind of connects me to my real home, or I should say, knowing it's available if I need to call helps, somehow." Lately, he'd felt like he lived on the moon or some other planet, a captive far from where he belonged.

"We'll keep the line open for you, son," the clerk said with a wink. "It ain't goin' nowhere, and the missus always pays the bill."

Nate thanked him and walked over to Y.T.'s mercantile store. Before he touched the door, Y.T.'s voice yelled his name.

"Hey, hey, we got young Nate," Y.T. said, his belly filling the space on the other side of the screen door, so unlike all the other, lean, farm people around here. "Glad to see you. Where's your grandpa?"

"Working on your brother's boat."

"Oh, what in the world?" Y.T. ushered him inside, laughing. "There's maybe two lakes 'round here, and both are hours away. Manmade ones, too. This ain't Minnesota. So, what's he going to do with that thing?"

Nate shrugged. "Don't know, but I'm helping build it. She's beautiful, too."

"My younger brother has more money than brains." Smiling, Y.T. opened the cash register drawer, setting off a loud ringing sound.

Grandpa had said Y.T.'s family owned several businesses and the biggest farm around. They even hired men who lived in a bunkhouse during the busy season. If Hartsville had royalty, it would be the Andersons, and Nate got to call Y.T. a friend.

Nate took a nickel from his pocket and walked fast across the small store. He stopped in front of the faded green pop machine, a four-foot-long rectangular chest about waist high. Before Nate could insert his nickel, Y.T. ran over and slid one of his own into the slot.

"Go ahead, kid," Y.T. said, waving at the full-length door that opened across the whole top like a toolbox.

"Thanks," Nate said, smiling, then pulled the lid open. Of the many times he and Grandpa had spent in Y.T.'s store, never once had Y.T. let him pay for his bottle of cold pop.

Nate looked down at the neat rows of glass bottles spaced between metal divider bars, and he scanned the brand names on their caps. When he found his favorite, he followed the line of bottles to the end of the row, reached in, and pulled one straight up. Invisible metal fingers let go, and the bottle sprang up and out, the others sliding between the dividers to fill its place.

Nate grinned up at Y.T. "No wonder you don't need a lock on the lid. Without the money put in, those powerful fingers hold on so tight, I bet even that Charles Atlas, the Build Big Muscles guy in the back of the comic books, couldn't pull a bottle out, even with both hands."

"Sure couldn't," Y.T. said, heading back to the register. "Hey, listen to this one. It's funny." He waved toward the radio he always kept playing.

Nate carried his cold bottle over and took the stool next to the cash register stand as a new song about a flying purple people eater filled the store.

Y.T. sang along. "It was a one eyed, one horned, flying purple people eater. Pidgeon-toed, under growed, flying purple people eater. Sure looked strange to me."

They both laughed while Nate tried to figure out whether the creature ate purple people or was purple himself. Ah, well, enjoying this with Y.T. was the important thing.

Without warning, Lotty intruded on his thoughts again.

He squeezed the countertop's edge, hoping she'd be there when he got back.

"Maybe they'll play that new Conway Twitty one, too," Y.T. said. "He grew up around here, you know. He's about a millionaire by now. I'll tell you that."

While the radio played, Y.T. reported on local happenings, then started his usual round of questions about big city life. "So, every house really has a telephone?" He shook his head. "Amazing, but you're going to miss supper if you don't get going."

Thinking of Lotty again, Nate bought two candy bars, a Three Musketeers and a Milky Way, then made a silent promise not to eat them himself.

"Hey, just remembered to tell you," Y.T. said as Nate turned to leave, "keep an eye out for a runaway negro girl. Some folks from south of here are looking for her. The sheriff came by and gave me these papers." He reached behind the counter. "Here, take this one home and keep an eye out. There's a reward, too. You seen her, maybe?"

"Uh, right," Nate said, taking the paper. "I'll be looking for her, count on that. See you next trip." He smiled, then rushed to the door, hating to lie, especially to Y.T.

"Can you hold up a bit?" Y.T. yelled. "They're going to play that new Everly Brothers tune again."

Nate stopped partway out the door and shouted, "Gotta go," as he waved the paper like swatting flies. Then, he entered the street, yelling, "See ya next time."

Before heading back, Nate needed to do some exploring. He started behind the shabby old buildings but found only junk tires, rusty metal items, and an old metal boxspring mattress.

Back on the gravel road out of town, Nate admired Stony's craftsmanship. The surface was smooth and clean, he resisted the urge to kick at rocks again. He couldn't leave pock marks in Stony's beautiful handywork.

Halfway to the farm, thoughts of the candy bars tortured him. He'd never possessed two at one time. "She'd never know if I ate one," he whispered.

A clear vision of her sad face and shabby clothes filled his mind. He left both unopened in his pocket.

Chapter Three

During the walk back to the farm, Nate thought mostly about Lotty. Would she be there? If so, what could he do?

As he shuffled up the driveway, Grandma's car came into view, parked alongside the house near her small vegetable garden. The shrieking of a power tool told him Grandpa was still in his shop. No windows would give him a view of Nate, and the old man wouldn't quit working until Grandma called him to supper. All Nate had to watch out for was Grandma, so where was she?

Nate walked toward the branch, keeping an eye on the house. Lotty had to be in the root cellar by now, if she was there at all. She'd no doubt be tired of fighting spiders and countless other nasty bugs that inhabited that underground, dirt-walled cave. He hurried his pace.

The rusty spring of the screen door on the far side of the house screeched, announcing Grandma's location. Nate ducked behind a nearby walnut tree and heard the water slosh from her direction and splatted to the ground. Grandma, throwing a bowl of dirty water out the back door like usual.

Nate tucked in against the tree trunk. Good, she was in the kitchen and wouldn't see him on this side of the yard. Everything was working out...if Lotty had followed his instructions.

Making his way along the corn rows to the hillside, he looked back again to be sure nobody had entered the back yard. Sneaking toward the root cellar door, he smiled. Fresh footprints dented the ground, and the door stood ajar a sliver. "Yes!" he said, louder than he'd intended. She'd made it.

"Lotty," he whispered through the door's crack. "It's me, Nate." Pulling the door open, he looked in, and there she stood, leaning a little to her right, her cloth case in hand. He tilted his head. "I'm surprised you aren't sitting."

She took a short step back.

"Ready to run?" he asked.

"Where you been?" she said. "It's creepy in here. Why didn't you tell me? There's a million bugs everywhere, and maybe something alive back there with red eyes. Get me out of here, but quick."

"Easy does it." He lifted a hand toward her. "We'll head for the barn as soon as Grandma calls for supper. It'll be safe then, so just wait up and keep quiet. She'll ring the bell soon. You'll see." He backed away a little. "Well...okay... c'mon out of there, but keep tight to the hillside. That way, no one can see us."

"What kind of a plan do you have?" she asked, edging through the door. "I'd rather be in that cornfield than this dirt dungeon."

"I have a hideaway in the barn that's cozy and dry. Looks like the big rains I promised are on their way for tonight. For sure, they'll be hitting us hard. Check out that sky."

She didn't look up. "I don't like strange animals. What's in there?"

"Nothing, honest. All we have are some piglets, and they're outside in a pen. Grandpa quit keeping cows years ago, so don't worry." He kept any mention of the mice to himself.

Grandma's bell rang, announcing supper.

"Watch this," Nate whispered, flattening himself against the hillside and motioning for Lotty to do the same. "Grandpa's going to beeline it to the back door in...five, four, three, two... Ha! See his backside? There he goes in the door." Nate grinned at her. "Stay close to me, now, okay? And be quick."

They moved at a half trot toward the back of the barn. Nate stopped at the corner, catching a deep breath. They were well out of sight.

He laughed and said, "So far, so good. C'mon in. I'll show you your new room. It has a real roof, too."

They climbed the steep, wooden stairway to the hay loft. Across from tall rows of sweet-smelling hay bales, many still shaded light green, a door opened onto a small room that had once been used for a hired man when this was a much larger farm.

"Hmm," Lotty said.

Nate crossed his arms. "Aw, c'mon, will ya? I could've left you in that field to drown tonight."

"Okay, all right then, thanks for this," she said, shuffling into the room. "Sorry. It's just been rough since I left there."

Nate leaned on the doorframe. "Where were you before? I mean, where is *there*?" Before she could answer, he said, "Wait up. Tell me about it if you want to, but not right now. I better get inside, or they'll be wondering. Oh, here's a candy bar. Uh...I mean, here's both candy bars. If I can manage it, I'll sneak you out some real food later."

"Something to drink, too, please," she said, taking the candy. "Really thirsty."

"Grandma always keeps lemonade. I'll get that for you." He bounded down the stairs two at a time, then sprinted across the yard and into the house.

"Where you been?" Grandpa asked the second Nate entered.

"Uh...haircut." Nate rested his hands on his knees, panting. Maybe he should tell them. Then Lotty's fearful eyes burned through his mind. Yeah, maybe not.

"Oh my, don't you look handsome," Grandma said. "You might need one more just before going home. Can't let them folks up north think we turned you into a hillbilly." She chuckled, setting dishes on the kitchen table. "You clean up nice, Nate. Maybe you could talk your grandpa into a visit to the barbershop once in a while. Anything fun happen in town?"

Nate's brain churned, still not used to keeping up with Grandma's habit of asking several questions in a row and never pausing for answers. "Oh yeah, sure was," he said, sitting at the table. "Or um...sure did, I mean. Met Stony. He gave me a ride in the road grader. He says 'Hi' to you both."

"Good, golly," Grandma said, pulling out her chair. "Looks like I owe him a *thank you* or at least some cookies or bars or something. I'll see Sylvie after church. Maybe this week, Stony might be with her, too."

They all began eating, and Nate relaxed. No more questions peppered him.

After dessert, Grandpa settled into his big chair and adjusted the electric rooftop antenna for the best T.V. reception. He could usually pull in two channels from the nearest stations. After dishes, Grandma went outside to pick some vegetables.

Nate made a quick meatloaf sandwich and poured lemonade into an empty root beer bottle. "Plenty still left," he whispered. No one would miss this little bit. What a dinner for Lotty, candy bars and meatloaf. "I'll be outside, Grandpa," he called.

The old man just mumbled something Nate couldn't make out. When his nighttime T.V. shows were on, only they would command his attentions.

After sliding along the side of the barn to the back door, then rushing up the stairs to the hay loft, Nate entered Lotty's room. She blinked up at him from her seat on a blanket spread on the floor.

He swallowed hard. "You're crying?" Unsure what to do, he thrust the food toward her. "Here you go, something good to eat." She took it, but tears kept sliding down her cheeks, and Nate fumbled in his pockets in vain for something to wipe them with. "For breakfast, I'll bring something, too."

"I may not be here," she said, sniffling.

"I can't listen to your crying," he said, folding his arms, "so give it a rest. Will ya, please?" That had sounded too stern. He forced a smile and gave her a thumbs-up sign. "Stay here, okay? You'll be unhappy if you go, and you are the safest here, too. That's a for-sure fact. Tomorrow, we'll figure out something best for you, or at least better. Honest."

Lotty said nothing, so he waved and closed her door. While he worked his way down the stairs in the dark barn, then across the long back yard and into the house, Nate tried to figure out how he could make sure she wouldn't run. No useful ideas came.

"Bedtime, Nate," Grandma yelled from the living room.

Nate froze. How'd she know he was back? He let out a breath. Oh, right, that noisy screen door.

"What're you doing in the barn?" Grandma asked.

"Just looking for Butch." Wow, that lie had popped out fast.

"He's with your grandpa in here," she said, "snoozing on his rug."

"Okay. Goodnight." Nate climbed the dark stairway to the attic, hoping she wouldn't call him back to brush his teeth. "Don't want to talk to them," he muttered. "Too many questions."

He glanced around his attic room and said, "This is no nicer than the one in the barn. Just bare wood walls, and I bet it's even hotter." At least the gaps in the barn siding would let some air pass through. All he had was a tiny square window set just above the floor. "I hope Lotty's more comfortable than I am and doesn't take off in the dark," he mumbled, changing into night clothes. He pulled the chain on the bare lightbulb hanging from the ceiling. In an instant, darkness filled every space, crack, and corner of the room.

He flopped onto the narrow bed, atop the covers. "Now I lay me...aw, I'm way past that one," he whispered, "but I have to ask for help. This is my biggest problem ever, so, Lord, please don't let Lotty be afraid of us. And keep her here where she's safe. Amen."

Nate's face heated, more from praying out loud while alone than the temperature. He reminded himself no one could hear him up here, but he'd always whispered his infrequent prayers, just in case. His family might be church-goers, but nobody talked much about religion. That stuff was private. Maybe those Baptists and Church of Christ folks down here were rubbing off on him. They could be much more outspoken than the up-north Lutherans he was used to.

Turning on his side, he stared through his tiny window. Facing the back yard and barn, it might give him enough warning if Lotty tried to leave. He'd stay up to keep an eye on her. This adventure had already given him more excitement than he'd had all summer, and his heart pumped hard as he imagined the consequences that might come from it.

He yawned as rain pattered on the roof. The patters turned to pounding, lightning flashed, and the wind whipped strong enough to blow the rain sideways against the house. A storm this big could surely keep him awake.

His eyelids drooped, then closed.

The next morning, Nate stretched and scowled. "It's still so hot up here. Did I dream that storm? Maybe it missed us." He knelt to peer out his window. Fallen leaves and a few broken branches in the yard explained everything.

Grandma must have left for work by now, and that whoosh in the walls meant Grandpa was in the shower. Nate dressed fast and scampered down to the kitchen. He made two pieces of toast for Lotty, one with peanut butter and jelly, and the other with a slice of bologna. He had to keep track of these little thefts. "They'll never notice anything missing." He smirked. "Not like a whole pork chop or a turkey leg, at least. Who counts bologna slices?" He shook his head. "Sorry, Grandma."

He filled another empty bottle, this time with milk. He had to remember to bring back the bottles. Grandma would figure it out if he left them. Time to see if Lotty was still out there.

He juggled the bread and bottle while walking over the uneven path to the barn, the whole time reminding himself not to yell her name and scare her. He'd wait till he was halfway up the stairs, and keep it quiet then, too.

Nate fumbled with the barn's side door handle and managed to open it without dropping or spilling anything. He climbed the stairs as fast as possible, praying, *Show me she's here, Lord.* He hadn't prayed this much in a long time. When Lotty's face peeked from the edge of the doorway, he said, "Oh, thank you again, great Father."

"What are you saying?" she asked in a whisper.

"You're here, and thank goodness. You hungry?"

"Plenty. Whatcha got?"

"Nothing fancy. Take a look."

She took both pieces of bread, and Nate set the milk bottle on a ledge jutting out from the wall. He grinned, happy her eyes shone brighter as she started eating like a hungry puppy.

"Thank you much," she said. "This is delicious."

A whine from the bottom of the stairs announced Butch's presence. Lotty jumped and scooted backward on her bed as the aging collie stared upward, looking for them to appear.

"He's friendly," Nate said. "Don't worry. He just wants some attention, and he's too old to make these stairs anymore. Well, up maybe. He's done that, but not down. He knows it, too. Last few times, he tumbled halfway to the bottom." Nate gave her a sideways grin. "I'll introduce you two when you're able to be in the yard." Then, a thought struck him, and he looked away. "Uh, what are you doing about...well, you know, about..."

"Just you never mind, that's all," she snapped. "You don't need to know.'

"I'll tell you what, then, when you hear Grandpa's power tools zinging in the shop next door, hustle yourself across the back yard and into the house. If you see a shiny green car in the driveway—along the far side, that is—come back here right away. That's Grandma's car. The rusty old pickup truck is his. But if no car is there, means she's gone, so sneak into the house and find the bathroom, and don't take too long. And if you hear anyone come in the side door, get out the front door fast. Then, hustle back alongside the house. You know, where you walked by it the first time. Along the edge of the cornfield, I mean, then get back in here but quick. Okay?"

"Believe me," she said, "I can be fast as a deer if I have to. Plenty practice. A good hider, too. And thanks for this. I haven't eaten this much in days."

Nate nodded. "You're safe here. Grandma's great, but I'm not as sure about him, so let's just keep you hidden a little longer. Not sure what to do yet. We have plenty figuring left to do."

The screeching of a power saw penetrated the walls.

"Hear that?" Nate said. "He's in the shop, and he'll be looking for me, so I have to go. The house is yours, for a while, that is. If you want to be outside some, stay on this back side of the barn. You know, the hay field side. No one will see you. They never come over here." Worried, he shook his head, recalling the squeaky door. "No, wait a minute, I tell you what, just go in and out the front door of the house—it's never locked—and skip the side door. Keep to the cornfield side of the house. Then, nobody'll see you. Promise me."

"I will," she said. "I promise. Best you get moving."

Nate ran to the house, ate a bowl of cereal, then hurried toward the shop. Maybe Lotty really would listen. That storm had been all he'd said it'd be, so maybe she'd trust him now. And maybe tell him her story.

He skidded to a stop in the doorway. "Grandpa!" he yelled over the screeching of the power planer.

The old man looked away from the work for an instant, nodded as if to say, "I see you," then looked back and finished passing a board across the cutter. Turning off the machine, he said, "Where you been? Get a new girlfriend? Hmm, or hanging around with that Pistol? That'd be okay, I'll say so. He's a good boy. Glad you two made friends."

"What? You kidding me? No girls around here, Grandpa. Just slow today because it's so hot in the attic. Don't sleep like I should, but no girls, that's for sure." Nate hated to lie, but figured this was one of those exception-to-the-rule things his sister had tried to explain.

"Never seen you comb your hair so good. That's why I ask," Grandpa said.

"What's the plan today...for the boat, I mean?" Nate asked.

"Make her sea-worthy, son. No sinkers coming out of this shop."

Nate relaxed and admired their handywork.

The rest of the day came and went as usual. Nate brought Lotty a small dinner but didn't stay long in case his grandparents asked why he spent so much time in the barn. Lotty smiled and thanked him for even that little bit of food and company.

Chapter Four

The next day, when Nate went to help work on the boat, Grandpa said, "C'mon out to the barn. Something out there I need to investigate. Got a strong hunch about your reaction to this deal, too."

Nate's heart hammered. "The barn?" He rushed to beat Grandpa to the door. "Hey, shouldn't we be working on the boat? Nothing to do in that empty old barn, anyway. Just all that hay you're selling."

Grandpa raised an eyebrow. "Let's take a look. There's something out there, and it's important. Surprised you haven't mentioned it." He stepped outside. "Let's go see."

The old man walked toward the barn, then slid open half of the wide main door on the front, turned sideways, and motioned to Nate. "Give me a hand. Might be tough to drag her out of here. I sometimes wish we could still have slaves."

Her? Nate stumbled to a stop halfway there. Grandpa knew.

"Quit dawdling, son," the old man said.

Nate forced his feet to move. "Slaves? Grandpa, you serious? That's not funny."

The old man laughed and walked farther into the building. "You should know, by now, when I'm kidding."

Nate followed him in, looking up toward the loft. He found no sign of Lotty. No doubt she'd heard them. He hoped she could hide as well as she'd claimed.

"Help me drag this out into the aisle," Grandpa said, bending over a large lump by the wall.

"What's that?" Nate asked.

"Your new house. Or let's say, my old tent from long ago. Grab that wheelbarrow, too. We'll load it in and go outside. It's terrible heavy."

"For me?" Nate said, pushing the wheelbarrow toward the wall. "Nice, really nice. That attic's way too hot."

They tugged, pushed, pulled, then lifted the heavy bundle of army-green cloth and poles onto the wheelbarrow. They'd worked together enough to have become a team, listening to and respecting one another, but lifting the weight took much of their strength.

"How big is this thing?" Nate asked, wiping his sweaty face on his shoulder.

"Hope there's no new holes in it," Grandpa said, scratching his head. "Oh, how big, you ask? Could park a tractor in her. Big tractor. Maybe a truck or two, as well."

Nate shook his head. *New* holes? Grandpa liked to exaggerate, but Nate never dared to call him on any of his bold bragging or tall tales. He was getting good at picking the truth out of those stories, and mostly enjoyed them, too. "Where we going to put this?"

"Over on the east side of the barn, by the branch." Grandpa pointed. "There's a flat spot there, so you can sleep easy without rolling out the door."

They chuckled together, then moved their load in an awkward shuffle toward the door.

Backing out of the barn, Nate looked up again, but still no Lotty. She couldn't have missed all their grunts and groans and the few cuss words from Grandpa. "Good girl," Nate whispered, so quiet Grandpa couldn't have heard. The old man was half deaf, anyway.

After moving carefully downhill, they stopped on a spot Grandpa said was just right, removed the heavy canvas from the barrow, and started unfolding it. The poles tumbled out. Nate's job was to match them by size and length.

He smiled and whispered, "We made it. Gonna like this a lot." Then, louder, he said, "Ugh! Whoa, does it always smell like this?"

Grandpa chuckled. "Let's air it out a day or two before you use it. Been sitting in there too many years." He glanced over his shoulder. "Did you hear something? Was that a sneeze coming from the barn?"

"Nope, didn't hear a sneeze," Nate lied all in a rush. "Could've been Butch. He makes those watery-sounding noises sometimes."

"I s'pose he does." Grandpa shook his head. "Can only hear out my right side, these days. Left side's shot."

Nate held his breath, waiting for Grandpa to question his own senses again, but nothing further came of it. "So far, so good. Still lucky," he mumbled. The fresh hay up there could bring on an instant sneeze attack or two, no matter how hard you tried to stop it.

Grandpa barked orders, spun about, groaned, and huffed as they tugged, lifted, set poles, and let huge sweat drops plop onto the canvas floor.

"Grandpa, it's good you know how to erect this giant,"

Nate said between huge puffs of air. "I appreciate this. I could never figure it out. Not the first time, at least." He grinned at the old man. "By the way, maybe a small tractor could fit, but *really* small. No truck, though. That's for sure. Probably not even your John Deere B."

"I'll have to teach you how to measure better, young man." Grandpa laughed. "Watch Butch, now. See what he does."

The dog poked his head a few inches through the tied-back doorway flap, looked about at the inside, sniffed hard, then backed out slow while shaking his head side-to-side and up-and-down. He sneezed hard, twice.

"He's grown careful in his old age," Grandpa said. "Time was, he'd have charged in there to terrorize any real or imaginary devils or critters and drive them out."

"Can he stay in there with me?"

"Of course. It's hot in the house for him, too. He's becoming more yours than mine, anyway, and I'm glad to see that."

Nate took one last look around for his hidden friend, and hoping it wouldn't be too long before he could move in. "Grandma might put the stop to this, ya know," he said. "What'd you think about that? It does need a cleaning."

Grandpa grinned, grabbing the handles of the wheelbarrow. "She might come down here with a spray can or some fancy, schmancy cleaners. She'll be okay with it. You'll see. Ever since we got that T.V., she's buying cleaners I've never heard of. Good place here to test 'em, I suppose."

"I'll take that back to the barn for you," Nate said, reaching for the barrow handles. He hoped they'd let him move into the tent soon. It'd make a good daytime hideout for Lotty.

"I hear from Y.T. there's some runaways around here,"

Grandpa said, backing away from the barrow. "Butch is pretty useless if they show up, but he'll at least bark up a ruckus and scare them some. So, don't worry. We're safe enough back in here. No one ever wanders back this far from the road. Besides, if I see one, I can still plink 'em with the twenty-two."

"Careful it ain't me, Grandpa."

Chapter Five

A few evenings after they pitched and cleaned the tent, Nate sat inside, arranging things for his first night.

Grass crunched outside, and a shadow darkened the closed canvas door flaps.

"Nate," a high voice whispered, "you in there? It's me, Lotty."

Butch snorted and wiggled about in the tent as Nate cleared his throat. "Hey, keep it quiet," he hissed, then crawled to the door and untied the drawstrings.

A short way back on the lawn, Lotty perched on her knees with her hands flat on the ground like a four-legged critter. Any sight line from the house to the tent door should block her from his grandparents' view.

"C'mon in," he said.

"I can't."

"Don't be afraid. I couldn't hurt you. Don't you know that by now? Best friend you've got, really. C'mon, now, before they hear us."

"I really, for sure, can not," she said.

"Stop goofing around. What's the problem?"

"That crescent moon's over my left shoulder, with a large star just over its point at the top. Haven't you seen it? Should never enter a strange new house like that. Would bring terrible, bad luck—awful, nasty bad luck you couldn't believe."

"Phooey. Where'd you dream up that kinda thing? Just get in here before they—"

"Nope, can't, and everybody knows it. Don't you? I can't be havin' more trouble than I've got already, so I'm staying put."

"Okay, tell you what," he said, scooting back a little. "It's simple. You just turn halfway around. Then, with your back to the door, sit up straight on your hind end, and that puts the moon on your other side. Next, you shamble yourself backwards through the opening and, *voila*! You're in here. C'mon, now, no time to waste. They're sleeping up there, but we're plenty noisy, so get yourself inside."

Lotty sat still with her eyes closed, then scratched her head while balancing on the other hand. "Should be okay, I guess. Better be, cuz here goes." She turned around, then used her hands and heels to lift and push herself backwards, and slid onto the canvas floor.

Butch blocked her in the doorway, wagging his tail and trying to lick her hair.

"Go on, silly dog, get away, now." She pushed him with her elbow. "Good boy. That's right."

He wiggled and sniffed and turned around twice in complete circles.

"Welcome to my summer house," Nate said, grinning as he reached around her to close and tie the door flap.

She turned and glanced around. "It's a nice big tent. Smells good, too, like flowers."

"That's Grandma's work. She cleaned it with some stuff

from a T.V. show. Supposed to smell like flowers, I think. Shoulda smelled it first day we put her up." He wrinkled his face. "Was awful."

"I like it," Lotty said, wiggling to sit cross-legged. "Beats my room in the barn. I heard you two working on it the other day, and I wanted to come out here and see it better."

"Glad you did. You hungry? I've hidden a few things in here."

"A little hungry. Whatcha got this time?"

"Donuts, some slices of tomatoes, and a bag of crackers."

"Tomatoes on crackers sound like heaven. Can you spare 'em?"

Nate nodded, then opened an old tin box and produced the treasure. Butch rose on all fours, ears perked and sniffing. Trust the scent of food to perk him up. Nate gave the dog two crackers. Butch barked his *thank you* and moved to the doorway.

Butch barked again, then growled low and serious.

"What is it, boy?" Nate whispered, straightening. "Who's out there, fella?" He gestured for Lotty to move to the dark, back corner of the tent and pull his sleeping bag over herself.

"Nate, you in there?" a deep but youthful voice asked. "Wake up. You here?"

Nate and Lotty stared at each other, making not a sound, then he said, "That you, Pistol?"

"Sure is. How do I open this door?"

Nate squinted at the flap. "What in the world? Hold on, I'll do it." He looked toward the back. No way in this darkness could anyone see Lotty under the fluffy bag. He threw his pillow, which landed perfect at the head of the bag and looked like it belonged there. She'd get what he was doing. Then, he hid the flashlight under some nearby clothes and said, "Hold on, man, I'll untie this door." He did so and poked his head out. "What're you doing out at this hour?"

"Came to get you. We're going to have some fun. Create a little havoc, you might say."

Just the other day, Grandpa had said Pistol was "a good boy." So, Pistol's plans tonight couldn't be too serious. Maybe just stealing a few watermelons or something.

Pistol entered the tent, and Nate told him to stay toward the front by the door and talk quiet. Butch sniffed him over, wagged his tail, and lay down on his new favorite spot. Good thing Butch was between Pistol and Lotty.

"Old man Fletcher didn't pay my brother even half for all the work he's done there," Pistol said, narrowing his eyes. "Him and our cousin Freddy, too. But the old man just bought himself a new truck and a shotgun. He's bold enough to be showing them off to the guys he owes money to. So, we'll fix that. We're getting a few friends together to go and let his fancy horses out the barn. Then, we'll wrangle them out to the road and get 'em as far away as possible before that criminal knows they're gone. Maybe take one of his fancy saddles, too. We can sell it later and get paid what he owes. He deserves that. You in?"

"Uh, sure. I'm in, I guess. I mean...when?" Nate tried not to fidget, more concerned about getting Pistol away from Lotty than helping right some wrong old man Fletcher had done. The tent was feeling too small for a change.

"Right now," Pistol said, opening the tent flap. "I've got my car down the road a-ways, so I wouldn't shake up your grandpa. Down by the Ellis place. Let's go. Gotta pick up somebody else, too."

"Okay, uh, you head to the car," Nate said. "Gimme a few minutes to get some other clothes on, and I'll be there."

Pistol punched Nate on the shoulder, then crept from

the tent into the side yard and disappeared into the darkness.

Once Nate figured Pistol must have made it far enough, he whispered to Lotty, "Okay, you heard it all, so do what you want here. Stay in the tent or the barn. You pick. I don't think we'll get caught, but it may be a while before we're back." As Lotty poked her head from beneath his sleeping bag, another thought hit him. "In fact, best you go to the barn, just in case he comes back here with me."

"Don't do this," she said, the whites of her wide eyes shining. "Really, don't go. Bad idea, cuz that moon I tempted tonight will not be happy."

"C'mon, get real," he said, chuckling under his breath. "Nothing to worry about. We won't get caught, and that old geezer deserves it. I've heard of other tricks he pulls, too. Word gets around a place like this." When Lotty hung her head, he said, "I'll make it back okay. I promise. You never seen me run."

"You'll end up in jail or shot dead. I just know it." Her voice broke. "Then, I'm lost here without your help."

"Nah, not a chance." Nate gave her knee a gentle nudge. "There's only one cop anywhere around. He's miles away and don't work most nights. Plus, Pistol's almost fifteen and been driving since he was ten. These country kids have little use for a driver's license, and no one cares. He can drive these dirt roads with his lights out, like a shadow in the night moving across a picket fence. Would just make a person dizzy trying to catch ahold of him. Nothing can see or stop him. I wish you could come, too. You could use some fun!" Could she tell he was just bragging?

Lotty just shook her head.

Nate pulled on a dirty work shirt and slipped into his

tennis shoes, lacing them tighter than usual. "Take this food back to the barn. If you'll feel better, I'll come up and see you when I'm back."

"Just throw a rock on my wall," she said, pushing the sleeping bag away. "Make it two or three in case I fall asleep. Except I don't think I will. When I hear the rocks, I'll tap-tap on the boards so you'll know I heard you."

"Deal," he said.

Nate showed her how to tie the doors shut from the outside, but not so tight down low that Butch couldn't get in and out when he had to, then he slinked over to the far side of the yard by the cornfield. He slowed down and ducked under his grandparents' bedroom window, then crept out to the road.

When he reached Pistol's old Chevy sedan, he shuffled to a stop. Somebody's silhouette filled the front passenger side window, so Nate slid into the back seat.

"Nate, this is Fuzzy, my big brother," Pistol said, starting the engine. "He's the guy the old man cheated first. We'll go get Cousin Fred next."

"Hi, Fuzzy," Nate said. "You guys have actual real names? I mean, like Tom or Bill?"

Both brothers laughed, and Pistol said, "Maybe we'll tell you the real ones sometime. You might not believe what they are, though."

As they drove in the dark, Pistol swung the car side-to-side with the steering wheel, then he and his brother started jumping around on the seat, punching the roof, and kicking the door panels.

Nate sat back, Lotty's worries filling his mind. Why were these guys so happy to be taking such chances? He sure wasn't. His hands and arms shook a little, and he had to look sideways out the window rather than at his two accomplices. What was he afraid of? He and his pals back home had become old pros in their apple raiders club. No one ever caught them sliding between houses with those heavy bags of fresh-picked red and green fruit. But this was bigtime compared to that. If they had to run, he sure hoped he could keep up with these guys and not get lost, caught... or shot.

The thwack of a rock hitting the barn wall woke Lotty. Nate! Was that the first, second, or third rock he'd thrown? She sat up, holding her breath and waiting for another. When none came, she scampered down the stairs. As hard as she'd tried to stay awake, she must've fallen asleep fully clothed and missed the first two thrown. She sprinted to the tent, glancing in every direction, then knelt by the flap and whispered, "Nate, I'm here. Let me in."

"Hey, sure, c'mon in," he said, pulling the flap aside. "Thought you were sleeping hard when I threw the rocks. Didn't hear you tap on the wall. I bet that mean ole moon's moved away, too. No worries now."

"Was too sleepy to remember that part about knocking back," she said, yawning as she scooted inside. "You okay... safe? Did you guys raid that old man's farm? That fella with the new shotgun?"

"No sweat," he said, grinning and making more room for her. "Those horses are out and about, plenty far down the road, too. We left them drinking in a pond. Maybe tomorrow after he's upset plenty, they'll wander back in when they're hungry. Were you really worried?"

She stared at him. "Of course. Why wouldn't I be? Folks here can get dangerous."

"It was no problem, except I broke Grandpa's sling-shot," he said, shrugging. "I'll need to make up a good story to tell him. Used it to zing the horses on the rump and get them going."

She gasped and covered her mouth. "Shame on you, Nate! A story? Just call it a lie, cuz that's what its gonna be."

He shrugged. "You'd tell one, too. You don't know his temper."

She glared at him. "I prayed to God every minute you were gone, and that's who brought you back here safe. And now you want to make up lies?" She crossed her arms. "Don't you know there's more than one kind of trouble? This mean world is one kind, and there's plenty trouble here, but losing His favor over you? Ya know, God's blessings?" She shivered. "That's way worse. Don't be telling your grandpa anything but truth."

"Oh, c'mon. He'll never know."

She huffed. "Your creator will. He's made everything here just wonderful for you, *especially* you, so don't be spitting in His eye." She wagged a finger at him. "Not ever again."

Nate leaned back, eyes wide. "I didn't know you were like this. I mean, I been to church plenty and all. Most every Sunday and a few Wednesday nights, too. But how is it you know these things so strong? That He will turn against me? They teach us back home that God is love."

"Says so. Don't you know that?" She tilted her head, studying him. "Don't they read the Good Book to you? Says so just clear as spring water." She scooted closer. "Think about this. How come no one's caught me? Except just you, I mean. And you're the only one, I believe, who would try to help me. You brought me to this safe place, and that's no accident. He put me on your road. I know it, cuz many times I stood at a crossroads and didn't have a clue which way to turn...left, right, or straight ahead. Lonesome and scared, that was me, but every turn I made led me here. Where I'm from, that's called fate, and His help makes it so. You know what I mean? A good fate, one where He makes it work out for you. It's way more than just plain luck."

Nate sat still, just staring at her. "You sound like a preacher...but better," he said at last. "Okay, one thing's for sure. I won't be lying to Grandpa."

Chapter Six

The next mooring, Nate drummed his fingers on the door of Grandpa's truck as they drove to Y.T.'s Mercantile for fasteners, sandpaper, and other items they needed for the boat project. Grandpa might hang around long enough to have a pop with Y.T., but he'd never waste a trip just for amusement. What if they ran into Pistol and he gave away last night's adventure? Nate rubbed his palms on his jeans. Steve and Tommy and the other guys back home could be careless, but no doubt Pistol would keep a cool head.

When they arrived, Grandpa went to the hardware department at the far back end of the store, so Nate sat by the counter with Y.T. and his cold bottle of pop, listening to the radio playing the newest rock and roll tunes.

"D'you hear about old man Fletcher's horses and some missing tack from his barn?" Y.T. asked. When Nate said nothing, Y.T. shook his head. "That old cuss was the first one in here today, buying two boxes of twelve-gauge shotgun shells."

Lotty's scolding filled Nate's mind at once. He couldn't lie to Grandpa, so it stood to reason that he couldn't lie to

Y.T., either. Now what to do? He swallowed hard and said, Uh...nothing. Nobody's told me a thing. No sir, not a word. Haven't heard a thing. Been home all morning except here." Nate sat straighter and looked Y.T. in the eyes, grinning at his clever way not to lie. No one had said one word about it. Besides, was not answering a question the same as lying? He stared at the floor, hoping Y.T. wouldn't ask anything else.

"Never kid a kidder, my young friend," Y.T. said. "Let's start over. I'll put it this way. Do you have any idea who may have done something to Fletcher's horses?"

Nate thought fast. He'd either be in trouble with Y.T. or with Pistol, or both, so what should he say? Telling on Pistol might cause him more trouble than having Y.T. think him a liar, but both choices could cost him. Again, he said nothing.

"C'mon, Nate," Y.T. said, moving so close you could barely slide a piece of paper the thin way between their noses. "I'm thinking you know more than you're letting on. In fact, I'll bet on it."

Nate leaned back, swallowed hard again, then said, "Mister Y.T., uh...here's the thing. You've put me on the spot but good. So, my answer is this. Who should I be most afraid of? And by the way, none of it was my idea, I want you to know. I can't win here, no matter what, so I'll tell you all about it if I have to...but I'm hoping we can still be friends."

"Hold on, young man, and settle down," Y.T. said, stepping back. "You've just answered my question, so we'll let it go for now. Done deal, it's over, so far down the road I can't hear it, see it, or smell it. I appreciate your honesty. We are friends, you know."

He walked behind the counter again, turned, and leaned his elbows on it. "Old Fletcher, by the way, is no friend of mine. He's been coming in here for years and always harps about my prices. Does all he can to squeeze me down to rock bottom, then smiles that awful, smart guy, 'gotcha' look of his if I ever do give him a bargain. Which is rare, these days. I'll tell you that." Y.T. uncurled and fiddled with the receipt tape sticking out of the register. "Yes sir, no friend at all. Keep your secrets when you have to, son. That's what I'll advise you. None of my business, anyway, and sometimes letting a thing go is the best way. No one's angry here. We'll keep it that way, too, you and me."

He reached for Nate's hand, and they shook on their first ever shared secret.

Nate grinned, but his insides tightened. Would Lotty be in favor of or against this kind of a deal? He hadn't really lied, and he'd started to tell. He let go of Y.T.'s hand and wrapped it around his cold pop bottle, wishing he knew the rules better. At least he was in Y.T.'s good graces and had kept Pistol in the clear.

"Just don't ever get caught," Y.T. whispered across the counter, "whatever it is you guys are up to. No true friends of mine ever get themselves caught."

Nate and Y.T. smiled at each other as sounds from the dusty, ancient wood floor reached them.

"You two hand-shakers making some kind of bet?" Grandpa asked from behind. "Anything I should get in on?"

"Find everything you wanted, Henry?" Y.T. asked.

Nate winked. Y.T. could be clever, too.

Grandpa set his purchases on the counter. "You're changing the subject, but yes, I did. Here, you can ring it up. Still want to know what the hand-shaking and head-nodding's all about." He turned and eyed Nate. "You tell me now, Mister Nate. What's up around here?"

Nate swallowed. "We're talking about that business

with old man Fletcher's horses. You hear about that yet?" When Grandpa shook his head, Nate kept going with his tale. "Some rascals run off his prize ponies, and me and Y.T. agreed to split any reward if there is to be one. Maybe we'd spot them along the road somewhere and help each other chase 'em down."

Nate forced himself not to glance at Y.T. Would his friend take the cue and keep him out of bigger trouble? His heart pounded, a little in pride and a little in shame over how quick he'd come up with his answer. Now, those were fantastic lies, no question about it.

"Count me in, then," Grandpa said. "Could always use some extra cash, but don't hold your breath with Fletcher's promises. He's tighter with a dollar than a preacher's wife."

Everyone laughed, then Grandpa pointed at his goods on the counter. "Add it up, now. We need to get back. Your brother's boat isn't going to build itself. And speaking of rewards, how about that runaway negro girl? Any truth to the rumor there's a reward out for her?"

"Heard about it," Y.T. said, tapping buttons on the register. "Sure it's true. Also heard from the sheriff she maybe was spotted a good bit north of here, just across the Missouri line."

"That'd be fine," Grandpa said, pulling cash from his wallet. "Then, she's not our problem anymore."

Y.T. nodded, took Grandpa's money, gave him his change, then turned to Nate. "You seen anything like her on your travels?"

"No sir, but then I don't get around much," Nate said. "Home to here, mostly. Maybe it's all gossip." Nate looked away, recalling one of his mom's rants. Rumors got around this small town even faster than back home, and here he was making his original lie bigger.

Tiny Hartsville didn't have a newspaper or its own radio station, so Y.T.'s store was the center for most news-gathering—be it true or not. Nate could've stopped some of the rumors, since he knew Lotty wasn't in Missouri. His mom was always saying people would talk about anything, especially things they knew nothing about. Maybe it was best he kept quiet.

Leading the way back to his old Ford pickup truck, Grandpa asked over his shoulder, "You want to practice shifting the gears again?"

"Sure do," Nate said, relaxing. "It's fun, and I've pretty much got it figured, now."

"Be sure not to hit reverse again when you're aiming at second, okay? It makes that awful grinding sound," Grandpa said, tossing his bag onto the floor of the bed.

"Yes sir," Nate said as they climbed in.

Grandpa pulled out of the parking spot, then pushed in the clutch pedal. Nate moved the floor-mounted shift lever down and back to the left, into first gear. Grandpa worked the gas pedal and steering wheel, moving the truck to the middle of the gravel road. Then, he pushed the clutch pedal down again, signaling Nate to slowly move the lever straight forward, over to the right, then forward again into second gear. When the noise of the accelerating motor reached its peak, it was time to shift into third, so Grandpa put in the clutch again and Nate pulled the lever straight back. Since they wouldn't need to shift again until they turned into their yard, he let go of the shiny black shift knob and sat back.

"Nate," Grandpa said, "if you do ever run into that colored girl hiding around here, get the heck away from her, first thing. You never know with them if they're carrying a knife or a gun. I mean, most are just fine folks, like anyone else, but the chances of trouble, especially from one on the run, can be high. Be careful. You hear me?"

"Sure, Grandpa," Nate said. "Stop worrying about me getting hurt. Let's go work on the boat. You said you'd teach me about the mahogany."

"That's our plan, boy. I hope you can use these lessons in your life."

"The ones about wood or about people?"

"Good question. Both would make me happy. What the heck, put each one into practice, and they'd make me proud.

Chapter Seven

"Quiet down," Lotty hissed the instant Nate poked his head through her door in the loft. "They'll hear you!"

He laughed, almost bouncing as he swung her door wide. "Nah, they're—"

"Stop it, now," she said from her perch on the floor, wrapping her arms around and gripping her shoulders. "You're noisy as a cannon."

"Not to worry, missy miss. They're gone. Don't ya remember? Grandpa and Grandma both. They left early this morning for the whole day and won't be back until dark tonight. Take it easy. The whole place is yours. Saturdays here are great."

She ducked her head and shook it. "You come storming up those stairs like a herd of elephants, yelling my name so loud, and all I can think is, big trouble is here. Something's coming, so I better get running."

"Sorry."

"Then, I look around for my bag to grab quick so I can take off," Lotty said, then glared up at him. "Don't do that to me again...okay...never."

Nate could only stare at the haunted look in her eyes and her hunched figure. He wanted to give her a hug but didn't dare. "Sorry, really am. I'm just happy right now and didn't think."

"What day is it, then?" she asked.

"Saturday, for sure."

"What makes you think they won't be back till dark? Why should I believe a noisy, thoughtless bugger like you?"

"Because they always do this every couple weeks. You know, when it's their payday." He smiled and leaned closer. "Listen, now. They drive about thirty miles to the big city and buy all the stuff they can't get at Y.T.'s store. Then, they have dinner at that famous chicken place they like so much. So, go ahead and scold me, but remember, I've always been on your side, and I still am."

"I know, I know," she said, uncrossing her arms, "and thank you. I'll try to do something nice for you someday...if I ever can." She straightened and braced her hands on the floor. "So, what do they buy? Looks like they got everything already, at least from how I'm living."

"Well, you know, everything from clothes to jewelry to fancy things like cloth and ribbons and all the what-nots Grandma likes. Grandpa, too. He buys a case or two of that Busch Bavarian beer he likes, more tools, and sometimes parts for his old truck. Mostly that kind of thing." Nate laughed. "Shiny and nice for her, greasy and black for him."

"Okay," Lotty said, blowing out a noisy breath. "I hope you're right. I'd like to be outside this barn, for a while. Maybe I could wash some clothes and my hair. Feels like I been living in a ratty old doghouse or a dirty, nasty chicken coup. Probably smell as bad as I look."

"The house is yours today," he said, standing. "Let's get you fixed up."

"Breakfast, please," she said, jumping to her feet. "Can we do that? Something fried. Cooked hot, you know? And that bath and washin' my clothes. I have one clean dress to put on, so I'm not getting back into old barn-smellin' rags after I'm clean for the first time in who knows how long." She grabbed her canvas bag but froze. "You really sure they won't be back?"

Nate gave her the thumbs-up sign and led the way down the stairs.

At the bottom, Lotty stopped and said in a low voice, "When do you leave for home...how much longer?"

"Um, not sure. Two, maybe three weeks. Gotta find out."

Lotty wore her sad face again, the one he hated to see. His usual energy left him, and for a moment, he couldn't move.

Without speaking, they left the barn and walked into the house. Nate opened the bathroom door for Lotty. She'd been there before, but never for a bath.

"Use that clean dark blue towel over there," he said, pointing. "It's mine, so Grandma'll just think it was me if it's still a bit damp."

Lotty nodded. "I have my own soap and shampoo. I'll use that. She won't notice anything's short, but I bet her stuff is better."

"Right," he said, backing from the room. "I'm going to start a nice breakfast for you. Only thing I know is fried eggs. My mom taught me. That got her out of making them, I guess. There's ham, too. Hope you like that."

"More than I could tell you." Lotty closed the door, and the muffled swish of running water soon followed.

Nate guarded the house from the living room, keeping watch where he could see if anyone drove into the yard.

The kitchen faced the back, so he wouldn't be able to tell from there. He grinned, finally able to do something *real* to help Lotty. She looked so thin, though. His puffed-up chest deflated. He wasn't sneaking her enough food. "I'm going to dish up as much as I dare," he whispered, to himself or God or just the empty air. "I can handle a little less for myself to keep Grandma from wondering where it all goes. She says I've reached my next growing stage, so if I eat extra, shouldn't be too much of a problem with her."

Lotty started singing in the tub.

Nate strained to hear her words. Was that in English or some down-south Arkansas lingo? "Wish I knew what to do about her," he said, heading to the kitchen to cook breakfast. Grandpa would for sure pull something nasty if he caught her. With his sometimes mean streak, things could go a little bad for Nate, but worse for her.

Nate sat on a hay bale in the upper barn, enjoying the sweet smells of the fresh cut hay while Lotty hung her clean clothes on a tight-stretched rope line they'd rigged by her door. He sneaked short peeks at her when she wasn't looking in his direction.

She was pretty, especially with her washed hair, clean fresh clothes, and the first real smile she'd worn since they'd met. *Shiny*, that was the word for her today. Still too skinny, but maybe their breakfast would help that. She'd eaten the ham and eggs like a trucker just back from three days of icy roads, and she'd hummed the whole time they'd cleaned the kitchen.

Lotty finished hanging her clothes, turned, and said, "That was a great breakfast. Thank you, thank you. Hey, let's sit outside. Beautiful day. Blue sky, the birds are singing for us, and there's just enough breeze."

"Sure," he said, standing and brushing off his shorts. "I can snatch another chair, and we can sit by the tent. That way, if anybody drives in the side yard, you can hightail it away before they see you."

"Aw, c'mon," she said. "Don't spoil this for me. You worry so much. I'm looking forward to an outdoor day."

He swallowed and blurted, "Tell me some about your life. I mean, why'd you run away?"

Nate looked her in the eyes. She stared back but kept her face straight. She moved her head in a slow, side-to-side shake, then her arms fell limp and her chin dropped.

"Sorry," Nate said. "You deserve a nice day, and I don't really care about your problems. Well...I mean, I do. I just want to know things. Somehow, I think I'm supposed to protect you. Can't explain why, but I do know I'm proud you're here and safe, thanks a little to me, of course." He lifted his chin higher than normal.

"C'mon," she said, not looking at him. "Outside, let's go. You're even slower'n I am sometimes."

Nate skipped fast down the stairs, turned, looked up, and said, "Comin', turtle lady? Time's a-wasting. I want to see you movin' fast as a dog just let out of a car trunk."

Lotty's laugh echoed off the highest barn rafters. She bounded down the stairs and sprinted out the door toward the tent. Halfway there, she stopped and turned to him. "I can tell you a few things, I guess. You better keep quiet about them. Promise me that. You hear me?"

Nate nodded and touched one hand to his heart, the other to his lips.

They walked to the tent, and Nate grabbed his chair from inside, then went back to the barn for another. Lotty spun around like a dog chasing its tail, her arms raised toward the sky. She smiled wide and twirled without stopping. Nate's chest grew warm again as her eyes twinkled and she hummed a pretty song he didn't know.

"The sad girl from the cornfield is feeling better," he said, still smiling. He watched her twirl while he set the chairs on patches of level ground where they wouldn't rock or sink.

Nate and Lotty sat facing the cornfield. The large cherry tree veiled the harsh midday sun, but its rays kept the horseflies hiding wherever it was they went to escape the heat.

"So, you want to know why I ran away," Lotty said. "Have you ever thought why you never asked me before? I mean, you just brought me home and cared for me without knowing a thing. Who I am or what I may have done. That surprises me. Does it surprise you any?"

Nate shrugged. "Not really. I guess I never thought about it that way. You looked sad and scared, and I wanted to see that change. That's all it was. Makes enough sense for me."

"Believe it, I'm still sad, but a little less afraid...since being here, that is."

Nate stared at his knees. "I've been taught not to be snoopy about people. You know, 'live and let live,' they call it. My dad, especially, says don't ask folks too many questions. Particularly about money, right? Like how much a man makes." He shot a glance at her from the corner of his eye. "Do you even want me to know about you? Why you're a runaway, I mean?"

"Yes, yes...now, I do. I just hope it doesn't make you regret your kindness and want to send me back there."

"I think I know you by now," he said. "I can't imagine

anything so bad where I'd get you in any trouble. Like you're a murderer or something. Don't you know me better, too?"

Neither spoke for a few minutes, but to Nate, this silence felt like friendship.

"I had to escape," Lotty said at last, her eyes lowered and hands clasping tight to each arm of the chair. "I wouldn't let those two get me, and they were ready. They'd already tried once. I was alone, too, and had no one left could help. Running was the only thing."

Nate swallowed hard. "Can I ask you something?"

"You can ask."

"What about your parents? Where are they?"

"Dead." Tears circled her eyes. "Daddy died when I was six. Mama just this spring. In May, it was."

Nate reached over and touched her cheek. Moisture rolled across his finger, then she took his hand and rubbed it with hers.

Letting go, she said, "Thank you."

He waited, torn between asking about 'those two' she'd mentioned and not really wanting to hear that part of her story. Whatever they might have been planning to do to her seemed clear. He needed to change the subject. "Where were you living?" he asked.

"On a large farm just east of the Oklahoma border," she said. "South of here forty or fifty miles, or so. Not exactly sure. Never lived anywhere else. My parents had always worked there, too, and we had a house. Well...a shack, really, but Mama made it nice."

Nate relaxed into the new topic. "What about school? How'd that go?"

"The only school was miles away, real far." She shrugged. "I could go there if I wanted to. Some of our people did, but it was too far, and Mama didn't drive. The law just changed about negroes going to public schools, and nowadays I could go there or anywhere. I think it works that way now." She looked up at him. "You heard about that mess, didn't you? I mean, the fight in Little Rock so we could go anywhere to school."

Nate nodded. "Sure, we knew about that in Minnesota where I live. I asked Grandpa about it, too, being he knows about this state. He said no one should have hate in them like some folks here do." He squeezed both fists tight. "So, how'd you learn anything, then?"

"Mama taught me everything," she said. "To read, write, add, subtract, the Bible, and just everything there is. It was easy. And we went to church a lot. We got rides from neighbors."

"Tell me how they died...if you want to," Nate said, tensing a little and hoping what he learned wouldn't be too painful for either of them. "You don't have to, you know."

"Daddy died in an accident. Some kind of farm machinery hurt him." Lotty stared into the distance with a sad half smile. "I remember him well. He was nice to me and seemed like a giant. Mama had a stroke, they said. She went fast, and I'm glad for that part. Seen a few people get sick and live in pain a long time. You know, screaming and all. She left me real fast." Lotty sat up straight and looked him in the eye. "Nate, whatever I tell you now, I have to be truthful, okay?"

"I suppose so. I mean, sure. I try to be, too, except sometimes when I just can't."

"I'm not sixteen like I told you. I'm fourteen, and that's the truth." She stared at him, as if expecting him to get mad.

He laughed and slapped his thigh, then yelled, "Well, call me dumber than an old flat tire. So, you are about my age, then. I thought so. I'm going to be fourteen soon, in the fall, so close I can see it."

Lotty smiled and shrugged. "There's something about the law, about being sixteen or more. I told you that so you wouldn't try getting me in trouble, cuz sixteen makes me old enough to be on my own. Ain't that right?"

"Sure, I guess. Don't worry, okay?"

Butch wandered down to the tent and snuggled his chin down onto Lotty's crossed ankles. He settled in and sort of whinnied a little the way horses do. Every muscle in his stretched-out body quivered, then relaxed.

"The old timer is down for the count," Nate said, laughing. "You've won him over."

"Dogs are lucky," Lotty said. "They have a simple but sometimes beautiful life. We have struggles, and that's a fact." She glanced from the dog to Nate. "Should I keep talking?"

"I s'pose," he said. "There's really two things I've wondered about. Not just why you ran, but where do you plan to end up? You told me enough about the why part, so what's next?"

"I was okay staying there after Mama passed," she said. "Sometimes, the folks were like grandparents in a way, almost always kind. Well, except Mama told me once the mister had ideas about her. And the boys—the twins, that is —they were rotten. Mean, too, and a little dangerous."

"How so?" Nate swallowed hard and turned his eyes away from her, bracing himself for what he was sure she'd say.

"They tried to have their way with me," she said in a flat voice. "They're older and ready for that kind of thing. Too ready. I think I was some kind of experiment to them, a place to get started. I was able to fight them off that one time and run to the big house. This was when I was still by myself in our house. They don't care about nothing, and to them I'm just nobody."

"I'd have smacked them good with a baseball bat, or took a chain to 'em," Nate said.

Lotty's voice lightened a little. "I believe you would. You're as big as them, too. Bigger, actually." She sighed. "They did get their success with the negro girl on the next farm over. I knew all about that, cuz word gets around. And after, her parents sent her off someplace. Nothing happened to those two. Not nothin'." Her chair creaked as she fidgeted. "The problem, as I see it, is their parents don't have the gumption to straighten them up. They got away with everything. I watched that for years, y'know. Their backtalk and then stealing their parents' money."

Nate fought the rage growing inside him, not wanting Lotty to see it. At the thought of them hurting her, he squeezed the chair arms till his hands turned white, then made them relax.

"The folks moved me up to the big house," she said. "Had a room and a cot in the attic that was right over one of the boys' rooms. I heard them through a grill in the floor, planning to take me the next weekend when their parents—that's the Waldcotts to you—when they were leaving for a trip somewhere. I packed my old bag, put all I could in there, took the hidden money left in Mama's poke, and out the window, I went. Middle of the night, it was."

"Glad you did," he said, then forced a smile. "Things have to get better now, and if I can figure some way or another, they will. I think about that all the time." And he'd remember that name—the Waldcotts. He repeated it over and over in his mind, just in case.

Lotty forced herself to ask what she'd been dreading. "With you leaving, what do I do?"

"Let me study on that a day or two," Nate said. "We have that much time, for sure. I'd like to get you somewhere safe. I'd also like to talk to Grandma about it, but I don't trust Grandpa to keep you a secret. He wouldn't listen to her wishes, either. He almost never does, and I know he'd be razzed something fierce if some of his friends ever knew he'd hid you here."

"I don't have any kin, or any close friends anywhere near here," she said, then snapped her gaze to his. "Except you, that is. I'm praying every day in that barn, all the time." She fiddled with a ribbon on her dress. "Waiting for the Lord's answer is worrisome. It's not supposed to be. I been taught that way, but it is a terror having to wait. Can't seem to help the worrying part."

Nate stared across the hay and cornfields. "I could be better about praying." He shrugged. "We mostly always let the preachers at our church do that sort of thing. I mean, it seems all the other Lutherans we know, and our family, never talked about it much at home."

Lotty folded and unfolded her ribbon. "Nate, why're you so good to me?"

"What? Uh...well, you looked so sad back in that cornfield, and I—"

"Stop," she said, lurching forward in her chair, heart pounding. "Stop talking, right now. I mean it." She clapped her hands and hurried her words to undo the damage she'd done. "The Good Lord set me up to be right here, with you, safe. I just now saw it clear, and I'm being a fool to take the risk of looking outside of His gift. Worrisome, that's exactly what I am right now, but I shouldn't be."

"What do you mean?" he asked, his forehead wrinkled. "I'm not—"

"I said stop, okay?" She gulped in warm air. "I mean, please listen. I'm going to jinx myself, for sure—maybe you, too—with such unfaithful talk." She twisted in her chair to face him full-on. "Do something right now. Just think of something you can picture in your head, something good. Anything. Think of it right now. Something you like a lot works best. I'll wait."

"Um...sure, I guess," he said, frowning. "Am I supposed to tell you?"

She nodded. "So, what's in your picture?"

"An apple pie right out of the oven."

She laughed. "Perfect. Now, concentrate on it. Look close and describe it to me."

"For real? You being serious?"

"Yes, tell me now. Describe it."

"Okay, then." He closed his eyes. "It's got one piece missing, cuz it's on my plate. The bottom crust is soft and looks kinda chewy, and the upper crust is perfect, nice color and a bit crunchy." He opened his eyes and stared into hers. "Is this what you want me to say?"

"It's exactly what you want," she said. "I mean...really, it's what we both want." She tapped her temple. "Keep that perfect picture in your mind, because if you ever get a thought again about what I just said"—she dropped her voice to a whisper—"you know, about doubting Him, you just flip it gone." She flattened her fingers and twisted her wrist like turning a pancake. "Erase it with that picture." She leaned in, holding up one finger. "Never, and I mean *never*, think of what I said, about being unfaithful. You should never think doubts about a person who is good to you, so don't do that to Him. We've come this far, so let's not get jinxed by me showing a lack of faith. I'm sorry I said it."

"Okay, I suppose that should work, huh?" Nate laughed.

Lotty sighed and wiped her damp face. "Please, Nate, I'm not kidding. We're taught to get those bad thoughts from our minds, right away. Take them captive like the preacher always says. It's some kind of sin not to trust the blessings He gives us. So, throw the bad out, and for sure invite the good in."

Nare shrugged. "Makes good sense, but where do you get all this?"

Before Lotty could answer, Butch got up slow and growled deep and long, gave them an over-the-shoulder, pitiful look as if to say, "Sorry I'm so old and worn out," then turned and walked toward the house.

Nate stood and craned his neck, looking toward the driveway. The nose of a car peeked out past the edge of the house, just the grill and headlights visible.

"Lotty, in the tent. Now," Nate hissed. "And stay put. If you hear me leave in a car, just get this chair back to the barn, then tuck into your room and stay there."

"Nate!" a boy's voice yelled as Lotty scampered toward the tent. "You around here somewhere?"

"Hey, Pistol, that you?" Nate shouted. "Coming up there. Just wait a sec."

"'Course it's me," the other boy said. "What do I sound like, a bullfrog? Hey, I've got us another adventure to go on. Just came up kinda sudden, so c'mon, quick."

Lotty ducked under the door flap as Nate yelled, "No way. One adventure with you was dang near one too many."

Safe inside the tent, Lotty flopped onto Nate's sleeping

bag and curled into a ball, trying to make herself invisible among the shadows. She should have let Nate describe more about that pie. The apples, the flavors, all of it. She shivered, despite the heat. The jinx was right here in front of them, standing right up there by that car, just waiting to get them.

"It showed up fast, too," she whispered, then offered a silent prayer. *Protect us, Lord. I'm truly sorry for my careless words. I know I'm taught better, and I'm tryin' not to be so afraid of the world and to trust you more. Please keep Nate safe from that young-dickens friend of his.* She lay frozen, listening to the sound of Nate and Pistol driving away.

Chapter Eight

"Where are we headed?" Nate asked, glancing at Pistol from the corner of his eye.

Pistol just stared straight ahead, driving fast.

Nate clenched his jaw. What was his friend angry about?

They turned onto a neglected side road a mile or so from the farm, then hit a faster speed at which the car's tires didn't chatter as much on the ragged edges of unplowed gravel.

"Looks like Mr. Stony hasn't been here," Nate said. "I guess these side roads don't count during an election year."

"I hate that shaking they do to my car," Pistol said. "I've seen mirrors and hubcaps just go flying off and disappear."

Nate turned toward him and smiled. Finally, he was speaking! "So, what's up?" he asked. "Where we going? I mean, why aren't you—"

"I saw her, man," Pistol said. "And you know exactly who I mean. *Her*."

"Saw who? What're you talking about?"

"C'mon." Pistol's voice dropped to a growl. "The negro girl sitting by your tent. That's who. So, what's the deal?"

Nate gripped the edge of his seat. "You what? Saw what?" He shook his head and forced a laugh. "C'mon, you having a bad dream in the light of day?"

Pistol shot him a glare. "Nice try, but don't be kidding with me. I know what I saw." He took the next turn fast enough to skid the tires. "I looked along the side of the house when I was on the road, drivin' by slow, and there she was, sittin' on that chair. I have a good idea who she is, too. Word's around on her, ya know. It's everywhere. The sheriff's looking too, pal. So, tell me straight, and no lies between us."

Nate turned his whole upper body away and stared out the window. Some kind of flying bug was stuck to the outside of the glass. Just how he was feeling. Stuck.

"You ever think of yourself as a jinx?" Nate asked. "I'm going to have to tell you about her, I suppose, but you best keep this a secret. You ready to swear on it? I'm serious here, cuz you could jinx everything I'm doing. Mess it up bad."

"Swear to what?"

"Keeping this quiet," Nate said, giving him a hard stare. "Not only that, but helping me to get her out of here, too. Maybe north to my city. She's a good person who needs protection. I'm not kidding. I know some things you don't."

"You sure she doesn't have you snookered?" Pistol asked, then pointed at Nate's face. "Maybe she's a rat, or a snake, something dangerous that bites."

"Get your old finger out of my face," Nate said, waving Pistol's hand away. "Listen, she's an orphan, and the rats and snakes are the folks where she lived, and that is a fact. Especially the kids there. Well...and the old man, too. She's as nice as anyone you've ever met and is scared bad. Trust me. I'm telling you all this because she's okay."

"Hmm, all right. I guess I could do it." Pistol smiled and squirmed about on the seat. "You want me to pinky swear it?"

"Yes, I do. So, show me."

Pistol curled his little finger on his right hand, and holding it about chin-high, he said, "I pinky swear I won't tell anyone about her. That is, if you tell me some more on what this deal's all about."

Nate's heart banged against his ribs. What if Pistol told on them? He wanted to trust his friend, but this could hurt Lotty way more that it would hurt him. Her earlier words about faithless beliefs and that apple pie filled his mind, stopping those thoughts before they could get traction. He let out a breath through his teeth. Amazing. It worked just like she said it would. His negative thoughts just flat disappeared. Smiling, he turned toward Pistol. "Okay, I'll tell you."

Pistol nodded and slowed the car a little, then waved for Nate to go on.

"She's in trouble and is hiding here until I can figure out a way to get her somewhere else. No clue where, but you don't ever mess with that, okay?" Nate softened his tone. "Be a buddy."

Had he sounded too harsh? Pistol could wring his neck anytime he chose. Nate had seen him throw a whole bale of hay from standing flat on the ground, up at least fourteen feet and through the barn's open upper doorway and into the loft. He'd made it look easy. Plus, Grandpa had warned Nate never to pick a fight with him.

"What's a pinky swear worth if you don't believe in it?" Pistol said. "We go by it around here, bigtime, you know.

Maybe not so much where you're from, huh? Around here, it's gospel and has powers, and we don't be foolin' with it. Not the cops, our parents, or even the school principal can get a word from us once it's been rightly done. It's carved into our hearts just like the words on a granite tombstone. Cut in there deep, strong, and forever."

"It's worth plenty where I'm from, too," Nate said. "Except, some kids I know don't honor it right. That's the only reason I mention it. I sure go by it, and I'm counting on you for the same, so I do believe you. Besides, terrible things can happen if you break it, so better be careful, or as sure as stink follows dog-doo, you'll get jinxed."

"I know that. Trust me." Pistol raised a closed fist high and bumped it against Nate's. Another of their contracts was now sealed.

Nate told Pistol how he'd found Lotty, then what he'd done to keep her a secret and somewhat well fed. "But I'm leaving in a week or so. We're running out of time."

"Why you doin' this?" Pistol asked.

Before Nate could answer, a train's whistle blared, announcing its speeding entrance through the crossroads in nearby Hartsville. "How much is a train ticket to Minnesota?" he asked.

"Who knows?" Pistol said, tapping the steering wheel. "Twenty bucks, maybe more. I sure don't know. Rode the train once with my parents, all the way down to New Orleans. We had a sleeper car, too. That's gotta be more than a coach seat." Pistol kicked the car door, sat straighter, and whispered, "I'm not sure they'll even let her on the train. I mean, she's a negro, you know."

"We better find out," Nate said as Pistol turned donut-style and headed back the way they'd come. "I've got some money, maybe enough to do it. I'm just not sure what to do.

So, we heading home? Hey, what happened to this adventure thing you talked about?"

"We're on it, dummy, right now," Pistol said. "When'd you get thick headed?"

"Oh, you mean we're figuring on how to help Lotty? You and me, that is?"

"Sort of," Pistol said, spraying more gravel as he shot down the road. "It didn't start that way, but yes, looks like now it's you and me. Tell me more. What's she like? Anything like those other negroes I've met? A little crabby and kinda shabby?"

Nate gritted his teeth. "Don't talk about her like that... not ever."

"Sheesh. Take it easy. I'm just asking." Pistol pulled the car to the side and stopped.

Nate stepped out of the car and said, "Mother nature's calling. Don't be running off on me."

"Maybe my sister could help. Let's take a drive over there."

"Not right now," Nate said. "I need to get back before Grandpa comes home. Can you come over tomorrow or the next day?"

"We'll do it, Sport."

As they drove back toward the farm, Nate squared his shoulders, breathing easier than he had since he'd first found Lotty.

Chapter Nine

The next morning, with Lotty well fed, Nate entered Grandpa's shop. "Whatcha gonna teach me today, Grandpa?" he asked.

"No time for any of that," Grandpa said, laying out tools on his workbench. "We're finishing the last parts and pieces. Have to be extra careful."

Grandpa was always fussy, so that was saying something. "Cuz this part's harder?" Nate asked.

"Nah. Because this is what the people will see."

Nate walked around their project. It was only a sixteen-foot speedboat, built for a friend, but Grandpa, who had been a high school shop teacher, wouldn't allow careless workmanship on anything he set his hands to.

"I know it's not a piano, and it's not a church," Grandpa said, eying Nate over the boat, "but it's ours. Has our names on it, too, so let's get it right. First off, climb inside the boat and get yourself under the bow. Take this block of wood with you. Once you're under there, I'll tell you what to do. My old bones don't bend too well these days, but you can get under there easy."

Nate climbed in, then slid on his back, moving to where his head was close to the front of the hull, the spot where the two curved sides met and formed the sharp point of the bow. His nose was only inches away from the underside of the mahogany deck. "It even smells wonderful inside here," he said.

"Nate, look for the tiny pilot hole I started on the boat's left side," Grandpa said. "That's the boat's left, your right side. Got it yet?"

"Yup, got it. There's a sliver of light coming through it." Nate wiggled around to make his backside more comfortable. The hull's wooden ribs dug into his skin. "Now what?"

"Use your thumb to hold that wood block tight over the hole, and be sure the hole's lined up to about the middle of the block. I'm going to drill down through the mahogany with a bigger bit, and if we miss where your block of wood is, the drill bit will punch through and splinter the wood on your side. Don't want that. Got it? I want the bit to bite into the block instead. That'll stop any splintering."

"Okay," Nate said, pressing hard on the block. "I'm holding it tight over the hole pretty good. Now what?"

"Just stay put, and when I start the drill, hold it tight... real tight, because the bit will push against it and spin it around if you don't."

The electric drill whined to life, then slight pressure pushed at his thumb as the bit cut through the wood deck and started biting into the block. Suddenly, the sharp spinning bit ate all the way through the soft wood block and started cutting into his thumb.

Gritting his teeth against the slow-motion, electric shock sensations thrumming through his hand, Nate didn't dare yell, and he sure wasn't letting go. Damage to the boat and Grandpa's wrath would be way worse than any hole in his thumb. He held tight until the sharp tip of the spinning bit pressed onto the back of his thumbnail, trying to cut through it. "Stop, Grandpa!" he yelled. "It's stuck in my thumb."

The drill stopped instantly, and Nate pulled his thumb straight down and away from the bit. He kept his eyes on the wood block. It stayed put, holding itself tight around the shiny silver and partly bloody bit shaft, which protruded a half-inch or more past the block's face.

Pain shot through his thumb, and he finally glanced at it. "Oh man, look at this. What in the world?"

"You okay?" Grandpa asked.

"Uh...sort of," he said, fighting to keep his voice steady and matter-of-fact. "I'm bleeding pretty good. Should be okay, I guess. The bit went through my thumb, so hand me a towel or something," He reached out his good hand. "I'm bleeding on the wood down here. I'll just keep it over my T-shirt."

"Hold on," Grandpa said, his voice strained as if he was stretching. "Can't let this drill tip over and scar the deck top." He reached around and under the dashboard and dropped a clean shop rag into Nate's outstretched hand.

"Thanks," Nate said, pressing the rag to his thumb. "I'm going to hold the block by the edges with my good hand, so you can reverse the bit and pull it out. Okay?"

"Okay, if you're able to do it. We going to need stitches on you?"

"Nah, it's a small hole," Nate said. "You'll see. A band-aid will do, maybe two of 'em. I've got the block tight, now, with my other hand, so go ahead."

The drill bit backed out easy. Holding the rag around his thumb, Nate shinnied out from under the bow, pushing with his non-injured arm. He sat upright in the open space where the seat would be when they finished. Letting out a long breath, he leaned his back against the dashboard.

"Let's have a look here," Grandpa said, leaning over the side of the boat.

"Hang on." Nate unfolded the rag. "Okay, here it is. See it?"

"Not too bad," Grandpa said, nodding. "No sir. Seen worse. No stitches, either. Sit there, and I'll get us the first aid kit."

Nate grinned, proud he hadn't overreacted. "I don't want that mah-mah-mah-cura-chrome stuff."

Grandpa snorted. "Big baby. You just took a drill bit through your thumb, and you're a scaredy-cat of a little tickle from some medicine?" He shook his head. "Hold that up here. Keep the rag under it, too. This'll hurt me more than you."

Nate huffed. "Everyone says that. It's some kind of joke, you know." The instant Grandpa dropped red liquid onto his thumb, he flinched at the sharp sting. "Ouch! Oh, that smarts." He tried to pull his hand away. "That's enough of that stuff."

"You want to get an infection?" Grandpa asked, grabbing his wrist. "Want to get that thumb chopped off? Lose that one, and you could only hitchhike in one direction. You'd never get anywhere. You'd just travel round in circles."

"Very funny," Nate said. "Okay, fine. No, I don't want to lose anything."

"What's all the shouting about?" Grandma asked, walking into the shop. She looked over the situation and said, "Who's hurt? I could hear you from the clothesline."

"Not to worry," Grandpa said, wrapping a bandage

around Nate's wound. "Nate's got a little cut on his thumb. No big deal, old lady."

"I'm fine, Grandma." Nate climbed out of the boat, glad she couldn't see the real damage. She might scrub it raw till it bled even more, then cover it with stuff from one of her brown bottles. The scary ones with a human skull and crossbones printed on the front.

"I'll bring your dinner down here," Grandma said, moving to the door.

Nate stared after her. How could he get Lotty some if Grandma served lunch in the shop? He'd have to sneak her extra from supper.

Grandma stopped in the doorway. "Nate, did you see that paper flyer we brought back Saturday? The one about that runaway negro girl? I'll go get it." She hurried out toward the back door of the house.

"Why'd she want me to see that?" he asked Grandpa, unable to look him in the eyes.

"She thinks you'll find that girl on your trails," he said, putting away his kit. "You and Pistol, cuz you two drive around a lot. I think she's long gone, though. Probably up north somewhere. Your grandma wants to help her. She's built that way." He shrugged. "I'd just as soon send her packing."

"Watch it, old man." Grandma said from the doorway, giving him a nasty look. She gave them each plates, then pulled a folded paper from her apron pocket. "Here it is, Nate. Read it over."

She held it toward him, but he glanced down at his plate, balanced with his bad hand, and a fork in the other.

"Oh, don't drop your dinner," she said. "I'll just tell you about it." She started reading. "'Fourteen-year-old negro girl has run away from a farm near Center City and could be in our area. She is slender, tall for her age, and would be carrying an old canvas bag. Her name is Lotty Pickle, and her adopted family wants her returned safe. There is a two-hundred-dollar reward. If you see her, call this number or your local sheriff.' There you have it," she said, then eyed Nate. "So, any chance you and Pistol seen her around here?"

"No, ma'am, not us." He looked toward Grandpa, hoping he hadn't noticed the flutter in Nate's voice, and for the flash of a moment, thought of that warm apple pie.

"I hope you don't," Grandpa said. "No good for you to get mixed up in this, anyway. Stick to your own kind of folks. Who knows what she's done? Doesn't say on that paper, but you can bet she's a problem to somebody, and probably runnin' from something she's done."

"Henry," Grandma said, "You shouldn't ever talk that way. You don't know if she's a good girl or not. She may have reason to run, and you know that can happen. You forget about little Sarah Brown?" She rolled the paper into a tube and poked it at Grandpa's nose. "Don't be putting those thoughts in Nate's young head, either. You tell me what the Good Lord would say."

"I'll say whatever I please, Marvella," Grandpa snapped. "The lad needs to learn certain things, too. I'm telling him the truth. They are plenty different from us, and sure, we don't want to hurt anyone, but we do need to protect ourselves. That's my rule, first and foremost. The Lord knows that part, too. He didn't make us a bunch of fools to open the door to trouble."

Grandma turned, walked to the door, then stood there a moment with her back to them. Facing them again, she said, "Nate, your grandpa knows a lot of good things, and mostly will set you straight every time. But on this subject, he's a long ways from the truth. A real long ways." She left the shop.

Nate and Grandpa looked straight at each other.

"Let her go," Grandpa said. "She means well. She's like most ladies around here. Thinks with her heart, not her head." He winked. "You see that girl, you tell me, and we'll shoosh her on back and split that reward."

Nate turned away and set his plate on the workbench. He had to get Lotty out of here, and soon. But how? Maybe Pistol could help. He squished a roll thin and shoved a slice of roast beef inside. The instant Grandpa turned to his own food, Nate coaxed the sandwich into the back pocket of his blue jeans. "I'll be right back, Grandpa."

Chapter Ten

"Nate, you need to listen to me," Pistol said, leaning against his car. "Have you pictured what happens when you get caught hiding her? And maybe worse, how the folks around here are going to give your grandpa the nasty business? And they will...believe me. Plenty of 'em, too. You don't know this place like I do."

"I have no clue where to go from here," Nate said, kicking loose some hardened dirt clumps stuck on the edge of Pistol's tire. "I mean, I'm just trying to help someone who's in trouble. That's how I'm raised. For sure, I'm not trying to hurt anyone, especially my own family."

He stared at Grandma's garden, searching for a way to change the subject. "Everything looks ready to harvest," he said, pointing. "I'm tired of digging up those little potatoes, though. Especially with all these flies hovering around. They bite right through my socks."

"Did you hear me?" Pistol asked, then thumped him on the head. "Hello, anyone home? You best be listening. I know your game."

Nate ducked out of reach. "Sure. I'm thinking. That's all I do."

"About what?"

"Nothing. Well, just potatoes and what to do about her. You got any ideas?" Nate looked quick toward the barn, then smiled at his silliness. Lotty couldn't be listening at this distance.

"One," Pistol said. "Hop in the car. We're going to my half-sister's over in the next county."

They drove some miles on dirt roads Nate hadn't seen before, past tiny, rundown farms. Tired, that's what they looked like. Worn out and shabby. Old, ragged-looking couches and rain-soaked stuffed chairs sat in the front yards, and hound dogs snoozing in the shade of large, drooping trees. Just what Nate had imagined hillbillies' homes were supposed to look like...hungry and poor. Long-time poor. Cartoons he'd seen were close to right.

"Didn't know you had a half-sister," Nate said, keeping his gaze glued to the window.

"Sure do. Suzanne's a good bit older than us, and her husband ran off somewhere a few years back. Maybe that's a good thing. Can't say. It was back when the twin boys were born. Maybe was two too much for him. Get it?" Nate could only offer a weak smile. "I haven't seen her since Christmas, and I'm hoping she may be willing to help you with your problem. She's, uh...well, let's just say this: she's okay in her own way."

"Listen up," Nate said, "I'm not sure I want her or anyone I don't really know to learn about Lotty, especially where she's hiding. How'm I supposed to know we can trust her?"

"You're telling me about your grandpa and what he'll do if he finds her...right? I mean, then she's gone, outta here, *adios*. And he will find her sooner than later, so don't be kiddin' yourself." He gave Nate a serious look while shaking his head. "At least I'm thinking about your next move, even if you're not, so gimme a break. Let's keep ahead of this. You been lucky a long time. Maybe too long." He kicked the side of the fender well and slapped the edge of the steering wheel with his open palm.

"Right," Nate said. "Thanks." All Lotty's talk about fate ran through his mind. Maybe this was supposed to happen. "Okay, let's just drop in and take a look. I'll let you know if I'm okay with doing this. I understand your concerns, honest, but so far, you gotta admit, I'm doing all right."

"True. Okay then, it's a deal," Pistol said, making a sharp turn. "We're here already, so let's see if she's home."

They bumped and jostled into the yard and followed the two parallel dirt tracks tires had dug over time and now served as a homemade driveway. Nate stared at the house, which probably hadn't seen paint in a hundred years. Two naked little boys were throwing water at each other from an old wooden bucket. The blond-haired boy turned and pitched water from a long-handled metal cup, drenching a scrawny cat. It let out a loud, scratchy squeal, then ducked under the sagging front porch.

"She's got four kids and could use some help," Pistol said. "Maybe if she had someone around to look after them, she could get fulltime work somewhere. There's a cannery and a poultry processing place nearby. Maybe she still has that old car."

"I see what you mean by needin' help," Nate said. "Anyway, remember our deal. I'll do the asking, or better yet, I'll clue you in if any asking gets done."

"Don't waste too much time figuring things out," Pistol said, opening his door, "or you'll both end up sorry. You won't be askin' anymore. You'll be kickin' yourself."

A young woman in a thin summer dress came out the side door and ran up to the car. Grinning, she shouted, "Hey, you! My goodness, this is more welcome than ice cubes in lemonade. Getcherseff outta this car but quick. I got hugs for you I been holdin' onto forever."

"You're a sight, too, big sis," Pistol said, climbing out.

Suzanne embraced him. "We're hugging like two old souls finding themselves again in heaven," she said.

"Nate, get over here and meet my sis," Pistol said, releasing her. "She don't bite. Except for her husband, that is."

Suzanne slapped Pistol's shoulder with an open hand and hugged him again. Nate took his time walking around the car, hoping she wouldn't grab onto him the same way.

She did just that. "Any friend of Pistol's be a friend of mine," she said, gripping Nate in a bear hug he couldn't possibly get out of.

The sweat from the back of her dress stuck to Nate's hands, and there was nowhere he could reach to politely rub it off.

"C'mon in, you two," she said, letting go at last. "Plenty hot today, and I've got soda pop and a few ice cubes I hope haven't melted yet. The icebox isn't on anymore. Quit running this morning."

Nate followed her and Pistol inside. The seat of every chair held clothes, empty boxes, or household items that should be stored anywhere else.

Suzanne flicked a few of these items to the floor, placed

the rest on a table, then said, "Sit on down, now. What brings y'all out this way?"

"Nate's getting ready to go back home to Minnesota," Pistol said, perching on a ratty chair. "So, I thought I'd introduce him around a bit, cuz he's always at his grandparents' and hasn't had much chance to meet anyone. Been here all summer, too."

"Sure, I heard about you, Mister Nate," Suzanne said, emptying another chair. "Sylvie, that's Stony's wife, told me. You maybe met them. They're busy bees. She comes around here sometimes with gifts from her church ladies. Kids' clothes and what-not. Was a box of peaches last time. Good to see you, and now I got a face pictured with the name. When you heading home, then?"

He sank onto the sturdiest-looking kitchen chair. "Not sure. A couple weeks. Maybe less."

She tousled his hair with one hand while patting his shoulder with the other.

Nate squirmed, but grinned. She was nice. Real messy, but nice.

"Pistol, will you look at the icebox for me?" she asked. "Everything's going to melt or spoil. Can't afford that."

Pistol walked over to it and opened the door. The light didn't go on, and he quick shut the door, to keep cool air from floating out. He slapped one side down low with his open palm, but nothing happened. "That works sometimes," he said. Looking around the back, he laughed. "Oh my, big sis, I'd charge you repair man money for this if I thought you could spare it. What'd you say if I just plug it back in for ya?"

"C'mon, tell me true," she said, walking toward the icebox. "It's just unplugged? Halleluiah and praise the Lord! But dang those nasty cats." Everyone laughed as

Suzanne clapped her hands over her head while dancing and twirling about in circles. The compressor started to hum.

Remembering their mission, Nate looked around at everything he could see from his kitchen chair. Every inch held layers of clothes, junk, and all kinds of debris. A window shade in the living room hung crooked, attached at the top on only one side. Dishes formed high piles in and around the sink. An image of how neat Lotty kept her humble barn room filled his mind.

One section of a large coffee table in the living room stood out from the overall mess. Two dolls lay in neat, toy-sized cribs. One, a Raggedy Ann, and the other a freckle-faced girl wearing only a doll-sized diaper. Tiny kitchen toys stood next to them in a perfect row—a stove, refrigerator, and wringer washing machine. A stack of neatly folded doll clothes sat across from them. No dust or dirt covered the shine of the tabletop on that side, and a vertical cardboard barrier fastened down with tape separated it from the other end. A few stacked books behind the cardboard, sitting flat on the messy side, kept it propped straight up like a wall.

Nate stared at the table, the only place in the house where someone seemed to care. Who would that be?

Suzanne eyed Nate, then she called out, "Angel, you and Little Sister get in here. Got someone wants to meet you. C'mon, y'all leave those cats alone and bring yourselves 'round here. I mean now, not tomorrow sometime."

Two young girls stepped into the kitchen doorway. Nate guessed they must be about six and seven. They wore only adult-sized T-shirts that had once been white. One hung to the girl's mid-calf, the other almost to the floor.

"Ladies, stand up straight and meet Mister Nate,"

Suzanne said. "He's your Uncle Pistol's friend, and he lives in Alaska."

"Minnesota," Nate said.

"Oh, right, Minnesota. What's the difference?"

"Hi, girls," Nate said, ignoring the joke. "Nice to see you. Whose beautiful dolls are those on the table over there?" He pointed. "And no, Minnesota isn't Alaska, but people think it is because it's got a long cold winter with lots of snow. But we don't have Eskimos, and Santa Clause doesn't live there, either."

"That's mine," the tallest girl said, pointing to the coffee table. "And nobody better touch it, neither. No sir, not nobody ever dares."

"I won't, I promise," Nate said. "What's your name? and the babies' names?"

"Elizabeth and Itty Bitty," she said. "And I'm Angel. They're mine, you know. Just mine and not hers." She pointed at the other girl, who must be Little Sister.

Hanging her head, Little Sister stepped back a bit and turned sideways to Nate, never looking straight at him.

"You two run along, now," Suzanne said. "We have grownup talk to do." She opened two bottles of pop and handed them to the boys.

The girls scampered away fast.

Nate stared in that direction even after they disappeared back to wherever they came from. What did the rest of this place look like? "Pistol, time for me to get back," he said. "It's Wednesday, and we'll be going to Anderson's farm for the midweek party. I have to change into clean clothes, or Grandma will be upset." He paused, hoping he hadn't offended Suzanne.

"You sure you don't have more time?" Pistol said. "You thinking about it?"

Nate snuck a quick look at Suzanne to see if she might have a clue what Pistol was talking about, then scowled at Pistol and said, "Well, yes, I have, but it's time to get going. Nice to meet you and your kids, Suzanne. Thanks for the pop, too."

"Big sis," Pistol said, "Nate's got a question for you. Have you seen that runaway negro girl around here?"

"No, but I heard plenty about her. Why you askin'?"

Nate kicked Pistol's shin under the table.

Pistol frowned. "Oh, never mind. We drive around a bit, but only Nate's seen her."

"Where's that, then?" She looked at Nate and waited.

"Uh...just a ways from our place," he said, thinking fast. "She ducked into an old empty shack one time. Last week. Long gone by now, for sure." Nate rubbed his hands on his pants. Another lie. He did want to stop that, but sometimes...

"I've never seen her," Suzanne said, "but I'm told of a big money reward if you catch her. Keep your eyes open, boys."

As they all walked out to the side yard, Nate stuffed a hand in his jeans pocket. Maybe he should have left a few nickels on her table for the pop. Someone likely wouldn't be having theirs today. Probably Suzanne.

When they reached Pistol's car, Nate glanced back. Angel peeked out from behind a curtain that partly covered a cracked front window, the Raggedy Ann doll cradled in her arm.

"God bless you, little lady," he whispered, looking straight at her and waving. "Take good care."

Suzanne bear-hugged Pistol again. When she finally let go, he and Nate escaped into the car and started back. They both waved out of their windows until out of sight.

Fighting the steering wheel on the roughest stretch of back road, Pistol kept the car steady. "I know it, I do," he said. "She's a train wreck, and that's for sure. But her heart's real good, and she wouldn't hurt a rattlesnake."

"I see that," Nate said, "but you scared me there for a minute. It helps me figure out what to do, though. I want to see Lotty living a really good life. You know, not being somewhere that's not hers, or...uh, a servant and maybe always afraid. I don't know exactly what's possible. Really wish I did. So, anyway, that means getting her up north by us somewhere." Nate tapped his fingers on the dashboard like a drummer, hoping the broken radio would come back on. "Hey, I have this letter in my back pocket to send to Margo, a church lady I know up there. She might have some ideas. I need to get to Hartsville on our way back, so I can get a stamp and send it."

"That's a lot of pasture to cover," Pistol said, turning onto a better road. "Not Hartsville, but I mean up to Minnesota. I'll be thinking on it, too. How it could work out, I mean."

"In spite of your big mouth sometimes," Nate said, grinning, "you're a real pal. Nice not to be alone in this."

Chapter Eleven

Back home from Suzanne's, Nate ran into Grandma in the kitchen.

"Time you get ready," she said. "I want you lookin' good for the Andersons' party."

"Do I have to dress up?" Nate asked, trying to hide a scowl. "Like for church?"

She laughed. "No, no. Shiny, clean, and simple wins over fancy around here."

Nate blew out a breath, nodded, and hurried to change into his new blue jeans and a fresh white T-shirt. Then, he slipped back into the kitchen to see what he could sneak out to Lotty.

Grandpa sat in the living room, watching T.V. as usual, and the sound of running water in the bathroom told Nate where Grandma was. Safe enough. He put an apple, a white powdered cake donut, and half a summer sausage sandwich in a paper bag, then walked down the hill to his tent, grinning. She'd like that donut.

He stuffed the bag into the knapsack he'd told Lotty he would leave for her, since he wouldn't be home for supper.

After tying its drawstring closed, he hung it from a strap in the center of the tent's roof, high enough off the ground to be out of reach for Butch.

The moment he returned to the house, Grandma said, "Nate, you look almost as good as Lavonn Dollar, when he owned that clothing store up to Springdale, I mean. If he's not there tonight, likely you'll be the handsomest and shiniest-looking of all. That new T-shirt's as white as angel feathers, so try keep it nice."

"Glad you're happy, Grandma," he said, his face heating. "So, how come the Andersons do this every week? I mean, it's got to cost them a pretty penny and be lots of extra work."

Grandma paused in the middle of filling a basket with food to bring. "Did your mama and daddy tell you about the Great Depression of the thirties?" Before he could answer, she said, "Like all of us our age, the Andersons grew up in those times. Didn't they talk to you about it?"

"Some. Dad doesn't talk much, but Mom did a little. She told us once about how important it was to everyone to keep all their teeth, and how sometimes, if they were lucky, they could go see a Saturday matinee movie for a dime."

Grandma nodded and placed some fresh rolls into the basket. "The Andersons were hit harder than most. Stanley, the youngest, died from havin' no doctor around and no medicine. And even if there was one, it was harder to get one to come way out there. Mickey, that's our Mr. Anderson you know today..." She held up a finger. "And don't you dare call him that. Over time, he helped dig three graves on their old farmstead, the small place they had before this big farm today. Back then, you could do your own buryin' if you had the room for it. Not anymore. Country people called it 'the family plot.'"

"Three graves?" Nate asked, leaning against the counter.

"The first was his sister," Grandma said. "Only about age four or so, then his brother, Stanley, of course, and last his own mama. Then, the darned banker tried taking their place away." She rubbed her hands together in front of her face, shook her head, and let out a groan from her throat, quiet but deep.

Nate gave her a startled look. "You say *tried*. Did he get it? The banker, I mean. Did he take it away?" Nate stepped back as an angry expression crossed her face again.

"No sir," she said, plunking plates into the basket harder than necessary, "and let's not talk about that, neither. Things happened in those days that are best left forgotten. Why that banker backed off is one of those forgotten facts, so never mention it to anyone." She eyed him with both hands clutching the edges of the basket. "I shouldn't have brought it up. You just forget it, now. I'm not kidding." She closed her fist, then punched at the air while staring a long distance away through the window.

Nate smiled at the twinkle in her eyes and relaxed a bit. "Did Mr. Anderson shoot him or something?"

"Shoot him? Ha! No chance. Bullets were expensive."

"Then, what?" Nate asked, resisting the urge to laugh at the fire in Grandma's eyes. She was like a dog growling but wagging its tail at the same time.

"Let's just say, Mickey and his papa had enough strong rope to tie around that banker's ankles and drop him head-first down a dried out old well.," she said. "Way, way down there, real far he went till it's terrible dark. It's been told, they tied off that rope and left him down there a good long while before hauling him up again. I wasn't there, you see, but it's a known fact just the same, and the Andersons aren't folks to spin tales. Now, let's get ready to go. You get your grandpa away from that dang T.V. set of his."

"Yahoo!" Nate yelled, picturing the scene around the well. "Old Mr. Anderson," he shouted, "what a guy!"

"Pipe down, now," Grandma whispered and motioned Nate to come closer. "The way I heard it, every now and then, Mickey would tug on that rope real hard, cuz he liked to hear the banker's screams echo off the stone walls. Tug the rope up a little, let it drop, hear the screams. A beautiful thing, yes sir." She grabbed a spatula from the drainboard. "Okay, enough, young man, and I'm still not fooling. Just forget that and never bring it up around here again. Not to anyone. It's your secret now, too, so respect keeping it private." She thrust her spatula toward Nate's chest like a sword.

"Careful with that, Grandma!" he said, stepping back. "And thanks, that's a great story, but it doesn't answer my question. Why do they do this party thing so much?"

"They're celebrating how these days are better, boy. And all of us who remember the old times appreciate it, too. The Andersons, all of 'em, they've done real well for themselves and are happy to share it." She dropped the spatula into her basket. "Okay, time to go, so get your grandpa out that darn chair."

Inside the barn, Lotty smirked, imagining Nate's face as his grandma yelled at him to slow down and not drop the food basket. The car doors slammed, their voices carried across the yard, then the car started and crunched onto the gravel road.

Yes! She had the place to herself, as Nate had promised.

After waiting several minutes to make sure it was safe to leave the barn, she scurried into the tent and checked to see what Nate left her in the knapsack. "A powdered sugar donut," she said, grinning. "Oh, lovely. nice, nice!"

Carrying the food bag, she prowled up the hill to the house, catlike, scanning every direction. When she entered the kitchen, she looked in every corner. Through a side window, a shadow moved, and she ducked behind a wall. She peeked through the gap in the side of the curtain. A car had stopped next to the house, in the spot where Nate's grandma usually parked.

Her heart hammered in her chest. They'd come back. She had to get out the front door, and quick. Staying low and scurrying toward the living room, she almost tripped as two voices she didn't recognize approached the house. It wasn't Nate and his grandparents. She froze and held her breath.

"Let's go in the shop," a man's voice said, growing fainter as he was walking away from the house. "Henry says it's almost finished. I want to have a look. Been waitin' all summer."

"Hold your horses," the other man said, coming closer. "Let's see who's home first. His truck's here."

That had to be the owner of the new boat. Lotty peeked out the living room window, then a knock at the back door made her jump.

"Henry?" the second man called. "You home? Anyone here? I see your truck's out here."

Lotty sidled to the front door and wrapped one shaking hand around the handle, then tried to hold it still by pressing down on it with the other. Holding her breath, she waited.

Again, the men's voices grew quieter as they walked

away. Letting out a breath, she craned her neck to peek through the sheer curtain in the kitchen window. Two grown men entered the workshop. They wouldn't see her from their angle, so she crept through the front door, then ran deep into the cornfield. She had to get in there so far no one could see her. She rushed between the stalks until she couldn't see the house.

Her heart beat so hard, they could probably hear it all the way in that shop. Sitting between the rows, she tried to catch her breath, then prayed in a soft whisper, "Lord, protect me." She snapped her head up. "Oh my, I left that dinner bag somewhere in the house!"

Chapter Twelve

Nate sat straight, bouncing on Grandma's back seat. He stuck his head out through the open window, looking for any sign of Pistol. Smoke from the Andersons' barbecue grills floated above the treetops. Pulling into the long driveway that led into the yard, his grandpa looked around for a parking spot. Dozens of cars sat side by side, stretching the long distance from the road to the house, with a few others parked on the lawns to either side of the driveway.

"Half the county is here," Grandma said. "This time, let's park somewhere that we'll be able to get unparked from before midnight. Remember last time?"

Grandpa nodded and laughed.

"Free barbecue and perfect summer evening weather," Grandpa said. "Can't beat this."

Nate scanned the cars again for Pistol's old Chevy. "He's here," he said, smiling. "How big is this place?" he asked as they all climbed out.

"Largest in the county," Grandpa said, grabbing the basket from the back seat. "Twenty-six hundred and twenty acres, with a bunkhouse that's the summer home to at least ten hired men." He shut the door and handed the basket to Grandma. "Anderson hired a professional company to put in that volleyball court in the side yard. Made it from some fancy clay base that's extra firm, and covered it with short, special grass he keeps trimmed like a fancy golf course."

"It sure looks perfect," Nate said, following his grandparents to the nearby manicured lawn. Beautiful as a putting green, for sure, dotted with picnic tables under colorful canvas awnings. Lights on tall poles would illuminate everything after sundown. Early arrivals had already claimed their spots for the evening at many of the tables.

Grandma carried her basket over to one of the last empty tables and spread out a fancy cloth. She placed heavy plates on the ends to secure it from the breeze. Stony and Sylvie arrived and began setting up across from Grandma.

"Great timing, Sylvie," Grandma said. "Glad you're filling out this table with us. Last time, we had to listen to the Bellton widows chatter all night about their good ole days a million years ago. Not to mention everything wrong with them. Too much for me, I can tell you."

"Sure smells good. It's chicken, this time," Sylvie said as smoke drifted over all the tables from three hot and busy barbecue grills.

Folks everywhere were laughing and talking. Just like at Nate's family parties, all the men gathered tight in their little groups, the ladies together in theirs. He grinned. And here he'd thought that was only an up-north, back home, Norwegian thing.

Some of the younger crowd drifted over to the small barn where the horses were kept. Nate decided to join them after supper. Two young girls bounced a volleyball off the hard court like a basketball, waiting for others to take their hint and join in.

"Nate," Grandma called. "Over here, now. Food's ready in two minutes."

Nate turned his back to her, wishing she wouldn't yell his name so loud. He looked around to see if anyone from his age group might be thinking she was bossing him. Since nobody stared at him, he walked to their table and found a large display of steaming chicken sitting proud on folded, brown, grease-stained paper bags.

"Sit here next to me," his grandma said, pointing to the plate she had fixed for him.

Since Stony sat directly across, Nate took the seat before Grandpa could arrive and rearrange the placing. "Stony, hey, remember me?" Nate said.

"Sure do, kid. We had a good ride into town that day. How's your summer going?"

"Uh, good. Learning a lot of things. I'm driving the tractor, the truck a little, and shooting the twenty-two rifle. How's things with you?"

"Just fine. Except there's one thing I don't know the answer to, but I think you do."

All but bouncing on his bench at the prospect of Stony asking him a question, Nate leaned closer across the table. "What is it?"

"That time I picked you up, there was something I saw in the cornfield, and I have to wonder...did you see that same thing?"

Nate sat back and stared at his plate, wishing Stony wouldn't talk so loud. Turning his head just a bit, he glanced at Grandma, who was deep in conversation with Sylvie. He relaxed a little. She hadn't picked up on anything Stony was saying.

"Nate, you hear me, son?" Stony asked.

"Uh...yes, I do. Only, not sure I follow you." Nate looked at Grandma again to be sure she was still occupied. When he turned back, Stony was glancing at Grandma, too.

Lowering his voice, Stony said, "After I picked you up, you were looking backwards a lot, back where you'd been before. I can see fine from up in that cab, and that's the area I'd swear I saw someone hiding in that cornfield. You do get my drift, now, don't you, boy?"

Nate's stomach tightened, and he didn't trust his voice enough to speak. He looked again at his plate and set down his chicken leg.

"Nate, relax," Stony said. "I think I know what happened, and maybe who found her." He pointed with his fork. "Maybe, that is, and you don't have to speak up if you don't want to. Just be careful around here, because some don't feel the same way as the folks from up north might." He tilted his head. "That's how I hear it, anyways. Two different worlds, especially in these times of desegregation and all. So, be smart and be careful. If you need to be, that is."

Nate picked up the leg again and took a big bite. Stony couldn't expect him to talk if he was chewing, after all.

"Our secret, kid," Stony said, winking. "Finish your supper and go have fun. Not to worry, either. Trust me on this, okay?"

Nate nodded, offering him a weak smile, certain Stony knew everything.

"Nate, over here," Pistol yelled, just in time. "Let's take a ride. Meet me at the horse barn."

Stony winked again and said, "Go, and don't worry."

Nate swung his legs over the bench and stood. These were amazing people, but now another one knew about

Lotty. *Can't keep nothin' secret,* he thought as he left the table.

"Have fun," Grandma called after him, "and be careful of that clean shirt."

Nate glanced down. How was that supposed to work? Still wanting more chicken, he hurried away before anything else could surprise him.

At least the early night air was sweet...and cool, finally. Should be dark in another hour. He took a deep whiff of the moist, clean breeze, wishing they had big parties like this back home, and that he could sneak some chicken back for Lotty.

Grandpa and Mr. Anderson were walking toward the horse barn on an angle that mirrored Nate's path. They all got to the barn's open door at the same time.

"Nate," Grandpa said, "c'mon over here and say hi to Mr. Anderson. You've met him once before, I believe, over at Y.T.'s store."

"Mr. Anderson, yes sir, hi there." Nate shook his hand, which was like sandpaper glued to the edges of a metal bench vise. How did a man get so strong?

"You having a good summer, lad?" their host asked.

"For sure. Should be heading home sometime soon."

"You ride horses up there, do you?"

Nate shrugged. "I have. Not here, but home I have...a few times." He peered through the doors into the dark barn, hoping Mr. Anderson wouldn't put him on one of those Tennessee horses like his. Ones that stood a mile taller than he was. He'd heard talk about Anderson's champions.

"See these kids over there with Pistol?" Mr. Anderson asked. "Any one of 'em can ride better'n that Roy Rogers or some Hop-along Cassidy actor. Thinkin' we'll send you along with them tonight. Got a horse is just right, and she's about your size, too. You okay with that idea?"

"Uh, sure. I'll, uh, I'll do my best." Nate glanced toward the other kids. Three riders besides Pistol. So, five when Nate joined. He grinned. This would be great.

Grandpa patted Nate's back, then they all entered the barn.

"Dusty," Mr. Anderson said, "get Midnight saddled for young Nate, here. He's been riding at home and wants to join y'all on your moonlight ride."

"She's saddled already, sir."

"Good, good. Bring her 'round this way, then. We'll size 'em up."

Dusty escorted a somewhat heavy-looking horse over to Nate. She was so short, he could look her eye to eye. "Should be okay," he said. She had a nice gray beard and had to be old, maybe kind of slow, too.

Once they got all five horses out of the barn, everyone mounted up, including Nate. Midnight had her own mind and turned about in circles.

Nate pulled back on the reins and said, "Settle down, girl," and "Whoa," several times.

"Too quiet, Nate," Grandpa shouted. "Better to let her know who's boss."

Mr. Anderson grabbed Midnight's bridle under her chin with both hands and stood firm, face-to-face with her, until she stopped fussing. He stared into her eyes, telling her something Nate couldn't make out, then she settled down and stood still.

"How's he do that?" Nate said as the man walked away. He'd heard stories about Anderson riding his champion without a bit or reins. He only had to talk to the horse.

The other riders moved together in a line across the

yard, then turned onto the road. Nate, now moving straight, tried to catch up.

"This should be interesting, Henry," Mr. Anderson said. Both men laughed and walked toward the tables. Grandpa gave Nate a quick glance over his shoulder, and Nate waved.

The other four riders turned left at the gravel road and broke into a trot as if of a single mind. Midnight refused to turn at first, but with enough shouting and rein-tugging, Nate finally got her going.

"They're way up ahead of us," he said, then yelled, "Let's go, Midnight!" while digging his heels into her sides.

She just strolled along, refusing to trot. Nate yelled and kicked, but the road dust from the pack ahead had settled before he could catch up, and they were no longer in sight.

"C'mon, girl, let's go." Again, he kicked his heels into her sides.

She took off so fast, his body snapped back from the waist up and bent so far backwards, he almost tipped over.

"Whoa, now. Whoa!" Nate yelled. Midnight had carried him far enough that he couldn't see the farm lights, and the others were still way ahead, but he could faintly hear them now.

Midnight slowed and stopped. She whinnied, then turned fully around and began walking back the way they'd came.

"Stop it, you dumb horse. C'mon!" Nate yelled. He pulled on the reins, but Midnight only gained speed, heading back toward the farm. "You want the barn, you old nag?" he grumbled. "C'mon, now."

Midnight picked up speed, and Nate yelled his loudest. The bright farm lights came into view, along with the long string of cars in the driveway. At this speed, how would they make a tight enough turn into the yard?

"Hope this beast can slow down quick," he called out. There was little room between the last row of cars and the edge of a fence. Even a horse just walking would find it a squeeze getting through such a small space. "Whoa!" he shouted. "We're gonna smack into one of those cars." Squeezing his legs as tight as he could to keep from getting thrown off, he yelled, "Okay, horse, I give up. Do whatever you want." Pulling the reigns one last time did nothing helpful.

Nate shook his head and held on tight to the saddle horn. What else could he do? Her stubborn power was stronger than his beginner's skills. The distant party sounds mixed with the horse's heavy breathing and hooves pounding the gravel in fast repetition, telling Nate he had no hope. Brisk winds streamed past his face. Giving in to the bouncing up and down on the leather saddle, he let the useless reins hang limp. This was like skiing on glare ice, nothing he could do to stop. He could just drop the reins, and it would make no difference.

Midnight slowed only a little when they reached the turn at the end of the driveway. The overhead lights glinted off the parked cars. Nate fixed his eyes on them, and... *smack*. He slammed sideways into a four-door sedan's flank, denting its door and smashing his left leg.

Thinking it had broken, Nate yelled, "Dang it, horse! That hurts!"

Midnight turned toward the barn, picking up a little more speed. A few people around the tables stared as they passed. When they reached the barn, the horse finally decided to stop.

"Look-it this, Henry," Mr. Anderson said as he and Grandpa neared the barn.

"Better see how bad off he is," Grandpa said, walking toward Nate. "Can't send him home with anything broken." Both men chuckled.

"City kids," Anderson said.

After making sure Nate wasn't too hurt, Grandpa helped him over to the edge of the volleyball court, where he sat alone on a lounge chair. The yard light gave him a clear view of the players. He hoped everyone would leave him alone. What would Pistol and the rest think if he was gone when they returned?

Chapter Thirteen

"I was hoping to have some fun tonight, and this isn't it," Nate said, watching the volleyball game from his lounge chair. Should be the stupid horse who got hurt, not him. He squinted at the players. What an odd numbering. Three on one side, two on the other. Too bad he couldn't play. That would even things up. He leaned forward, trying to adjust the chair's back to a more vertical position. "Ah, ouch!" He moaned. This wouldn't work.

"Need some help?" a dark-haired kid asked.

"Sure, thanks," Nate said, turning to him. How had he not met this boy before? "Hurt my leg pretty good and want to raise this chair so I'm not laying back so far. Got this yard light right in my eyes, too."

"Okay, can you sit up a little more?" the boy asked, reaching for something near the seat of the chair. "Then, I'll flip this metal thingy and make the back come up to meet yours. Ready?"

"Go for it."

The boy's plan worked, and Nate eased back into a more comfortable position.

"Nice," he said. "Much better, for sure. Thanks. I'm Nate. Sit down a bit, if you can."

"Yeah, you're the guy from Minnesota." The boy grinned, pulled a lawn chair over, and sat next to Nate. "I'm Wally Anderson, one of the grandkids around here." He held out his hand. "How's your leg?"

Nate shook his hand, sitting as straight as he could. "Did you see it? Crashed into a car while riding a dang horse. Hurts like crazy, too."

"Didn't see you, but sure did hear it." Wally smirked. "That's my sister's car. Old piece of junk, really. That door was maybe the last piece of metal she hadn't put dents in." He gave Nate's arm a gentle punch. "By the way, she don't care about it. Told me so."

Nate relaxed against his chair. "Good to know. I did wonder if there was more trouble coming. I'll say I hope the horse is okay, too...but you don't have to believe it."

Wally chuckled. "Stubborn old nag, she is. Did you know that car is an important history car?"

Nate turned to face him, moaning as little as he could manage. "Ah...ouch. Sorry. A history car? What's that mean?"

"You've heard about that runaway negro girl, haven't you? My sis met her about fifteen miles south of here, down in Harris. They were both at a vegetable stand down there and got to talking while waiting in line."

Nate swallowed hard and tried to keep his face blank. He must not give anything away.

"My big sis offered her a ride," Wally said. "That's just like her, and if I figured this right, she dropped her off within a turtle's crawl of your grandpa's house. Real close. She described it to me." He leaned back and looked straight at Nate. "So...you seen her yet?"

"Um, no...not really. We're indoors a lot lately. Heard about her, though." Nate took a deep breath and looked anywhere but at Wally. The overhead lights glared more than ever, and he shaded his eyes with his palm. He was tired of lying all the time, but what else could he do?

"She's probably long gone by now," Wally said. "Nobody's seen her north of here, though, and that's what makes me think she's maybe still around somewhere. Sure can't be walking and bummin' rides and nobody doesn't see yah. Especially a colored gal."

Nate made himself nod and said all in a rush, "Me and Grandpa are building a boat, so we're in the shop a lot. Noisy in there, too. Wouldn't see an elephant if it walked by, and don't hear a thing."

"My Uncle's boat," Wally said. "Heard about that deal. Where's he gonna use it?"

Nate laughed. "You sound just like Y.T. He says the same thing, that there's only two lakes around here and they're both a good long drive."

"Y.T.'s my dad," Wally said. "Anyway, my uncle will figure out someplace to take it. My grandpa says he's nuts-o, too. But he says that about anything that ain't to do with horses. That's all he cares about."

Two more boys Nate hadn't met came over and greeted him and Wally. One flicked a shiny chicken bone into the taller grass.

"Get some chairs," Wally said.

They did, and all three sat on Nate's left.

Nate leaned back and let them talk while he watched flashes of the volleyball game. The night air and occasional breeze across his face lulled him. Sleeping right there could be a fine idea. Then, part of their conversation snapped him back to full attention. "What did you say?" he asked one of the boys. "Would you repeat that?"

"I said that if me and Walker caught her, we'd drag her off into the woods like we done to that other one, cuz that's all she's good for. You know what I'm sayin', don't ya?"

"That's what I thought," Nate said through gritted teeth. "Don't you know better than to treat girls like that?"

"She's no girl, and what're you gonna do about it?"

Nate sat straighter, and with narrowed eyes, looked them both over, wishing he could get out of that chair and give them some trouble.

"Hey, Nate, over here!" Pistol called from across the yard. "What'd you do to that horse?" Pistol and his friend Sam laughed until they doubled over.

"Hey back," Nate said. "I'm okay...I guess. Thanks for askin'. Just smashed in a car door, so my leg's a little sore."

"Looks like you can't pick a horse any better than your company," Pistol said, walking over. "You been ridin' a bum horse, and now it's even worse. Visiting with these two mountain monkeys. They giving you any trouble?"

Both boys stood, then looked at each other and, without a word, walked away toward the parked cars.

Nate smirked as he and Wally turned toward Pistol. Few kids around there would cross Pistol, and with his pal Sam nearby, none would dare start anything. "No trouble," he said. "Just their talk is nasty, that's all. Maybe they don't know any better. They're gone now, anyway. You and that funny-lookin' shirt you got on scared 'em off."

"They're rotten, and for sure they've never known any better. They'd sleep in a hog pen, 'cept the hogs would run 'em out." Pistol looked straight at Wally. "Wonder why Anderson even lets them on his property. Maybe he hasn't seen them yet."

"He'd run 'em off quick if he did see 'em," Wally said, "but he's too busy in the barn tonight."

Sam offered Nate his hand. Groaning, Nate extended his and shook it. If Sam was Pistol's friend, he'd best show him respect.

Pistol turned to Nate. "We heard your grandpa and Mr. Anderson in the barn, laughing about putting you on Midnight. I should have told ya myself. They get everyone with that old trick. She's short and old but ornery." He sank into one of the vacated chairs. "If you could have controlled her, you'da been the first to do it. She just loves the barn and only wants to be in there feedin' her face." He leaned his elbows on his knees. "They said you were a good sport about it all, and next time they'd be giving you a better horse. We'll have a swell time then."

"My, oh my," Nate said. "This night's been an eye-opener for me. Thought I was just going to a party."

Answering grandma's wave while walking toward their car, Nate wished he could have snatched some chicken for Lotty. Maybe next week.

Chapter Fourteen

On the way home from the Andersons', Nate sat with his throbbing leg stretched across the back seat of grandma's car. Grandma's driving could be unpredictable, so he kept his back upright, leaning against the door, and his right foot planted firm on the floor for balance. If only he could be riding with Pistol, who always kept his car riding smooth on these gravel roads.

Grandma divided her focus between her erratic driving and telling Grandpa all the new gossip she'd heard at the party. With each colorful bit she shared, Grandpa turned his head back toward the window and let out a strained but clear "Humph."

Nate hid a smirk. How many times had Grandpa said he didn't care to hear any gossip? Even the sign hanging in the workshop made that clear. It read, "Small people talk about people. Average people talk about things. Big people talk about ideas." When shop dust clouded that sign over the summer, Grandpa had given Nate the job of using a clean, dry paintbrush to whisk it back to a proud state of shiny. When standing back after the cleaning, Nate had appreciated the shine a little, but the saying a lot. He'd remember that one.

Glancing between his grandparents, Nate wrinkled his forehead. Their relationship was strange. They treated each other in a more coarse way than his parents did.

Grandpa had once explained this about Grandma. "Boy, the collar doesn't hurt so much if you don't pull too hard on the leash," he'd said.

As the car rolled side-to-side on the gravel roads, Nate tuned out their one-sided conversation and began wishing he was a year or two older and a lot stronger, so he could teach those two mountain boys a lesson.

He knew about the 'Law of Love' from his minister back home, and his mother's and grandmother's teachings, too. That knowledge felt right. He'd become a believer, and the beauty he'd discovered in the law's promise was real. Some people, however, could only change their ways if they received a heavy shellacking. Those two deserved that treatment, in his opinion, and he sure would volunteer to smarten them up, but he lacked enough strength at this point. A time would come, though, when he could right some wrongs. His visions of Lotty's tears hadn't yet disappeared.

"Grandma, what's wrong with so many folks around here?" he asked.

She kept talking to Grandpa, as if she hadn't heard him. Nate let his question go for now.

When they reached home, Nate heaved himself from the comforts of the car's flat seat and said, "I'm going down to the tent. I'll be okay. In fact, I'm feeling much better already."

"You can use the living room couch," Grandma offered. "No hills or stairs to climb."

"No thanks," he said, hobbling a few steps from the car. "I'll make it down the hill easy, and by tomorrow morning, should be okay to get back up here. Butch'll be looking for me, too. Goodnight, you two. The food was great. The horse...not so much."

Grandpa made a silent beeline into the house, probably to look for the late news on his T.V. set. Grandma gave Nate a gentle hug before going inside. As Nate eased his way toward the tent, he glanced back. Grandma watched his every cautious downhill step from her kitchen window.

When he made it to the tent, Butch greeted him. Nate's whole body sagged. By himself, at last. He slipped inside, checked the knapsack, and smiled. Lotty had taken her supper.

He wanted to tell her about the boys he'd met tonight, and explain that he now understood better what she'd been telling him about some people's potential treatment of her and others like her. Since there was no way he could climb the stairs in the barn, he lay atop his sleeping bag on the tent floor with his leg stretched out and soon drifted off to sleep.

From the second floor of the barn, Lotty looked out through her knothole. It gave a vantage of most of the back of the house and yard, but why hadn't anyone turned on the yard light over by the shop? The house was dark, too. Should be okay to sneak over to the tent.

Moving gently on the creaky stairs, she crept down to the solid floor in the dark and left the barn. The night air was a relief after the stuffy, heavy daytime heat still hovering in the barn. She still enjoyed the sweet smell of the fresh hay, but with each day, its aroma became a little less powerful.

Crouched low, she slunk the few short steps to the tent. She'd heard Nate greet Butch a short time ago, so they both should be in there.

"Nate, you here?" she whispered, loud as she dared. "You up? Nate...wake up, it's me. Hello?" She untied the bottom door flap strings and slipped in. "Hi, Butch old fella." She scratched Butch's neck and hugged him hard.

The dog might be too old and tired to pull away from her grip, but he did try. Nate lay asleep on top of his sleeping bag, his left leg straight out.

"Wake up, Nate," Lotty said. "C'mon, I gotta talk to you."

He started to turn over but only groaned, then lay back flat and still. When Lotty pushed against the round curve of his shoulder, he said, "Why aren't you stopping, you stupid horse?"

She stared at him, raising a brow. "It's me, Lotty, and I ain't no horse. Get up. I need to talk. Something happened."

"What time is it?" he asked. "What's going on? Are we working today?" He opened his eyes, yawned deep, and turned toward her.

"Goodness gracious," Lotty said. "You're awake now. Sit up. C'mon, I—"

"Oh, ow...this hurts," he said, propping onto one elbow. "I think I broke my leg."

She jerked back. "You what? You kidding me?"

Nate turned partway toward her and said, "Two guys at Anderson's party were talking about what they'd do to you if they found you, so I whupped up on 'em good and got my leg broken in the process. Shoulda seen me teaching the both of them." He smiled wide but didn't look her in the eyes.

Lotty shook her head and gave his shoulder a push. "If it's broken, why ain't it in a cast or something? I don't believe you at all, mister. Not a word."

"Smart girl," Nate said. "And no, it's not broken, but it is bruised plenty and hurts like fire. Worse, even. Hurts like a dozen starving wolves chewing on it. So...that part's for real." His playful smile convinced her he told something closer to the truth.

"Wolves?" she said. "Oh, please, stop with that kinda talk. So, what really happened?"

"This crazy old horse I was riding smashed us both into the side of a parked car. Of course, the stupid horse is okay, but my leg hurts plenty. Thought at first it was broken." Nate slumped back again onto the bag and sighed. "Think I'll just lay back like this for a bit. Doesn't hurt so much stretched out."

"What about those boys you said would hurt me? Any truth to that?"

"Yes," he said in a growl. "Two guys I'd never seen before. Pistol says they're mountain boys, I think. Where I'm from, we call 'em hillbillies. Anyways, there was talk about the runaway negro girl, and they said how they'd hurt you if they caught you, and turn you in for the money, too. Something like that." Nate shrugged, looking away. "Well... they said more than just hurting you. Oh...ouch." He closed his eyes and lay silent, his lips tightened around his mouth, making deep lines in his skin over his teeth, which bit hard against themselves.

"I don't think it was them," Lotty said.

"Them who? What do you mean?" Nate groaned again and tried to sit up. "Oh...blast it...this pain."

"You're pitiful, mister. Sorry to see it," she said. "So... after y'all drove off, I went up to the house. Two men drove in and knocked on both doors, back and side. Scared me plenty. I was inside, in the hall where they couldn't see me even if they did look in. They wanted to see the boat—I heard 'em say that—so, they went to the shop and were in there quite a long while."

Nate lifted his head, biting down on his teeth. "Not good. What'd you do? Did they see you?"

"No, cuz I sneaked out the front door and ran into the cornfield. I hid there, really deep in, too, plenty far. Couldn't nobody see me. I couldn't see the house, neither, so I figure if I couldn't see out, could nobody see in. That's a fact."

"Woulda been Freddy and a buddy, I'll bet," Nate said. "He's the guy we're building it for. He's an Anderson, too. Funny he wasn't at the party. For sure, they'd capture you if they saw you. No worries now, I'd think. They just wanted to see the boat. Otherwise, *zap*, you'd be gone."

"It scared me bad," she said, wrapping her arms around her middle. "So, I'm thinking about takin' off again. I'm feeling my luck's going to run out if I stay here much longer. It has too. Do you understand how that works?" She couldn't wait for an answer. "I'm thinkin' about getting up to the next state. Too many people comin' and goin' around here. I gotta go soon, too. I just know it. I'm thinkin' tomorrow."

"Easy, girl," Nate said, resting a hand on her arm for an instant. "We need a plan first. You can't be duckin' in and out of cornfields and counting on rides from decent folks, either. There's a lot of them, but plenty of the other sort, too. You're still safer right here until we work up a plan to escape you to somewhere good."

"Like what plan? You have any ideas?"

"One," he said. "And by the way, what're you talking like that for? Best be thinkin' about that pie or something good. That's what you tell me, you know. Bad things you say can come true."

She nodded. "I still think I need to change my place, though. Soon. Sorry to say that, but this time, it's the right thing. I mean, it's the message I'm getting, now, and real strong, too."

"I'm waiting for a letter," he said. "Could be here tomorrow, or today even. I mean, it's after midnight already, I'd bet."

"What kind of letter?" She folded her hands like when she prayed.

"From my church lady friend back home in Minnesota," he said, grinning. "I wrote her about you and asked could she help any."

"You told her about me?" Lotty yelled, bounding to her feet.

"Quiet down, for cryin' out loud," Nate hissed. "You're going to get us both caught. And yes, I told her everything and asked would she have ideas to help us. What else should I do? Have a little trust, here. And yes, I do know you can't live in the barn much longer, and of course I understand about luck. It's great when it's with you, and dangerous when it runs out. Right?"

Lotty just stared at him, then sat again.

Nate looked into her eyes. "I'm leaving soon, too. I gotta ask someone for help. I trust her, and you should, too. She'd never tell." He propped back up on his elbow, groaned, and gave Lotty a serious look. "Sometimes, you have to trust somebody. You're not alone in this world."

"You sound like my mama." Lotty rested her elbows on

her knees and braced her hands under her chin. Tears formed then rolled down both cheeks. She turned away from Nate, shaking.

"C'mon, Lotty," he said in a consoling voice. "Stop that, will you? We've come this far. Just a little longer, and we'll have you somewhere safe. I already tried to find a safe place close by for you." He paused, then asked, "Should I tell you about it?"

She sniffled. "Where?"

"Pistol's sister's place. Coulda been okay. I'd hoped it would be, but after checking it out, I didn't think it was even as good as right here. Kinda risky, maybe more than that."

Lotty wiped away the tears and dried her fingers on her sleeves. "So, now she also knows where I am. Well...does she?"

"No, no she doesn't. She just thought we were having a visit, and watch what you're thinking, cuz I don't deserve it."

Lotty's face heated as heavy raindrops plopped onto the thick canvas roof. She reached over to tie the door flaps. "Sorry, and thanks for that donut. It was wonderful."

"There's more," he said. "Better stick around. I think they're going shopping again tomorrow, so I'll ask for another box."

"Why can't everyone be like you?" she said.

"Most are, Lotty. You've just met too many that aren't. There's a bigger world out there you haven't ever imagined."

"Mama taught me that sometimes we have to look at things like they're a little caterpillar, or a baby bird in a nest. We can't just run up and touch them too fast. We have to step back and look them over for a bit. Just admire them first, I guess she meant." She threw both arms into the air and clapped her hands. "You have me thinking my future is that way, something to just look at right now...but not run after it too quick."

Nate closed his eyes while fighting the urge to sleep.

"I've had all this time to think," she said, "and I have so much to tell you."

He made not a sound.

"Hello...you in there?"

Again, only silence.

"I think I can trust you to make things work my way," she murmured, wrapping her arms gently around Butch. As the rain patted the tent's canvas, she said a quiet prayer, thanking the Lord for Nate and this safe place. Then, she whispered, "I think I'll just be waiting right here until all my own scary rains have stopped falling."

Chapter Fifteen

Nate breathed in the delicious smell of fried bacon filling Grandma's kitchen. He looked at the stove then the table set with only one place. Must be for him.

"Hope you're hungry," Grandma said. "You'll need extra today."

"I see what's cookin' this morning, but why this 'need extra' thing you're saying?"

"Pancakes, eggs, and bacon," she said. "Special, just for you. Your grandpa and I have to go over to Lewistown to see my cousin Gerty. She's in a bad way. Terrible bad, so I thought I'd feed you heavy so you can make it through till dinner. We'll be back by then. Might be just a bit late, and I'm guessing you don't want to visit a sick old lady all the day long."

"Are you going to check for mail on the way back?" Nate asked, then held his breath.

"Usually do. You expecting something?"

"Um...maybe. Just curious, mostly. That's all. Haven't heard from anyone in a while." He turned away quick. Hiding Lotty made him tell so many fibs. Not wanting to hear a long tale of bad news, he avoided asking about the cousin.

His grandparents loaded a few packages in the car, then Grandpa shouted his usual advice. "Keep an eye out for colorful strangers lurking about, and go slow with Butch."

Nate waved, saying nothing, then whispered, "Time to bring her some breakfast," as the dust from their tires rose, and the engine's noise and crunch of tires on the gravel road grew dim. "Let's see if any of those donuts are still here."

After stuffing a paper bag full of food, he entered the barn and shouted; "Hey up there, you awake yet? Plenty breakfast down here. Come and get it."

Lotty sprinted down the stairs. "Hey," she said, "you're walking okay? I mean, you must be. Here you are." She took the bag of food he offered.

"Grandpa and Grandma are gone for the day," he said, grinning. "And it's a beauty, too. Only a few clouds, cool breezes, real nice, so let's go down to the ridge. You can eat there. Great views of the valley, too. You've never seen it, I'd bet."

"Sounds good," she said. "I saw 'em drive off. Watched through my knothole."

Nate eyed her clothes. "You look fancy today. You sure you want to wear your beautiful dress down to the ridge? Could get dirty."

"I'll wear this to celebrate your walking." She twirled. "Where'd your grandparents go?"

Shrugging, Nate kicked at some dust on the floor. "Don't know. Some cousin of hers is sick or something. Glad I got out of that deal. So...this day's ours now. Let's explore some."

He led the way through the yard and across the dry branch, then they walked the spaces between tall corn rows and the cut hay field. He craned his neck to stare up at the tops of the corn stalks, now above his head. Yep, he'd be back home soon. "I like that crackle noise the corn stalks make from the wind," he said.

Lotty moved ahead since he was taking slower, cautious steps, favoring his bad leg. She turned to look at him every few paces.

"Don't worry," he said. "Keep going. It's a long way to get there, but worth it. I'll keep up." He swatted some black flies away and resumed walking, watching his footsteps on the ragged, rutty path.

They kept up a leisurely and quiet pace, enjoying the sunshine and cooler weather. Lotty switched her bag back and forth, from arm to arm.

Nate's chest swelled over how much he'd been able to bring her to eat.

After a half-hour hike, he said, "Hold up, now. Okay, look over there to the right. See it?" He pointed. "That's where we're going. The ridge is right there, so don't go walking too close, or...to the bottom, you'll go."

Lotty stopped so quick, he bumped into her.

"Ha! You're a hoot," he said. "Never thought a brave runaway girl who sleeps in cornfields would be a scaredy cat."

She rested her free hand on her hip. "If I had a switch, I'd shine your backside."

Nate chuckled and reached out to take the food bag.

She turned her back to him and cradled the bag tight between both arms. "No sir, all mine, and be nice or I won't share."

"Hmm, you think so?" He grinned. "Well, okay, then, you win that one. Follow me, and slowly, too, or I won't tell you the secret." He led her closer to the edge, then said,

"Right here is perfect. Set the bag down on that flat spot, then sit where the grass is thickest. Makes a nice carpet for us. I wouldn't put my legs over the edge just yet, either. Maybe you could after you're used to being up here a while."

They sat side by side and looked across the empty space to the hills on the far side of the deep green canyon.

"So, what's this secret?" Lotty said.

"The secret is...there is no secret. Just said that to keep you in line."

She elbowed him. "Nice try, mister."

"I'm not sure what you call that," Nate said, pointing across the valley. "A canyon, or a valley, or just what it's known as down here. It's deep, I know that much."

"I want to peek over the edge," she said. "Can I?"

"Have a care," he said, tensing, "but sure, go ahead." He straightened, prepared to grab her if need be.

She leaned forward on her knees, placing both hands close to the edge. "Just a skin of grass covering solid rock," she muttered, then stretched her head past the edge and looked down. "Oh, my!" she shouted. "It's beautiful. Let's get down there."

"Easy," he said. "Don't fall, or you'll wish you'd brought that food with, cuz you'll be stuck down there a long time. Maybe forever."

"Is that a stream at the bottom?" Lotty asked.

"More like a river, I'd say." He glanced down. "Anyway, if we had horses or a Jeep or something, maybe we'd find some way down there, but walking? Uh-uh, no way. Then, there's the getting back up to consider." He smiled at the look on her face. He was right to bring her here. "See, it's not so bad around here," he said. "Actually, I'm always giving you great advice. You should keep listening to me."

Lotty nodded, then rummaged through the bag and started her feast with another powdered sugar donut.

Nate lay on his back and searched for clouds that might look like imagined characters or even cartoons from some Saturday afternoon kids' movie. Did he dare to ask her the question on his mind? Instead, he closed his eyes and drifted into a light sleep.

***

"Nate? Hey, can you wake up please?" Lotty said.

"Oh, yeah, I'm up," he said, propping onto an elbow. "Any food left?" He peered into the bag and took out half a sandwich. "Tell me some more about where you're from." He took a bite and said around it, "I mean, why's it so bad there?"

"I'd rather not," she said, ducking her head. "We talked this over before." She turned away and stared at the clouds.

"It's just so different for me to hear," he said between bites. "I'm happy with my family...well, pretty much, that is. Hard to imagine anything else. Tell me more, please."

"Mostly, it's those two boys," she said, crossing her arms. "You know why. I told you already."

"Mostly?" he asked, the sandwich losing its flavor. "What else happens?"

"It's the mister, too. He's done things. He'd been after Mama before she died. He's no different than the boys, or maybe they're same as him. Mama was plenty afraid of him after Papa died. He never messed with her when Papa was around cuz my daddy was one powerful man. After he left us, I once heard the mister telling Mama she better do what he wants or else he'd be after me pretty soon."

Nate turned and stared across the gap, fists clenched hard and teeth ground tight, unable to speak.

Lotty took one look at his face and whispered, "You sure you want to know these things?"

Without looking at her, he said in a soft voice, "No, not really, but seems I'm supposed to. Not sure why." He made himself meet her gaze. "One thing I'll swear to, one thing you can count on, I *will* protect you...much as I can."

This time, Lotty turned and stared across to the other side. "Wish my papa was still here. Mama, too. You could meet them." Her shoulders rose on a deep breath. "Nate, I know something in my bones. I know I need to get out of here. Can't say why. Can't say how, either, just that I know something's waiting, and I'm afraid that it's comin' soon."

"I'm still waiting for that letter," he said. "I think it's the key to getting you away from here. Might come later today, too. If it does, and if it's good news, I'll for sure tell you tonight."

"Why can't people leave me alone?" she asked, hanging her head. She popped up and turned to him. "I'm talking about the mean ones, Nate. I've known whites who could act nice to me, but never ones nice as you. Are all the people up north like you?"

"Ha! No. Well, I don't know, really. Some, for sure. Maybe even most, but who knows how many? There aren't any folks like you where I live in the suburbs, anyway. Some places won't let negroes live there, or so I've heard. They have some name for that. Can't remember it. Never thought I'd need to. Anyway, my folks aren't meanspirited that way. They hate that kind of thing, especially Mom."

She gave him a sad smile. "They must be wonderful."

"Whoa. Sometimes, maybe. What I want to know is, why would anyone try to keep us from being friends? I don't get that part. You and me, I mean. When we get you up there, we better stay friends, and let's don't care a lick about who says what."

"It's hatred," she said, "and throw in some fear, too, then mix 'em together. That's how I see things. Makes up a mean ole witch's brew. Seen it on folks a long time now."

Nate leaned back. "That's what Grandpa says. He's explained the hate part to me already. I asked him one time. Says I should never give in to it." He closed his eyes, picturing Grandpa's story. "Says you put a little baby negro kid and a little white kid together in a playpen, and they have a good ole time making friends. He told me the hate part is learned. Somebody's gotta teach a person to have it, to make it grow." He shook his head. "I just still don't get it. I mean, I know we're different, a little bit, anyway. Our color is, and some other things might make us different. I don't know, but we get along okay, you and me. Ain't that right?"

"We do," she said, "but you surprise me plenty. Do you know, around here you could get hurt bad for helping me?"

Nate looked away again and said, "It's crazy."

"Do you think I can get up north with you?" she asked. "Can we try for that, and I mean soon?"

Nate hesitated, the weight of a promise this big pressing down on him, yet he wanted to guarantee it. "We *are* trying," he said, "so listen good. When Grandpa is mad at me for goofing something up, Grandma reminds him of something. She tells him like this, 'Nate's responsible for the effort, Henry, not the outcome,' or something like that. You get it?"

She nodded.

"Well, I am making the effort and going for the good

outcome, here, but no promises other than I'm trying. Let's hope that letter is here soon."

"I been praying," Lotty said. "I almost ran into your grandma." Nate sat up quick, but Lotty kept talking. "She came stormin' into the barn the other day. I was just about to step onto the stairs but stopped fast because I heard her down there. I thought it was the Holy Spirit stopped me, and I really think He did. But it scared me good. I gave my own self a hug, just thinking He has me covered."

"Maybe we should think about Pistol's sister's place," Nate said. "Just for a week or so. I'll see if she can keep a secret. If Grandma sees you, she'll have to tell Grandpa, and that's the end of it."

Neither spoke, both looking across to the other side. Was she, like Nate, wondering what it would be like if they could get over there?

"What a magic place," Lotty said. "The clouds are making pictures for us, and looking across the valley makes me think about what else there may be to see in this world."

"Let's head back," Nate said. "I better find Pistol."

Chapter Sixteen

Nate exaggerated his limp as he helped load the truck with new hive boxes Grandpa had built for the beekeeper who lived just past Hartsville. The man had ordered more than usual, this time, for his growing honeybee business, and Grandpa would expect Nate to go with him on the delivery, but his gut told him to stay around the farm and keep an eye out for dangers to Lotty.

"Don't you want to come?" Grandpa said, as if reading his mind. "I could use your help." He slammed his truck's tailgate shut. "Won't take but an hour or two."

"Not today," Nate said, unable to look his grandpa in the eye as he hobbled more than necessary toward the driver's side door. Was he overdoing it? "Next time, okay? My leg's stiff. Makes me want to take it slow a while longer."

"I'm off, then," Grandpa said, getting into the truck. "Be back after lunch." He shut the door and winked at Nate through the open window. "Makin' green cash money today. Might stop at Y.T.'s, too. You keep off that leg, much as you can."

"Don't get stung, Grandpa," Nate said, grinning as the double meaning of his words sunk in. Grandpa had said the bee man could be what he called "a slow pay."

Nate waited for the truck to disappear down the road, then went in the house and made a breakfast for Lotty. He carried it out to the barn, then set it on the bottom stair and called out, "Hey, good morning! Food's down here, so come and get it. I'm not up to climbing stairs today. Woke up hurting again. No one's here now, either, so—"

Heavy truck tires crunched in the side yard, and an engine roared, then shut off.

"Hold on," Nate whispered. "Someone's in the yard, I think. Stay put."

After slinking to the wall beside the barn's open door, he peeked out. An adult stranger walked along the house, looking through windows, then peered into the screen door on the back porch. Nate crept away from the barn toward the tent. If the stranger saw him, he'd pretend he'd just came from there.

"Hi, there," Nate yelled, standing next to the door flap. "Who you lookin' for?"

Saying nothing, the burly man walked fast down the yard toward him.

Nate straightened, making himself as tall as possible.

"Looking for a runaway," the stranger said. "The name's Waldcott, from down south of here. First name's Otto. Spelled the same front-ways as back. Oh...Tee...Tee...Oh... Otto. Who're you?"

"Nate. I'm staying here with my grandparents. I'm from up in Minnesota. Nobody here, anyway. Just me, and no runaways, either." He clenched his other fist next to his side. *Why* had he said he was the only one there?

The man turned and walked toward the shop. Grandpa's expensive tools! No way did Nate trust this stranger to see them. He scurried as fast as his leg would allow, reached the shop door before the man, and blocked it with his body.

"Hidin' something, kid?" The man smirked. "Move aside. I'm checkin' in there first."

The door handle pressed into Nates back as he stretched his arms out wide and flattened both hands against the walls past each side of the door jambs. "Hold on, here. My grandpa'll be back any second. You just ask him your questions."

The large, muscular man grabbed Nate's left arm and pulled him from the door as if he weighed nothing, then pushed his shoulder hard, shoving him to the ground.

Nate levered himself up from his belly and turned over in an instant, brushed dirt from his mouth and jumped to his feet. Backing away from this menace, he tensed his muscles to run. He'd get away before the man could make another move on him, bad leg or not. He'd ignore the pain like he had with the hole in his thumb.

"Listen, mister," he said, "better get out of here before Grandpa's back. He's an award winner, you know." Nate clenched his teeth. What a ridiculous thing to say.

"Award for what," the sneering man asked. "being old and useless? I know who he is, kid."

Nate backed away another step. "For boxing in the army," he said. "Never lost a fight, so just git, now, before he's back. I won't tell him what you did if you get outa here."

Ignoring him, the man turned the door handle and walked into the shop. Nate followed but kept an escape distance.

"Nice place," the man said, glancing around. "Nice boat, too. Makin' that for you?"

"What do you think you're going to find here, mister? You're at the wrong place."

"She told me she dropped off a negro girl right here by this farm," the man said, bending to look under the workbench. "Right by your dang cornfield. She described it perfect. Right here, it happened, for sure, so don't be lying, boy."

"Never seen her," Nate said, folding his arms. "And I been here all day."

The man straightened. "Last week sometime, dummy, not today. Said she got out of her car right by your field, just across from that shiny road sign out there." He peeked into the boat. "She made a point to remember this place just perfect. So, you're hiding her, and if you know what's good for you, better tell me where and don't make me more angry than I already am."

"My grandpa's old, that's for sure," Nate said, "but that's why he has other awards, too."

"For what, spitin' beer through the space where he's missing some teeth?" Shaking his head, the man stalked toward Nate. "Quit trying to scare me, boy. We both know, by now, I could snap him like a dry twig. Don't be lying to me, either, or else I'll show you again what I can do, but plenty worse. Get my drift?"

Nate balled his hands into fists to keep them from shaking. All he had was words to fight with, and again he thrust them at the man like a sword. "For shootin', that's what. No one at any of these county fairs will shoot against him anymore. He never misses. Pistols *and* rifles. He'd shoot you anywhere he wanted to. Shoot the little hairs off the tips of your ears, if he wanted."

"I'm shakin' all over, kid. Take a good look. Ooh, I'm a fraidy cat." He shook his bulky arms, then peered over

Nate's head out the door. "So, what's with that tent? Who's hiding in there?"

Nate hurried outside before the man could and glanced toward the house. Maybe he could get inside and grab the twenty-two rifle by the door before the stranger could catch him. *He gets Lotty, and I'll do it. I'll blast his kneecaps off.*

A sudden chill ran over Nate's arms, despite the summer heat. Waldcott. The man's name had escaped him in all the excitement, but that's the people Lotty had lived with when she ran.

Otto looked into the tent, surprising Butch into letting out a pitiful growl.

Snorting, Otto eyeing Nate over his shoulder as he straightened. "Who's he kidding? Your dog's no scarier than you, boy, or your old grandpa. Now listen, I'm looking for that girl for my uncle. Two reasons, and I'll tell you both." He jabbed a finger toward the sky. "One, he'll be button-popping proud of me. And two, he'll pay me the reward before I even ask. I'll lock her in my toolbox and have her back there before your grandpa could even find his rifle."

Before Nate could respond, Otto walked to the barn. Heart pounding like a steam engine, Nate hurried to catch up. Afraid he'd give Lotty away if he made too much fuss, he kept quiet and observant. Time to trust, like she always said.

Otto looked around on the empty first floor, then took the stairs two at a time. Nate followed as quick as his leg would allow. Lotty's breakfast was gone, thank goodness. She better be hiding like she claimed she could.

"Looks like a room up here," Otto said. "Strange sight for a barn. Fancy schmancy, a real room. Let's look in here, shall we?" He stared straight at Nate, showing off his frightening grin.

The ugly leer made Nate's stomach sour, and he had to turn away. A length of two-by-four lumber caught his eye. He could swing that at the man if he had to.

Otto pushed the door open, then walked into the room. Nate's blood pounded so strong, he couldn't hear over the drumming in his ears.

"Hey…look what I see!" Otto yelled.

Nate's entire body tightened, sweat popped from his forehead, and his stomach threatened to spew out breakfast. He entered the room and let out a silent breath at what he *didn't* see. No Lotty or any sign of her bag and clothes. "What're you talking about?" he asked.

"This bed," Otto said, pointing. "Looky here, it's been slept on. That blanket's messy. Been slept on, for sure. You blind, boy?"

"Of course it has, mister," Nate said, thinking fast. "I sleep up here a lot." Wiping his sweaty forehead, he rushed his next words. "If it's storming, I come up here because I'm worried the tent's going to blow over again. That's happened before. Ain't you never seen the bad storms high up in these hills? The clouds and lightning come right down to the tops of the electric poles. That's my bed." He let his chest swell a bit, proud he'd told this kind of lie.

"Hmm…maybe, maybe." Otto glanced around. "No sign of her, anyway. Where you got her, boy?" He looked in the tiny, empty closet, then walked into the area where the hay was stacked almost to the long timber crossties that spanned the width of the barn.

Nate stayed close behind him, hoping all he'd notice was there were no other rooms or hiding places up there. Only a mountain of hay.

Otto turned his head side-to-side and raised his shoulders toward his ears. "What the heck? She some kind of magician?" he said.

Nate had to agree. She had to have heard all their ruckus before they'd come up here, but where'd she go?

Otto bounded down the stairs as fast as he'd climbed them. The moment he stepped through the wide, open doors, he looked in every direction—up, down, everywhere. Nate tried to keep steady on the stairs, but his leg slowed him. By the time he made it outside, Otto was walking toward the house.

Nate followed, but not close enough for Otto to get another grip on him. He was sure he could outrun the man if I had to. His leg didn't hurt too much right then. He'd get out to the road and fly down to the Ellis place before Otto could even start his truck. They'd help him. Nate smacked his hands together like boxers do.

Otto stood on the porch, looking in through the kitchen window again.

"Ain't no one in there, either," Nate said, stopping next to the porch. "I'm tellin' you, so you better get but quick. Grandpa's back soon, any second now. In fact, I think I hear his truck. Why don't you try the place next door?" He pointed. "She could be hiding there just as easy. Whoever told you they dropped her off around here could be right, but we haven't seen her. Grandpa wouldn't allow it anyway, and that's a fact." He nodded, forming his mouth into a serious line. "If she was here, he'd have the sheriff on her but quick. So check them out down the road, but be careful when you stop your car. If you don't see the old man, don't get out. Those three dogs will tear you up."

"Aw, phoey, kid," Otto said. "I don't buy your big talk at all."

"Okay then, you're a smart fella." Nate crossed his arms.

"Tell you what, just drive on in there and hop right out. There's a good idea for ya. Hop out quick and start yellin' real loud."

Otto smacked a closed fist into his open hand. "I'll make you feel the hurt in this, wise guy, and you know I could."

Feeling stronger, Nate said, "And if she's not there, about a quarter mile the other way—past our place, that is—there's another farm. No one lives there, of course. They lease out the land, so you'll see crops in the ground, but that old shack and other buildings are empty. She's maybe camping out in there. No one around to stop her." He grinned. "But be careful, though. There's rats the size of bulldogs. Six, eight of 'em at a time will jump out and take you down. Eat you alive, too." He widened his eyes as if telling a ghost story on a moonless night. "And they'll be smilin' and burpin', chewin' and spittin' all the time. They like to start with your ears and eyes. So, don't forget. Go check that place out, too. Just go see if I'm lying."

"You northern brats tell tall tales too good," Otto said. "You don't fool an old country boy, though. The only rats around here be anybody hiding that negro girl."

Shaking his head, Otto walked from the porch to his truck. After backing onto the road, he put the gear shift into first, then gunned the motor and popped the clutch. The tires spun and shot gravel under his fenders, making an awful clacking sound. The truck slid a little sideways before straightening out and accelerating away, leaving a curved rut in the gravel.

"I sure hope Stony doesn't think we tore up his beautiful work," Nate said. "Gotta tell him about this."

He ducked behind the corn stalks on the edge of the field closest to the road and watched Otto drive down to the Ellis farm. When the dim sounds of the angry dogs and

Otto's loud yells reached his ears, he pressed a hand over his mouth to muffle his laugh.

After waiting there a short while longer, he ducked deeper into the stalks, before Otto would be driving by him again. After Otto's truck passed, Nate looked down the road just as it drove into the abandoned farm's yard.

"I'm not moving until he's done there," he whispered. "He won't find her, and that's for sure. Maybe she tucked herself into the root cellar."

Ten or fifteen minutes later, Otto drove off, away from Nate's farm, heading west.

"I better find her," Nate muttered, weaving back through the stalks. How did she know about things like this before they happened? She'd been telling him someone was coming.

He hurried to the barn and climbed the stairs, then paused outside her room.

"I heard him leave," she whispered from the shadows. "You think he's comin' back?"

Nate jumped back a step, laughed, then said, "Yeah, he's gone, all right, and I hope never comin' back." He focused on her shining eyes. "Where'd you hide? I been worried all morning."

Lotty stepped into the light, smiled, and pointed to the top of the stacked hay bales.

"On top, way up there?"

She nodded and put a finger to her lips. "C'mere,'" she whispered, as if someone might be near enough to hear.

She led him toward the end of the barn along the narrow walkway between the tall, flat edge of stacked hay and the outside wall. Reaching the end, she touched a narrow piece of wood nailed horizontally across two studs.

Spaced every half foot or so up the wall, another and another had been nailed in solid.

"Makes a good ladder," she whispered.

"What about your stuff?"

"I always keep everything in my bag. Everything, just in case. Heard him, grabbed it quick, then up I went." She pointed at the top of the stack. "Then, I crawled to about the middle. Can't nobody see that far in. Way too high. And I could shinny down in between two bales, if need be, disappearing down in there. Then, I thanked God for keeping His promises. People forget about that part, you know."

"What part?"

"The thanking Him part, because they just be always askin', askin', askin' for everything and never thinkin' to thank, thank, thank Him."

Nate nodded, looked her in the eyes, and smiled. "Pistol's comin' here later, and it's time to figure things out solid. I'm gonna ask him to drive me to Fayettville tomorrow, to the train depot. We'll get things organized. I better ask Grandma what day I go home, so we can figure on it." He took a breath and squared his shoulders. "Lotty, that man's a Waldcott. You know him?"

"Sure do. He's a nephew and a mean one, too. He's the reason my sis took off a year ago. I know what he wants. Did he hurt you? I heard something but couldn't see much through my knothole."

Nate shrugged. "Nah. He could have if he'd wanted to, I suppose. Hate to say it. I think I'd be able to outrun him, though, if I slipped out of his grip."

She slumped against the wall. "I told you so. Said you might get hurt helping me, and I'll tell you this, it could get a lot worse, too. I appreciate you trying, but he's not the only one looking, so let's get me far away from here, and I do mean quick."

Chapter Seventeen

Nate waved to his grandparents on his way out the door, keeping his voice casual and hoping they wouldn't ask too many questions. "Going with Pistol."

"Be good, you two," Grandma said from the kitchen, where she started the supper dishes.

Grandpa looked away from the T.V. and winked. "And don't get caught."

Nate let out a breath and walked outside to wait for Pistol on the front steps. As the minutes stretched out, he tapped his foot and drummed his fingers on his knees. What if Pistol didn't show up? Nate had to go to that train depot tomorrow, and he sure couldn't ask Grandpa.

He tore his gaze from the road and watched a line of ants going in and out of their holes, pushing and pulling pieces of grass and twigs, each piece larger than they were. They had built the soft dirt into tiny, volcanic-looking, round mountains. How many families of ants lived down there? Or were they all from the same one? Their unbroken streaming in and out seemed endless.

Just above his shoulder, a large colorful dragonfly hovered, then zipped around a flower bush. Its high-pitched buzzing and sharp, *snap-snap* clicking sounds broadcast its every changing motion. The sun shone through the giant fly's transparent wings and illuminated them in a shimmering orange-red-purple glow.

"Wish I had wings," Nate mumbled. He was like those tiny worker ants, lifting and straining, while what Lotty needed was a giant, colorful flying creature that could pick her up and whisk her to safety, snapping and buzzing at anything foolish enough to interrupt their journey. "We need those wings, now, before it's too late."

A gentle tap on a car horn made him bolt upright. He looked toward the road, where Pistol's car had stopped. "Hey, Pistol," he said, jumping to his feet. "Great, let's get going."

"You asleep or just daydreaming?" Pistol asked.

"Just thinking. Sorry. Can we take off now?"

"Hop in. Got plenty of time." They drove away.

"Let's go over to the drive-in in Carson," Nate said. "I'll treat."

Pistol nodded, then hit the steering wheel with his palm while accelerating. "Something on your mind?" he asked, then flicked the steering wheel hard to the right, just missing a puffed-up dead raccoon.

"Good one," Nate said, craning to watch the lump disappear behind them. "Looked fresh, too. Would've messed up your tires something nasty." He turned back around. "Okay, what's on my mind? Plenty. We had a visit earlier today from a guy named Waldcott. He's looking for Lotty, but ran into me instead."

Pistol frowned. "The senior, one of the kids, or a cousin?"

"Not sure. Said his uncle would pay him the reward for her."

"Cousin, then," Pistol said, nodding. "Nasty bunch, too. I could tell you stories about how they drove off Lotty's big sister."

Nate snapped his head up.

"Didn't know I knew that, did ya?" Pistol said, glancing at him. "You get through it okay? Did he see her?"

"Didn't see her, but he got a little rough with me. Could've been worse. I was there alone." Nate stared out the window. "I need to get her out of here soon. She agrees. Things seem to be closing in. We can feel it. Ya know what I mean?" He eyed Pistol out of the corner of his vision. "We wait too long, and something's going to happen."

Pistol only said, "Right."

After a few quiet miles, they pulled into a small country drive-in restaurant. A young girl, close to their age, walked over to the car.

Nate couldn't take his eyes off her. She was the most beautiful girl he'd seen here all summer.

"Hey, Pistol, what brings you over this way?" she asked. "And who's your new friend?"

"Hey, Deloris, just driving around. This is Nate. He's from Minnesota."

She smiled and leaned closer to Pistol's window. "Hi, Nate. Welcome."

Nate offered her a crooked half-smile, but his tongue stuck in place like old, dried-up gum on the bottom of a shoe. Good thing Pistol was able to speak, since he could only stare, then look down toward his feet.

"What'll you guys be havin'?" Deloris asked.

Seeming to understand the hyper-shy mood Nate was

fighting, Pistol ordered two root beer floats. Nate only nodded, then Deloris left to fill their order.

"Can't you city boys talk to girls?" Pistol asked.

"Uh, sure, yeah...usually. She's nice. I mean...really, who is she?"

"Don't get too excited," Pistol said, smirking. "She's engaged."

Nate stared at him. "Engaged? How old is she?"

"Sixteen."

"C'mon," Nate said, shaking his head. "She should be like twenty-one or something for that. Can't believe she's only—"

"This ain't up north, fella," Pistol said. "Things are different here. Haven't you figured that out yet?"

Deloris brought their drinks over to the door on Nate's side.

Why was she doing that? He fished money from his pocket with clumsy fingers, then gave it to her without speaking or looking in her eyes.

"Where's Minnesota?" she asked.

"Oh, uh...well, a long ways up north," he said. "Pretty far. Almost to Canada. You know about Canada? That's another country." His face heated. Why had he said that?

"Oh, really? Of course, I do," she said, grinning. "This is Arkansas, not Australia. You know about that?" She winked at him. "Y'all come back soon, now." She walked over to Pistol's door and said, "Nate should meet my little sis. Would be just about right, those two." She walked slow over to the building, her skirt swinging gently side-to-side.

Nate stared after her. Down here, they'd have him married off before he started high school.

"Snap out of it, dummy," Pistol said.

"Can't help it. Haven't seen anyone like her all

summer." Nate glanced sideways at Pistol. "A little sister, she says? Tell me more."

"She's even prettier." Pistol snorted. "You'd probably shake your teeth loose and pass out or something." Resting his arm out the window and tapping on the roof, he yelled to her, "Hey, c'mere again. Gotta ask you something else."

She walked slowly back, both boys staring at her.

"Bring me a small French fry, too, will ya?" Pistol said.

She nodded and smiled, spun on her heel, then sashayed back to the building.

Pistol looked at Nate with a wide grin. "Watch what happens next."

Deloris brought the fries, Nate paid her, then she walked halfway back again.

Pistol yelled one more time, "Wait up, whoa, c'mere. Got one more thing."

"This is embarrassing," Nate whispered, wanting to sink into the seat.

Returning, Deloris said, "Now what? Can't you get your order straight? You're going more directions than a blind mouse steppin' on a hot griddle."

"Sorry," Pistol said, "but hey, forgot about something Nate will like. You still have those frozen Milky Way bars?"

She started nodding, but changed to shaking her head, then tilted her chin and glared at Pistol through narrowed eyes.

"Okay, then, two of those to go," he said. "Pretty please."

She gave Pistol another look that made Nate think he'd better not do that again, then returned to the building.

When she came back to the car with the bars, Pistol said, "We'll be good now, honest."

"We'll have to see about that," she said. "And don't

strain yourself too much. You haven't had much practice." She flipped her hair over one shoulder, then walked away.

"Did you enjoy the show?" Pistol asked Nate.

"Huh? Enjoy the what?"

"We got to watch her make all those extra trips."

"Yeah, we did." A slow grin lingered. "Nice, good one, really nice."

"So, never—and I mean never, ever—order it all at once when you like the carhop," Pistol said, opening the bag of fries. "That way, you get to see more of her. Brilliant, I'd say."

"A lesson learned, my good friend," Nate said. "I'll use this later whenever I get a car."

They leaned back, smiling while enjoying their floats.

"Finished?" Pistol asked a while later. "You ready to tell me what I need to hear so bad?"

"For sure." Nate slurped the last sip of root beer. "Do you know how to get down to that little river west of my grand-folks place? The one down from the high ridge at the edge of our fields, overlooking that deep canyon?"

"Rogers Little Canyon Branch, you mean?" Pistol said, starting the car. "Not a river, really. Just a big stream. We can get there, but we have to cross it further upstream. There's still a good bridge there, I hope." He glanced behind them as he backed out of the parking spot. "You sure we need to go all that way?"

"Would like to, if it's not too much bother." Nate shrugged. "Can't say why, just that I like it, and it may help me think. Up where I live, there's a creek across the street. I go down there a lot when I have something to figure out."

Nate relaxed when Pistol turned the right direction.

They drove to the bridge in silence, crossed the branch, and turned down onto a steep rocky road that ended at a flat grassy area. Halfway down, the car slid sideways. Pistol sliced at the wheel, spinning the rear tires a little, making the car straighten out. Nate wanted to grab onto something to steady himself, but he was holding both candy bars, one in each hand.

When they reached the bottom, Nate looked back toward the highest point they'd started from. "We getting back up there?"

Pistol nodded, grinned, then punched Nate on the shoulder.

Nate looked far up to the top of ridge, where he and Lotty had sat a couple days ago. "What a place," he said. "It's perfect."

They got out and sat by the water's edge, enjoying the quiet after the perilous drive to the bottom, and finished their candy bars.

Nate licked the last of the chocolate off his fingers. "I trust ya, Pistol, so here's the thing, I need to get Lotty out of here fast. That visit this morning scared us both. Can you drive me to Fayetteville tomorrow, to the train depot? Tomorrow and no later. I have to check on a ticket and a schedule. Gotta figure out my money, too."

"Can't go tomorrow," Pistol said. "Next day, maybe. When do you leave for home?"

"Not sure. I'll be asking Grandma tonight. Leaving soon, though. And maybe my letter from back home will get here, too." He glanced at Pistol. "You know, I told you about the church lady up there? Then, Lotty will be taken care of...if I can get her there, that is. If not, I don't have a clue what's next. Scares me plenty."

"Yeah, you better get her outta here," Pistol said, tossing a rock into the water. "Some ticked-off redneck is gonna catch you both, and no tellin' what happens then. You're not supposed to be doing this, you know. Sometimes people just disappear around here. Has happened, and I hate to say it. Not so bad as other places—other states, really—but sometimes can be. You got off easy this morning, and you better believe it."

Nate huffed. "You call that easy? Thought he was going to kill me."

"Real easy. If you weren't Henry's grandson, no telling." Pistol shook his head, then twisted around to face Nate. "Tell ya what, I'll spin by before lunch the day after tomorrow. Tell your grandpa I need you to help me with some chores or something. I do plenty for him. He likes me, too, and even pays me more than I ask for sometimes, so no problem there. Folks help each other around here. Maybe makes up for the few nasty ones that just don't care, like those Waldcotts."

"Thanks," Nate said. "Big thanks. I mean it."

Pistol shrugged. "Why you doin' this, Nate? You don't have to."

"Yeah, well...you didn't see her sittin' in that cornfield. Bug bites, bloody scabs, and those tears. Can't explain it, but I had no choice. Could be it's in my blood. Who knows."

"More likely in your heart." Pistol stared at the stream. "Still dangerous, though, but I get it. I saved a baby from drowning in the river last summer. Everyone else just yelled and ran around the banks. I jumped in and swam for it. You could say it was up to me, or maybe was my turn. I don't know, but same deal as your problem. No one else came along and did anything."

Their plans set, they sat in silence by the running stream, enjoying the music of the moving water, the cool evening breezes, and the strength of fellowship in becoming partners around something a little dangerous.

The buzzing and snap-snaping of another dragonfly drew Nate's attention. It hovered above him, darting about, then flew over his head and landed on the hood of Pistol's car. Nate smiled at the car, which appeared to be patiently waiting for them. Maybe he did have some wings, after all.

Chapter Eighteen

Just after getting home from the ride with Pistol, Nate stood in the kitchen, halfway between his tired grandpa, who was lounging again in his living room chair, and Grandma, who sat relaxing in her rocker on the back porch. He wanted to sneak Lotty some supper, but how could he manage it with both grandparents blocking the doors to the outside? He moved to the back door. Maybe he should join Grandma on the porch until she came inside.

"Nate," she called through the screen door in a high, sour voice unusual for her, "quit standing there and staring. You never sit out here with me after supper."

Nate cautiously stepped onto the porch, staying behind her where she couldn't face him.

"What have you and Pistol been up to lately?" she asked without turning around.

"That southern fried chicken you made us tonight was great," he said, still gripping the door handle. "Better than they do at that fancy restaurant you two brag about. Can I have a piece or two to bring to my tent...for a snack?"

"A snack, you say?" she turned sideways and gave him

one of her *Who do you think you're fooling?* looks, with her head tilted to one side and one eye partially closed. "Glad you like it, but first, I want to know what you're thinking about, young man. I'm waiting."

Not sure what she was getting at, he stared at the floor then out toward the shop. "Just thinking about the chicken, that's all."

Then, thoughts of Lotty and what Pistol said earlier about nasty folks around here gave him courage and just the distraction he needed.

"And maybe a little about this business down here with the negroes and schools and all," he said in a rush. "Been meaning to ask you about that." He let go of the door handle, then sat on the empty chair nearest her, certain he'd steered the conversation away from himself. "Back home, I saw it on the T.V., but I still don't get it. Grandpa says it's about hate. It shows on a few folks I've seen around here, but I just don't understand where it comes from or how it starts."

Again, Grandma gave him the severe look that threatened confrontation. "The simple explanation is this, the white folks in Little Rock don't want negro kids in their public schools. That's about it. What's it like in Minnesota?"

"We only had two negro kids ever in my school," Nate said, leaning back. "Twin brothers. Their parents worked for this rich guy, and they all lived together in that big mansion out by the lake. I think, for some reason or a law or something, they had to let them in. Only one of the boys was in my class, but they're both gone now."

"Gone? What happened?"

"I didn't do anything," he said, glancing at her from the

corner of his eye. "And anyway, it's kind of embarrassing. Do I have to?"

"I can take it if you can," she said, her expression softening. "So, go ahead, if you dare."

Nate relaxed some, but hesitated. This story would not be easy to tell to anyone's grandma. "Um...well, okay. One day, we had a test, so the room was quiet. The teacher always sits in the back for tests, to keep an eye on us, but you know about that kind of thing. The negro boy walked up to the front, and uh, he...well, you see, he turned towards us, then he unzipped and just peed right on that old wooden floor."

Nate studied his grandma's face. Her expression didn't change, so he took a breath and continued. "Then, he just lit out the door, but not fast, not at all. He didn't run off like a scalded cat, the way I expected. No ma'am, he just walked away slow, down that hall. Left his stuff in his desk, too. We never saw them again, either one."

"Terrible," Grandma said, then her voice firmed. "Nate, I hope you were nice to them."

Nate shrugged. "Can't say I was or I wasn't. Plenty weren't, though. Lots of name-calling and all. No fights, and they kept to themselves mostly."

The cooler night breeze brushed Nate's face as they sat quiet for a time. Nate thought through how to finish his story and show her he wasn't one of the troublemakers.

"I felt kinda bad," he said, "seeing them every day in the lunchroom, always alone at their own table. One time, I asked my friend if he'd come along and we'd sit with 'em. You know, talk to 'em, but he wouldn't, and I couldn't dare if I was alone. That's about it. I tried a little." He brushed invisible dirt off his pants. "So, what finally happened in Little Rock?"

"Finally?" She shook her head. "I'll tell you, but first you tell me something. Were you afraid? If you sat with them alone, what did you think would happen? Would your friends get after you?"

"Um...I don't know for sure, but I guess I was worried how my pals would handle it. Anyway, I chickened out. Not too proud of it, either."

"At least you gave it a thought," she said. "I'll wager most didn't. In fact, just the opposite." She started rocking again for the first time since he'd joined her. "So, Little Rock, you ask. It's not a hundred percent over yet. There was an awful mess to begin with. Governor Faubus made sure they couldn't let blacks into Central High School. Then, President Eisenhower made threats to Faubus, who ignored them, so Eisenhower brought in the Army National Guard, and they escorted those nine brave kids into the high school. Brave, for certain, but had to be shaking inside. They had no idea what was behind those doors. It's not like their big brothers or sisters had ever been in there before them."

"That's right," Nate said. "Saw it, I mean. I saw a picture of a girl holding her books, up high across her chest like how all the girls do, and she was walking with soldiers all around her. And the look on her face...couldn't tell if it was fear or courage or some of both." He stared across the yard. "Sounds silly, but I was proud of her. I couldn't help it."

Again, both kept quiet for a few minutes, the night sounds and soft air providing a friendly diversion.

"This hate thing is awful," Nate said at last. "Grandpa says he knows Faubus. Says he's from some town close by. Does everyone here agree with him?"

"Some do, some don't." Grandma turned to him. "I sure don't."

A noise drew Nate's gaze toward the barn. He tried to spot the knothole Lotty looked through but couldn't find it from this distance and in the dimming light.

"What're you looking at?" Grandma asked. "Something interesting down there? Tell me, young man."

"Thought I heard something by my tent. Coulda been Butch."

"You never told me where you and Pistol went," she said. "Get talking, now."

'Nowhere, just around. We stopped by the Rogers Little Canyon Branch, that's all." Nate scuffed one shoe across the floor. "Oh, we had treats from a drive-in. He's not working or anything, so we hang out more. And um, can I have some chicken to bring to my tent? It's too good to stop. Still a little hungry for more. Maybe two more pieces, please?" He glanced at her and grinned. "You make the best, Grandma."

She gave him a look he couldn't figure out, her eyes narrowing, her eyebrows rising and wrinkling her forehead. She stood and walked toward the screen door, keeping her head turned in his direction. While she stood sideways in the doorway, she scowled at him. When she went inside, the sounds of cupboard doors and the refrigerator opening and closing followed.

She came back out, carrying a paper bag, and held it straight out to him. "There's a breast and a leg, some carrot sticks, and a cookie," she said. "Should be enough for her supper."

Nate jerked back, tipping his chair close to the going-over-backwards point, his eyes widening to the size of half dollars. Looking away quick, He righted the chair. Its front legs thudded onto the wood deck so loud, he twitched. Grandma kept holding the bag within his reach, but he couldn't look at her or try to take it. "What're you saying, Grand—"

"Stop right there, mister," she snapped. "You're not much of a liar, you know. Figured that out easy enough, so let's face some facts. I know who she is and what's been going on here. Your turn to talk, now, young man. So, tell me all about it, and no fibs, either."

"Wait a minute," he said. "How do you—"

"I found her late this afternoon, around the back of the barn. I went to gather some flowers and surprised her but good."

Nate imagined what Lotty was doing back there, and his face heated again. She had to be embarrassed and afraid. "Did you tell Grandpa?"

"Not a chance," Grandma said. "No, sirree. You should have figured that out right away. If I had, she'd be long gone." She turned halfway around and looked through the screen door into the kitchen. Giving Nate a glance, she held a finger to her lips. "Take this bag. I can't hold it out like this all night. I'm not the Statue of Liberty."

Nate stood and took the bag. Unable to speak, he lowered his head and waited.

"Tomorrow is the last day of summer school for me," Grandma said, her chair creaking as she sank into it. "You'll be coming to help me pack up books, displays, and such. So, dress nice, and I'll be sure you get up early enough."

Nate jerked his head up. "But I'm supposed to help Grandpa in the shop. I can't be going to school." He really meant he was afraid to leave Lotty alone, especially now.

"You don't worry about the old man," Grandma said. "Right now, you just be worried about me. Understand? Be ready, and besides, we'll be home early enough. It's just a half day."

Nate nodded. "Okay, I trust you." He sprinted off the porch without another word, then ran through the yard and into the barn. He had to trust Grandma. It was all he could do now. Bounding up the stairs, he called to Lotty through her closed door.

"Shut up, will you," she hissed, "Just you wait a second, then I'll open the door."

Nate couldn't stand still, and he wished they were back outside in the cool breezes. The paper bag slipped from his hand and fell to the floor as Lotty opened the door, glowing with a smile he'd never seen her wear before.

"Howdy, old friend," she said. "Looks like you brought me something." She pointed to the bag, then they both bent to pick it up, knocking into each other's heads. Only Lotty laughed. "You okay?" she asked.

"Not so sure. Grandma just told me she met you today. What the heck happened?"

"It's okay. In fact, better than okay," Lotty said, hugging the bag to her chest. "She's on my side and wants to help, so relax, will ya?"

"We still have Grandpa to contend with," Nate said, rubbing his head. "I'm not so sure she can keep this quiet forever." His hands wouldn't stay still, so he clasped them tight, locking his fingers together.

Lotty smiled and tapped his shoulder. "She's nice. Tomorrow—I think she meant tomorrow—when your grandpa goes into town, we're going to have a talk and do some figuring about what I can do next. She plans to ask you to join us, too." Lotty peeked into the bag, sniffed at the chicken, and threw her free arm around Nate's neck, hugging him hard.

"We better keep quiet till then," he said. "If Grandpa finds out, it'll go worse than if she'd never known."

Chapter Nineteen

"Time to rise and shine," Grandma called through the tent's canvas door, rousing Nate.

"Okay, okay," he said, "I'm up. How much time?"

"Twenty minutes, and good morning. We'll have a good day together, so don't go back to sleep, now. And dress nice. Remember, we're going to my school, so make us proud."

"Too many instructions," Nate mumbled. He untied the straps, giving Butch an easy path out, then looked up and smiled at the cloudless, blue sky. "Dress nice, huh?" he whispered. He pulled on his best clean jeans and cotton shirt. "I hope Lotty's okay here alone all day." Then, he hurried to the kitchen.

"You do look good," Grandma said. "Maybe you're wanting to impress these country mice 'round here. Is that a good guess?"

"Most I've met don't seem to care too much about what they look like," he said. "I mean, the ones my age. So, when do you think we'll be back?" He glanced away, hoping his harsh tone hadn't offended her.

"I was hoping you'd be happy for a change of pace," she

said. "Besides, you're leaving soon, and we've yet to have some you-and-me time. I'm glad it's today."

"Me too. Sorry, Grandma. I'll quick eat then meet you by the car?"

She nodded and handed Nate a warm cinnamon roll for his breakfast, then worked on cleaning the kitchen.

Nate gobbled his roll down and, when Grandma turned her back, snuck another to drop off in the tent for Lotty. As he headed for the door, he frowned. Why didn't he just ask Grandma?

During their drive, Nate asked, "What's the class about today?"

"American history. We're taking the final exam, too, so there won't be much talk, and I'd like you to help me grade their tests." Grandma turned down another gravel road. "There's only twelve in this class, so if you help, we'll get back sooner."

Nate smiled. "Going from student to teacher's assistant could be fun."

"It just might," she said. "I'm proud of you for helping Lotty. You may even learn some history today, about slavery and how they've been treated. History I'm sure Lotty has lived through, in part."

Nate rubbed the back of his neck. "She told me about her life, Grandma, before she ran away. But I'm guessing you mean something else. Something older, way back there times."

She nodded. "We've tried—the Americans, that is— we've tried for over a hundred and fifty years to correct the inhumane legacy of slavery. We're getting closer, too. This was a worldwide problem, by the way, not just here. In fact, it still is in other countries."

"Didn't know that," Nate said, shifting in his seat. "Never thought of it that way."

Grandma smiled at him. "You have the right spirit about yourself, and that's what makes me believe things will keep getting better. Takes time, too. Generations, sometimes. So, don't forget that."

Nate had no response, but sat taller since his grandma considered his empathy for Lotty worthwhile. He prayed his friend would stay well-hidden while he and Grandma were both away.

When they arrived at the old brown brick schoolhouse, Nate said, "This building looks the same as my old grade school. It has those long windows, and those flat stone corners that look strong, and the round columns on each side of the front door make it look important." His was better, of course, but he kept that to himself.

They entered an empty classroom, also like his. Same amber blond wood floor and wide blackboard in the front.

"Will you pass out the test papers when the time comes?" Grandma asked, setting her bag on the teacher's desk.

"Sure," he said as two girls who looked about a year younger than he came in.

"Who's this guy, Mrs. Martin?" the taller one asked.

"He's handsome," the other said.

Nate's face erupted with heat, and he looked to Grandma for some help.

"He's Nate, my grandson from Minnesota," she said. "And yes, he is handsome, ladies. And guess what? He's helping me grade your exams, so do your best to show him we country folks can do as well or better than his big city friends."

The girls giggled and whispered with their faces close together, then sat side by side in the front. Several others came in, all eyeing Nate. Grandma then wrote on the blackboard, *Nate is my grandson. Make him welcome.* When those who entered asked about him, she simply pointed to the board.

After the bell rang, she settled the kids down, then Nate walked among them handing out the pages. He stood straight and tall, feeling important in a way he never had before. As the test started, he sat in a chair beside Grandma's desk. When Grandma caught a student looking at another's paper, he fought to keep his laugh inside. School was the same everywhere.

After the dismissal bell rang, a few kids wished their teacher well as they stood around her desk. The others said simple goodbyes while looking over their shoulders, then they all hurried out the door.

Nate looked at the stack of test papers. How long to correct all these? He didn't want to miss too much of the boat finishing work, and Grandpa had promised to loan him a clean white dress shirt as he'd explained the tradition of wearing white shirts for the last day of a project, when doing the final fancy finishing. It was "old school," he'd said.

Then, there was Lotty, alone there with only Grandpa moving about and Otto searching for her.

"Sit here," Grandma said, pointing to a table and chair in the corner. "These test papers are mostly multiple choice and some true-false. You know about that, I'd imagine. Here's the answer list." She handed him another paper. "Use this red pen when you find an incorrect answer. Just make a circle around the number, then add the scores when done. Just the number of right ones, please. There's twenty-two questions. Got this?"

"Sure," Nate said, hoping he really did. Then, he sank onto his chair and went to work. After reading the second question on the first page, he said, "Grandma, this isn't right. I mean, this question's answer choice is wrong." How could she not know this? It was so simple.

"What do you mean?" she asked, looking up from a pile of books she was stacking. "All those answers on your sheet are correct."

"Uh, no, look-it. The choice in this box says, 'The government legally ended bringing slaves here in 1865. True or false?' And that's supposed to be false, according to your answer list. Says here the right answer is 1808."

"That's right," she said. "The key word is *legally*. Our constitution let it continue, legally, only from the document's founding in 1789 until twenty years later, when it ended bringing people here and into slavery, per our newly crafted constitution, in 1808."

Nate scrunched his forehead. "I thought the Civil war ended it."

"Most folks think the same. This is kind of a trick question, too," Grandma said, adding a book to her stack. "Understand the old times, dear. The Constitution only let it continue a little longer...they did that so the southern states would join the union. You can see why, so they would all become the United States, all thirteen original colonies. Some didn't want slavery to end, maybe forever. I can't say for sure on that, but the writers of the Constitution were concerned they wouldn't join the union if the document uniting them stopped the bringing in of persons, or slaves, from day one. The founding fathers wanted one America, not a divided north and south. One union."

"No, I didn't know that," Nate said.

"Plus, the U.S. withdrew from the Trans-Atlantic slave trade in 1809, and all the states north of Maryland voted slavery out in 1804," she said. "Maybe you didn't know about all that, either."

Nate tapped his pen on the desk. "So, if it was illegal after 1808, how come it was still going on here for so much longer?"

She abandoned her books and leaned against a desk. "Wealthy northern folks bankrolled fast slave ships that could outrun the U.S. Navy's ships that patrolled the coast of Africa. Back then, our government had been using the Navy to catch the slavers and make them stop. They diminished as much slave trade as they could for forty-some years. Didn't they teach you anything about that part?"

"No," he said, setting his pen down. "Never heard of it in our school. They just tell us about the Civil War and that slavery was a scar on our country's soul. I remember that was said. Had to memorize it for a test one time. Never a word at all about trying to stop it earlier. Always thought it was still legal till the Civil War changed it."

"Well, those making the money," she said, straightening her desk, "they were still bringing slave prisoners to the south. That's when the Civil War started, and that is what most folks today think was the beginning of making it illegal. The northern states actually voted it out in 1804. They weren't waiting for 1808. But not the south. Importing persons had been constitutionally illegal for fifty-one years before the Civil War."

"Okay, I see it," Nate said. Why hadn't his teachers taught him the full story? They had to know about this. He turned back to the test papers.

As he worked, the birds' songs floated through the open

windows, and he wanted to sing back to a whippoorwill like he did back home. He often walked to the end of the block where his feathered friend lived. They'd sing together, just the two of them, on many summer days, even though Nate had never seen his singing friend in the large fully-leafed tree. He'd only heard its song.

He forced himself to focus. *Gotta finish these. Need to get back. No singing today.* Besides, Grandma might think he was goofy.

Once he finished the grading, they straightened the chairs and desks, then gathered Grandma's books, charts, and other items, and packed it all in the car. As they climbed in, she offered to treat Nate to the drive-in.

"No, thanks," he said, not wanting to risk Deloris or her sister seeing him with his grandma. "I have to get back to the boat." As Grandma turned toward home, he said, "Those slave ships, the fast ones you mentioned, they must have been something to see."

"Yes, they were," she said, "for a while. They called the fastest ones Baltimore Clippers, and they could outrun anything afloat. The U.S.A. passed a law that our navy could seize any one of them that looked to be a slave trader, and after 1820, it was considered piracy to bring slaves here. The penalties if they caught them included death."

Nate whistled. "Never knew that. So, America did try to stop it a long time ago."

"Correct answer. From the first day America became a country, in fact. You get an *A*." She flashed him a grin. "Don't forget, all major slave nations abolished it by 1836. There was still a big demand in South America for slaves back then, though, and even now, believe it or not. The problem is, to this day, some far off places still practice and get away with it."

"You might have to explain this to my teachers," Nate said. "I mean, what if I get a wrong answer on a test when I'm really giving the right one?"

"You know where to find me," Grandma said. "I teach some extra truths that aren't included in their approved textbooks. And I plan to continue. Nate...don't forget, our constitution doesn't magically create perfect people. What it does do is give us, by design, the opportunity and the paths to correct our mistakes once we see them. "

Nate smiled then stared out the window, thinking of Lotty. *I bet she doesn't know any of this, either.*

Chapter Twenty

Unlike most lazy summer mornings, Nate awoke minutes before the sun rose. He'd slept lighter than usual both nights after finding out Lotty had been discovered. Peeking through the tent's back window flap, he stared up at the house. Still dark inside. He'd wait for the sun's first bright rays to appear before going up there.

The wait was short. The rays traveled across the sky, illuminating the tops of the trees.

"Beautiful," he said, "and since they're still asleep, it's a good time to sneak some breakfast." He slipped out of the tent and turned back to look at Butch. Instead of joining him like usual, the dog chose to stay in the tent. "Too early for you, old man?" Nate whispered, resisting the urge to give Butch his customary vigorous morning rub.

Nate crept to the screen door and opened it, taking care to keep it from squeaking, then entered the kitchen. He slathered two slices of bread with butter and jam. Shabby breakfast today, but he had no time for risking anything else. He scratched out a note that read, "Went with Pistol. Back later." The less said, the better.

He ate one slice and put the other in a paper bag, along with two oatmeal raisin cookies. As he stashed a third cookie in his shirt pocket, an envelope on the kitchen table caught his eye. His name was printed on the front. He forced himself not to shout, "My letter I been waiting for." Grandpa must have picked up the mail late yesterday. He grabbed it, slipped from the house, and ran to the tent. Why hadn't they shown him this earlier?

The envelope's face bore the name of his church back home. He ripped it open, pulled out the letter, and read.

Dear Nate,

I understand your problem with your new friend. There's nothing we can do about it due to the laws and regulations from one state to another. I can't simply tell you to bring her here and we'll take over after that. We don't know anything about her family, or if she has one, and what troubles she may be having. We may have problems keeping her here without their permission.

I am sorry, and this is no doubt not what you want to hear. Now, if you do get her here, stop in, and I'll see if we can find a temporary family for her to stay with until we determine the legalities of her situation. No promises, though. I hope you understand this. I can't just tell you to bring her. That's too much like helping with a kidnapping. After all,

she's a child, and there are laws we're not
sure about, both here and there.

If she appears here without our help,
that's a little different. Our lawyer says we
can't encourage you, but I believe it's different
if she's already here. You have my phone
number, and I/we wish you luck.

It was signed, *Margo*.

Nate lowered his head and crushed the paper with his hand. He hid the letter and envelope under his pillow and put Lotty's breakfast in the knapsack hanging in the tent's center. "I'm still getting her out of here, and that's that," he said. "Done deal."

Butch raised his head at Nate's voice, but when Nate paid no further attention to him, he lay back down, groaned, and closed his eyes.

"No time to babysit you today," Nate said to his friend.

Nate slipped from the tent, walked to the road, and turned in the direction Pistol would be coming from. Why couldn't people just be nice and helpful? All this legal stuff was too much baloney. Lotty was in trouble, plain and simple, so couldn't they just get that part and do what was right for her?

Several rocks good for kicking lay in his path, but he couldn't see any fun in that. Besides, Stony's beautiful grading work still looked fine. Passing by the Ellis farm, he tried not to make a sound so those nasty dogs wouldn't be alarmed. As he turned the corner, a car approached. "Hope it's pistol," he whispered.

The car stopped beside him, and Pistol motioned Nate to jump in. "Hey, why you walking instead of waiting?"

Nate climbed in, weighing his words. "Cuz I can't just sit still and let 'em do this to us."

"Do what?" Pistol asked, turning the car around, then driving off.

"I'll get you caught up," Nate said. "By the way, thanks for picking me up so early." He held up a finger. "So first, Grandma knows about Lotty." He looked to see how Pistol reacted.

Pistol's expression didn't change, but he glanced toward Nate and said, "Told ya so."

Nate shrugged. "No sweat, though. Grandma's trying to help. At least, so far." He raised another finger. "Second, the church lady letter got here. In fact, just read it this morning. She says we can go ahead and get Lotty there, but no promises, cuz there's lawyers and something about laws that worries them. Horse doodoo, I say. Lotty needs some real help. Period."

"How'd your grandma find out?" Pistol asked.

"Just saw Lotty outside the other day, behind the barn. She's not telling Grandpa, though. Not yet, that is."

"We better get things working and quick," Pistol said.

Nate nodded, rubbing his hands together.

They rode in quiet for a while, Pistol driving faster than usual. The sun now lit everything up bright, and no clouds shadowed the blue sky.

"Nate," Pistol asked, "you going to tell the train ticket guy she's a runaway negro girl?"

Nate whipped his head around. "You crazy? What a question."

"Right, sorry." Pistol shrugged. "I'm not thinking straight yet. Too much to figure out, I guess."

"For sure. This has to work, though." Nate stiffened, balling his hands into fists. "If they catch her and she's back at that other place, no telling what happens. Then, what do we need to do if they're keeping her prisoner over there?"

"What you mean *we*, Kemosabe?" Pistol laughed.

Maybe it was infectious, because Nate couldn't help joining in. When he finally caught his breath, he said, "*The Lone Ranger* is my second favorite show, cuz *Superman* is the best."

"I wonder why Tonto calls him *Kemosabe*," Pistol said. "They never do say. Must be some Indian thing we don't know about."

"Yeah." Nate squinted through the dirty windshield. "How far to the train depot now?"

"Almost there. It's on the far side of town, though. Twenty more minutes, maybe."

As they entered Fayetteville, Nate craned his neck to take in the sights of the largest city he'd visited all summer. "Look-it, electric stop signs and buildings taller than the trees," he said. "Think I'll just ask the train guy how much to Minneapolis and maybe can we get a printed schedule to take home."

"You going to try gettin' her on the same train you're on?" Pistol asked.

"That'd be swell, but who knows. And how much is a ticket? That's the real worry.'

Pistol turned at another intersection. "When are you leaving?"

"Day after tomorrow. Don't know what time, though. Morning, I suppose."

"Let's see what the ticket guy says." Pistol pulled into a parking area, and they sat still and quiet for a short time.

Composed and ready, Nate said, "Okay, let's give this a try."

As they walked in, Nate smiled. No people were lingering about.

The ticket agent gave them a welcoming wave as they approached. "Where you gentlemen traveling?" he asked.

"Uh...well...uh, Minneapolis," Nate said. "Just one ticket."

"Sounds good. It should still be there, last I heard." The agent laughed at his own joke.

Nate grinned, relaxing some. This guy reminded him of Y.T. "How about day after tomorrow?" he said. "What's on your schedule?"

"Let's see." The agent thumbed through some papers. "Okay, the Kansas City Southern leaves at 10:35 a.m. and stops in Kansas City, where you'll need to switch over to the Rock Island Rocket." He glanced up. "That's a quick transfer, too, because you'll only have around twenty minutes to get across that huge depot to catch it. The Southern will be on time, though, because she's originating from right here. Their crew's good that way, always on time when they start out from here."

Nate grinned at how the agent said "dep-oh" the same way Grandma did. He'd learned his lesson and didn't try to correct him, though. Correcting Grandma that time had caused enough trouble. "Okay, then," he said, "how much for tickets all the way?"

The agent scribbled on a piece of paper and handed it to Nate, who scanned the writing. It listed both times and train numbers, plus the amounts for each.

"Thanks," Nate said. "We'll look this over and be back in a while." Keeping his tone casual, he asked, "By the way, do you let negroes ride, too? Kids, I mean. Teenagers, actually."

"Of course, we have to," the agent said, "but they belong in their own special car. Why do you ask? And are you age twelve or more? Got to be to ride if no adults are with you."

"Who me?" Nate chuckled. "For sure. I'm almost fourteen. Will be in October. Oh, uh, your question? Just thinking about someone who might be on the train with me. Kind of a neighbor, you see? Just wondering if I'd see her or not, that's all."

The ticket agent raised an eyebrow at Nate and leaned away a little.

Nate said, "Thanks," then turned fast and scurried toward a long wooden bench.

Pistol followed, and both boys sat.

"He's not buying my lie," Nate said under his breath. "I don't know what to do." He looked over the paper again. "I'm short enough money in my pocket right now—for her, I mean—but how're we going to sneak her in here, anyway?"

"We need to get home—to your place, that is—and see if your grandma will help us," Pistol said. "I'm figuring they will be taking you back here early morning. If I can pull into their place just after y'all leave, I'll drive Lotty here. Then, we'd all have to act like we don't know each other." He scratched his head. "I mean, uh...they'd know me, though, so maybe I just drop her off close by and disappear." Pistol shook his head. "I'm not making much sense."

"No, you are," Nate said, pocketing the paper. "That should work. I like it." He stood. "Let's head back, and I'll get you the money I have. It's hidden pretty good, so best I dig it out in case you can't find it that morning. Maybe Lotty's got some to make up the difference."

Chapter Twenty-One

Now heading back, Nate said; "Hey, let's stop at the drive-in. Could go for some of their tasty food again, okay? One last time?"

"Done deal, pal," Pistol said, grinning. "Maybe Delores will be there, too." He turned the steering wheel hard back and forth, swerving the car from lane to lane, using the whole width of the road. He laughed as the tires grabbed the edges on each side of the road, then he'd flip the car back into the other lane.

Now used to Pistol's erratic driving, Nate could only smile.

When they pulled into the drive-in, an old man was sitting in the shade along the wall where Delores would usually wait. The man walked over to their car and asked for their order.

"Where's Delores?" Pistol asked.

"Around back, taking her afternoon break." The man pointed. "Better shade back there."

"Well, no offence or nothing," Pistol said, "but can you tell her Pistol and Nate are here...please?"

The old man looked at his watch and said, "She's about done. Wait up a moment. I own this place, so I suppose we should do what the customer requests. Am I right on that?"

"You bet, sir. And thank you much," Pistol said.

The old man disappeared behind the building.

"Hope she's happy to see us," Nate said. "The old guy's okay, but he ain't nothing like her."

Delores appeared, then smiled and waved at the boys. Her hand spanked the top of the car's metal fender as she walked past, then she stopped at Pistol's window. "Howdy, you two. Here's the deal, no extra trips when you order this time. Unless, of course, you plan to leave me some plenty-big tip money. The green, folding kind. Not those pocket-clinkers."

"No, no, that trick only works once per carhop," Pistol said. "Forgot to tell Nate that part. A couple cheeseburgers, please. Two root beers, too. No onions, and thanks."

Deloris nodded. "Hi, Nate. I see you're still here. Get any new girlfriends over the summer?"

Nate again began to feel tongue-tied but was determined to show Pistol he'd found his strength. "New girlfriends? Uh, no, but I'm leaving day after tomorrow, so guess it's too late. Was hoping your little sis would be a possibility, but no chance now."

Delores turned toward the building and yelled so loud, a few blackbirds squawked at each other from their perch on the top rail of an old wood fence. "Bailey Rae, get yourself out here and quick! Someone wants to meet you."

Nate slumped a little into the seat, but sat straight again and looked toward the building.

"You sure you want this city slicker to be seeing your li'l sis?" Pistol asked.

Deloris smirked. "She's got to learn about these things sometime. Better with me around to chaperone."

Bailey Rae peeked her face past the corner's edge and held herself there.

"C'mon over here," Deloris said. "Nobody's going to bite you."

When the younger girl stepped out and walked forward, Nate had to force himself not to say anything foolish. Pistol was right. She was prettier than Delores, or anyone else he'd ever seen.

In silence, she stood close to her big sister and wouldn't look at either boy.

"Bailey Rae," Deloris said, "this is Nate. He's from up north, Minnesota, I think. You know Pistol already, but Nate wants to meet you. He's from out of town, so you be polite. Show him who we are."

The young lady left her sister's side, walked past the front of the car, and stopped by Nate's open window. She had to bend some to look in under the car's roofline. "Hi, Nate. I heard about you, y'know, that you were here and all. My sis says you're okay."

Nate could almost look at her straight, but wished he was out of the car, standing instead of sitting and looking up. He pressed his face partway outside the car window, which made her back up a step. "We're supposed to be the same age, I guess," he said. "Now, I wish I was staying longer, and anyway, gotta go home day after tomorrow."

"Well, come back next summer, maybe," she said. "You ride horses?"

"Last time I did I had a, uh...well...yup, I can ride."

Nate glanced back at Pistol and Delores, who were both smiling. Turning back to Bailey Rae, he gripped the door's edge with both hands, tight enough that his fingertips turned white.

"Bailey, why don't you take their order over to the window," Deloris said. "Will be good practice for next summer."

Bailey walked back to her sister and took the slip of paper with their order, then started walking toward the building.

"Hey, c'mere," Nate yelled. "I forgot to order something."

Bailey turned around and walked toward the car. She raised an eyebrow at Pistol and her sister, who were laughing. "What?" she asked, and their laughter grew louder. Nate thought about next summer.

As the two friends rode in silence after leaving the drive-in, Nate took in as much scenery as he could, knowing his visit to Arkansas was ending. The fresh air smells, the beauty of the hills in the distance, and the low rumble of Pistol's engine all created an enhanced sense of being alive. This summer's adventure was one he'd never forget. Would he ever get to come back?

"Hey, Pistol, you think you could ever come to Minnesota?" he asked. "You'd like it. We have drive-ins there, too."

Pistol snorted. "How'm I supposed to do that?"

"Stay with us. Plenty room."

"They going to let me drive my car up there...huh? I doubt it. Besides, next summer I'm signing up for the whole season on Anderson's farm. No taking off till the harvest on that deal. You cut out before it's done, and you never work around here again. Going to make a bushel basket full of ten-dollar bills, too. Maybe you should sign up."

"Don't know about that," Nate said, staring out at the hills. "I'm not much of a farmer, and anyway, I'd have to be back in school before fall harvest is over."

Pistol grunted. "Okay, then let's just solve one problem at a time. First, we need to get Lotty out of here."

"She's gotta be afraid big-time plus a million," Nate said, nodding, "especially with me leaving and all. But she's no chicken, ya know. I mean, how many you ever known could take off on their own like she's done? No sir, plenty brave, just needs a little help, is all."

When they got close to Hartsville, Nate asked, "Can we stop quick at Y.T.'s? Not sure I'll have time to see him tomorrow, and I want to say goodbye."

Pistol gave him another of his punches on the shoulder, which meant *okay*. "Been good havin' you around here," he said.

"Same here," Nate said.

They pulled up to Y.T.'s store, then went in. The air and temperature were heavier inside.

"Hey, you two incorrigibles," Y.T. said. "Nate, heard you're heading back soon."

"Hey, Y.T." Nate said, walking toward his usual stool. "That's right. Thursday morning. Taking the train home. School's starting soon."

Y.T. nodded, wiping his counter. "We've enjoyed you being here. Coming back next summer?"

Nate shrugged. "Kinda hope so. Not sure, but good chance of it. Got a job for me if I do?"

Instead of answering, Y.T. said, "Listen up. I saw your granddaddy today. Do you know anything about what he was doing?" He leaned forward, not looking straight at

Nate or Pistol. "Have you seen him in the last few hours?"

"What's up?" Nate asked, leaning closer. "Something wrong?"

"Well...he had a young negro girl with him, and they went into the drugstore—to use the phone, I'm told. Had her tight by the arm, too. Then, they drove off in his truck." Y.T. turned sideways, still not looking directly at either boy.

Nate went cold all over, then hot. "Who told you this? I mean, how do you know about—

"Something about that sight bothered me," Y.T. said, "so I walked over after they left. Found out it was that runaway, and your granddad called the number on the poster about her. He's taking her back to them straightaway. Probably there right about now, I'd guess. It's been a few hours."

Nate hit the countertop with his fist, walked fast to the door, then stepped out into the middle of the road and looked both directions as if he might still see them. The screen door slammed behind him, but Nate didn't flinch.

As Pistol walked up beside him, Nate flicked a glance his way, then kicked at the dirt along the road's edge, scanning again in both directions.

"Nate, hey, listen up. We'll get her back,".

Nate walked around in circles, mouthing silent words, then shuffled to the old wood bench under the awning, sat, and propped his chin in his hands. "Nuts!" he shouted.

Y.T. came to the screen door. "C'mon in here."

Pistol moved toward the door, but Nate stayed on the bench.

"Nate...you givin' up so easy?" Pistol asked. "Y.T. says get in there. Let's see what he's thinkin'. C'mon, now. You're not getting anything done sittin' out here."

Nate stood, then trudged toward the door.

"That's the spirit," Y.T. said, ushering them inside. "No doubt you're not happy, but maybe it's for the best. That she's back there, I mean."

Nate stretched his frame tall, like a bear showing he was ready to attack. Raising one fist in the air, he said, "She's in big trouble, and I gotta do something right now. Whatever it takes. You don't know why she ran in the first place. Well, I do. So, let's go. How far is it?"

"Whoa, slow down," Pistol said. "Maybe we can get some help and head there tonight. We can't go barging in like the cavalry. Those people are no cupcakes, and you don't want to learn that the hard way. Otto and the old man, especially. You don't know 'em like we do."

Y.T. nodded. "Pistol's right, Nate. You tried hard to do a good thing, but maybe it's best now to just let her go. You can get hurt, and I'm not kiddin'. Proud of you for what you've done, but don't be dreaming here, cuz there's two ways we can send you home on that train." He crossed his arms. "Listen to your friend's advice on this, not so much to your temper. Anger is only one letter away from danger. You know that?"

"Thanks for telling me, Y.T.," Nate said. "Gotta go."

As Nate and Pistol walked toward the car, Y.T.'s voice trailed them. "You two be careful." He thought he should head over to Nates grand parent's place.

Nate waved over his shoulder and climbed in. They could trust Y.T. with their secrets, and Pistol sure seemed calm enough, all Nate could think of was how to make a fast rescue.

Chapter Twenty-Two

As they drove away from Hartsville, Pistol said, "I'll be taking you home now."

"No way!" Nate shouted, clenching his shaking fist.

"You need to stay out of this," Pistol said, then glanced at Nate's hands. "Are you angry with me?"

"I'm angry at this messed-up world, not you," Nate said between his teeth. "And you're not taking me home, so you better believe it. Nothing's stopping our plans."

Nate paused, waiting for Pistol's reaction to the "our plans" bit. Was his friend on board?

When Pistol remained silent, Nate plowed on, sure to convince him. "No sir, we just pick up anyone you say can help us, then we head down there, or we go by ourselves. Don't matter either way, but we're going." He straightened to sit taller. "I can't leave her alone with them Waldcotts, and that's that." He jabbed a finger toward Pistol. "Plus, you agreed, so no turning back. She needs us both. You in or what?"

"Okay, all right, I'm in," Pistol said. "But we won't get back till late, you know. You'll be in plenty trouble just for worrying them two." He shook his head. "They'll be howling mad at both of us, really. And what if we do get her back? You can't take her to your grandpa's place again."

"Don't care," Nate said, his voice little more than a growl. "We gotta just get her, and now, not later. I'll put her back in that cornfield if I have to, or..." He drummed his fingers on his leg, looking at the horizon where the end of the road met the sky. "We capture her and take her to your sister's for a time. How about that idea? I'm thinking she'll hide her and then you get her on a train later. I'll even give your sis some money. Well, a little bits possible."

"I don't like this," Pistol said. "Don't like the odds, either, but..." He slapped the steering wheel. "Ah nuts, okay, why not."

Nate leaned back in the seat for the first time, took a deep breath, then watched the scenery. He stuck his right hand through the open window and tapped the car's roof in a staccato rhythm.

Pistol drove a bit slower than his usual pace and took quick glances at Nate. "You're really not kiddin'," he said. "Okay then, we need to get my older brother."

"Why?" Nate said, stopping his roof-drumming. "I mean, that's a long way back. We need to get there but quick. Like now."

Pistol nodded. "Right, but we'll need him. Someone's gotta create a diversion while the others snap her up."

Nate's thoughts tripped over each other, and after a moment, he said, "Yes, let's do it. Good to see you're on the job. I'm too ticked off to think straight."

"Did you ever think you'd be needing to rescue her?" Pistol asked. "You must have considered this happening somewhere along the way. Or did you just believe it would all go nice and easy for you?"

"Yeah...guess I did," Nate admitted. "I mean, this is the biggest mess I've ever been into. Besides, I'm not used to actually seeing how hateful people can be. That's plenty new to me."

They didn't speak for a time. Pistol quickened their pace and sat up on the steering wheel, his usual posture when in a hurry. His back never touched the seat as he held both hands tight while sawing back and forth on the wheel. Driving straight and fast on these gravel roads was challenging unless a person kept flicking the wheel side-to-side and trying to glide over the ruts.

Nate relaxed some since Pistol was now working their plan. At this speed, it was as if their tires were barely touching the tips of the gravel ruts, just gliding over them like a downhill skier...or that dragonfly he'd longed to become. "My Grandpa is a good man," he said, "so why didn't he just ask me what to do? I mean, Lotty had to tell him I'm her friend, so what's his problem?"

"He has to live here," Pistol said. "He can't be hiding a runaway negro girl and expecting that to keep quiet from his neighbors. They aren't going to just say 'Okay, old Henry's just being a nice fella.' It don't work that way." He shook his head. "Well, not with some, that is. Anyway, we all depend on each other around here. He'd be in trouble with at least half the folks, and so would your grandma."

"I guess so," Nate said. "Half sounds like too much, but I'm trying to understand this business. Somewhere, someone's got to turn this mess around. I mean, all people are people. All of us bleed red, ya know."

"No, they're not," Pistol said in a firm voice. "Not all the same, I mean. People here like to keep to themselves, and that means making sure to keep the others to themselves, too. Right or wrong, it's always been that way, and it don't matter what some high-minded law says."

"Okay then," Nate said, "so why do I see it so different? I know she's good people. I know she is the same as me, pretty much, in her heart and everywhere that's important."

"Not around here, she ain't." Pistol blew out a breath. "Maybe up your way it's different, but I doubt it. There's two sides of town. Ours and theirs, and you ain't going to change that."

Nate gritted his teeth. "So, why're you helping me, then?"

"I don't know. Maybe cuz you're a friend, or because I'd like to see things get better myself. Mostly I'm so used to things as they are, but listening to you has me thinking."

They remained quiet until they neared Pistol's driveway, then both said at the same time, "I hope he's home," and laughed.

Chapter Twenty-Three

The late afternoon sun was beginning its daily hidings behind a large tree. Nate tensed even more as he and Pistol exited the car. How much longer would it take to get dark?

Pistol's older brother, Fuzzy, walked toward them. "What's up, you two?"

After they explained the mission, Fuzzy agreed to help without hesitation or questions. He did say, "We're all nuts, you know." As they walked back to the car, Fuzzy was first to call, "Shotgun," so Nate hopped in the back. Then, they drove to the paved highway and turned south.

Nate could barely think over his powerful heartbeats. Why was Fuzzy so agreeable to go find trouble? "You know where they live, Pistol?" he asked.

"We do. Been there a few times. We've done some tradin' with old man Waldcott. Last spring, we picked up that John Deere B from him, like your granddad's tractor. Still a good machine, too, and we use it plenty when we don't need the big Moline."

Fuzzy leaned backwards across the front seat, pointing his finger straight into Nate's face. "Speaking of questions and such, you goofy or something? Why'd you ever get started on this in the first place?"

Nate decided he'd better not say too much. He hardly knew this guy, and Fuzzy had to be eighteen or so, old enough to deserve respect. In a quiet voice, he said, "Couldn't help it. Just found her alone and scared. Felt sorry... and still do." That should do it. Respectful, yet strong.

"Well, okay then." Fuzzy turned back around. "I get it, sorta. I'm getting tired of how they're treated, myself. Things seem to be changing these days, too. A little, anyway. I've worked with many of 'em, you know, and can even say I'm fond of a few. If they were in trouble, I'd probably help. Well, for sure I would if it was Bart, and in case you haven't noticed, I am here, and it didn't take much askin, either."

"Appreciate it, Fuzzy," Nate said. "So...you guys have some kind of a plan? I sure don't, besides busting in the door, throwing some fists, and dragging her out, that is."

"We kick some Waldcott butt. That's first thing," Pistol said. "You up for that?"

He and his brother laughed while Nate slumped into the seat.

"Not to worry, pal," Pistol said, eyeing Nate in the review mirror. "We're hoping for a better...well, let's say a cleverer solution. Besides, that'd be too easy. We like it complicated. Maybe we'll light one side of their house on fire and catch her when they all run out the other."

The brothers laughed again, Nate too. With these jokers to help, this really could work. They weren't afraid of anything.

"We best wait till it's dark before doing anything," Fuzzy said.

"For sure," Pistol replied. "I know the layout over there. The house is kinda set back from the road, so we'll be stopping by the edge of their cornfield. Should be able to hide the car pretty well back there and work our way up close. Corn's plenty high right now."

"Then what?" Fuzzy asked.

"Well...next, we sneak through the cornfield and get up as near as we can to the house."

"I dunno," Nate said. "Lotty tells me there's another house. A shack kind of place, it sounds like, the one where she and her parents lived. It's some distance from the main house, I think. She could be in there, too. I hope so."

"Not likely," Pistol said. "They wouldn't leave her alone so soon. She ran once, so they'll figure she will again. They'll be keeping her in their house, for sure. Only makes good sense. Besides, they got to do some scaring her, so she won't run again." He turned around to look at Nate as the car started moving toward the far edge.

Fuzzy grabbed the wheel and pulled the car back into the middle of the road.

Everyone laughed.

"Sorry," Pistol said.

Pistol's reasoning was so strong, neither Nate nor Fuzzy offered a challenge or any new ideas. While the car carried them over the smooth highway and conversation stopped, Nate sagged a little. All the frantic energy his anger had fueled dwindled as he squeezed the top of the front seat with both hands and pulled his head forward to line up as close as possible with the two in front. Images of Otto kept filling his mind...memories of how strong and mean he was. Surely, he wouldn't be there.

Turning onto a gravel road, Pistol said, "We're getting close. I'm shutting off the headlights in a minute, so keep an eye out for anything and everything in case I don't see it. You know, coons, dogs or deer."

Nate squinted into the darkened roadside. This trip had gone much too fast. He wasn't ready just yet. He longed for more time to get used to this idea, to get his courage up. He folded his hands and offered a short, silent prayer for their safety and success. Lotty would like that. *Bet she's praying, too. Never prayed so much in my life.* He tried to swallow but had trouble.

Pistol shifted into neutral, turned off the motor, and coasted slow close to the edge of the cornfield. He steered the car with care and gently tapped the brake pedal until he made certain the car lined up and was well hidden from view of the house. The tall rows of corn offered great cover.

"Nice work," Fuzzy whispered, as if someone in a house that far away could hear him.

The three sat still, adjusting to the quiet and letting the night sounds and darkness focus into their new awareness.

"Get the doors closed fast as you can," Pistol said. "Don't want the interior lights to stay on too long. Fuzzy, you duck into the stalks, then me and Nate will take the row next to yours. Let's not all be nose-to-tail together, like a train or something. Let's keep spread out a bit."

Nate and Fuzzy both said, "Okay," in harmony, then Fuzzy asked, "Hey, boss, who died and elected you president?"

No one laughed, but Nate wanted to.

They abandoned the car in a mostly soundless hurry. Fuzzy ducked into a row, then Pistol and Nate stepped into the one to his right.

Nate sniffed, relishing the smells of the cornfield, but wished his heart would slow down some. He took a deep breath, then wiggled his shoulders, arms, and hands and kept moving, keeping close to Pistol without bumping into him.

"Keep low," Pistol whispered.

Nate frowned. Why was that important? The stalks were a foot or more taller than he.

Fuzzy's movements beside them made little swishing sounds, but only partial shadowy hints of his clothing showed through the adjacent thick, green stalks. "Hey," he said. "Hold up a sec."

They all stopped as one.

"We started too far to the right of the house," Fuzzy whispered. "Let's all move over about three or four rows. We should be lined up better to see in the windows when we get up there."

"We gotta be quiet doing this, too," Pistol said.

Nate was sure Pistol was talking straight to him. After all, he was mostly only along for the ride. Happy to follow their lead, he respected any instruction they offered.

They moved slower than before, fighting sideways through the tight rows. The stalks had matured to their full size after the long summer and left little space between them. While taking care to keep noise to a minimum, they moved with focused effort. Once they'd gotten aligned where they needed to be, they stopped to plan their next move. The house was now only twenty five yards away.

"Easy to see inside there," Nate whispered. "It's dark in that shack over there, too. You're right. She's not in there. I'd bet on it."

"Keep really low, now," Fuzzy said. "And hey, he don't have the big yard light on. That's a lucky break. Let's move up a bit until we get just behind the first row. The edge, I mean. You got it? Should be able to see in the house real easy from there. The missus is using those sheer curtains the old ladies like. Can see right through 'em."

As if on command, they all started moving as one, having found an intuitive harmony.

When they reached the place where it was easy to see into the yellow-lit windows, Nate whispered, "She may be up in that top floor room. You know, the attic. She told me about that room once, but it looks like there's no lights shining on the third or second floors."

"Nobody up there," Fuzzy said, "so here's the deal. We just wait...right...here. When we see bedroom lights go on and off, we know they went to bed. Then, we wait some more, let 'em get settled down, then sneak in and find her." He paused. "Nate, you keep close to us, cuz she knows you. Be ready to make sure she sees you, or else we'll be scaring her. We don't need extra noise or confusion."

"Got it. Good plan," Nate said. His stomach tightened, his mouth was dry, and he was thankful for the light breeze that swept across the sweat droplets on his forehead. "Wish this was over," he whispered low enough that only he could hear it.

They all sat on their haunches and kept watching the house. The fluttery sounds of the corn stalks' tiny moves as cooling night breezes traveled through the rows soothed Nate's nerves. The cricket symphony was playing everywhere.

A back bedroom light flared on the first floor, then Nate nudged Pistol and pointed. Pistol poked Nate on his leg, then made an *okay* sign, joining his thumb and forefinger together into a circle. Nate smiled, figuring Fuzzy had seen it, too.

Nothing further happened for a quarter hour or longer. Nate fought to resist fidgeting about from tight, cramped muscles. He was excited to see Lotty's face. Hopefully, she could just run without that old bag she carried, but he'd bet it was right next to her. He'd carry it himself if these kidnappers hadn't stashed it somewhere to look through.

Another ten minutes dragged by, and Nate's backside was starting to hurt from sitting on the ground too long without moving. He and Pistol both twisted and stretched, then settled back. Low clouds began to shade the half-moon's silver glow, and the sky had grown as dark as it would get for the rest of the night.

The quiet, shadowy shape of a man glided from the back of the house, across the yard, and into the barn.

A dim yellow light came on, then Fuzzy yelled, "Get down!"

The report of a shotgun crossed the yard in an instant. Lead pellets tore through the leaves above them and only a little to the right of Fuzzy's row. Then, a second report and a burst of pellets tore through high and tight to the other side, close to Nate and Pistol.

"What a lousy shot," Pistol yelled. "Run!"

In the instant it took Nate to get turned around, another gunshot fired close enough to come from only a yard away, the loudest he'd ever imagined. This one was so near, the odor of burnt powder stung his nose. Then, a second blast rang out, as loud and near as the first. He looked toward Fuzzy's row. Pistol's brother stood tall, shooting a pistol into the air, as if trying to scare the other shooter.

As they ran, an old man's voice spewed curses into the darkness from the yard.

"Don't shoot him," Nate yelled, sprinting toward the car.

"Rotten thieves!" the man's booming voice yelled. "Get

runnin', you devils, or you'll be breakfast for my hogs. No one'll ever find ya. They'll chomp your bones down easy."

A door slammed at the back of the house just as the trio reached top speed through the field. The fully grown ears of corn hurt as their hands, arms, and faces bashed into them, some hitting their knees and shins. It took no time to reach the edge, unlike their first ghostly quiet trip to the dangerous end of the field.

At last free of the corn, Nate rushed toward the moonlight that shimmered off the car's chrome bumper and grill, making their getaway ride look to be smiling as it waited.

The instant they all piled inside the car, Pistol fired the motor, then floored it in reverse. "Not passing that house," he said, twisting in his seat to watch the road behind them over his shoulder. "Might be recognized...or worse."

He somehow managed to keep the old Chevy in an almost straight line, lights out and driving backwards as fast as it could move. When he finally stopped, he blew out a noisy breath and turned back around.

"Nice going," Fuzzy said.

"Shee-oot," Pistol replied, wiping his forehead.

"You always carry that thing, Fuzzy?" Nate had to ask.

"Only when I'm kidnapping someone from the Waldcotts' living room," he said. "Didn't you bring yours?" Both brothers smiled.

"What is it?" Nate asked. "It's the loudest gun I've ever heard."

"Smith and Wesson, snub-nosed 38, the kind the cops carry," Fuzzy said. "It's so loud, if the bullet misses you, the noise will scare ya to death."

Nate stuck his face out the window and pulled in as much cool air as his lungs could take, then turned sideways to look back toward the field. He relaxed some once they were out of view of the Waldcott place.

Settling in for the ride, he stared at the backs of Pistol's and Fuzzy's heads. Why didn't they seem afraid? Weren't they? Instead, they seemed happy, like this was an everyday thing they did for fun. Something else they didn't show was becoming clear to him. Under their tough guy swagger, they cared. He couldn't think of anyone else he knew, here or back home, who would risk this for him. That hurt some, but so what? These two were what he needed right now.

Chapter Twenty-Four

Pistol stopped the car in front of Nate's grandparents' home. After their goodbyes, Nate walked the driveway toward the house, listening to the familiar sounds of Pistol's car as it drove away. He turned, stood still and watched the taillights until they disappeared. "What a great friend," he whispered. "So...back to normal again."

The back porch light spread its silver glimmers onto the yard a short distance past the edge of the house. The sight of that light on at this late hour made his stomach tighten. Grandpa was probably waiting. They would never leave that light on after going to bed. He stiffened his back, trying to get ready for the storm.

"Nate, is that you?" Grandma's angry voice called. "Get over here. Where you been all night?"

She'd only used that tone once all summer, but at least it was her instead of Grandpa.

"Hi, Grandma," he said, stopping next to the porch. "Been with Pistol and his brother. Sorry I'm late."

"Not sorry as I am," she said, rocking her chair fast.

"You scared us half to death. Shame on you. So, out with it. Where you been this time?"

"Well gee, there's no phone to call in on. I mean, back home I'd do that."

"Nice try, young man." She pointed a finger at him. "Down here, you don't just disappear then try out your pitiful excuses later. We're old, we're nervous, and we're supposed to be taking care of you. How are we to know if you're alive or not?" She stopped rocking.

"Sorry. Should've told you, and I do know it."

She crossed her arms. "So, where you been?"

Nate glanced at the screen door. "Where's Grandpa?"

"Just never you mind. Where you been, I said for the last time."

"Is he coming out here?"

"Nate...no, he's asleep. We're all getting up early. Things to do. I'm not angry you ran off with Pistol. We trust you both. I'm angry because you scared us by not coming home on time. You should understand that."

"I do," he said, trying to calm his own temper. "Same rules as home. Said I'm sorry, and I am. So, if you really want to know, we went to steal back Lotty. Y.T. told us Grandpa took her back to the Waldcotts. That's what we did." He dropped his head to his chest but kept one eye strained open, watching her face. "Well, it's what we tried to do. Didn't work so well, though." He stepped onto the deck and sat next to her.

Grandma's face looked tired. When she swatted away some night bugs that were swarming toward the porch light, he jumped back a bit. Good thing she wasn't about to swat at him.

"That was an awful thing for Grandpa to do," he said. "Did you know about it?"

She lowered her head and turned sideways far enough that he couldn't see her face.

He remained silent, letting her know it was still her turn to speak. As he continued to wait, another question plagued him. Why hadn't she asked if they'd succeeded in rescuing Lotty?

Turning back to face him, she said, "There's things you're too young to understand."

"Whoa, I'm not believing that one," he snapped. "Been hearing it forever. You were on her side, and you were helping her, too. So please, please don't tell me you somehow changed your mind. I think what you're getting at must be something else."

"Your grandfather understands things in a different way," she said. "He knows where she belongs. Well...he believes she's too young to run away, no matter what." She sat straighter while again looking right at him.

Nate dropped his gaze and stared at the floor. "Nothing I can do now," he said, "but I did think we were on the same side. And she's in big trouble because she's not here anymore. The 'no matter what' part is something I see you don't know about yet."

"You'll understand things better as you grow, Nate." He glared up at her, but she lifted a hand. "You will. His intentions are good, even if you can't see it now."

He gripped the arms of his chair. "Everyone says that, but I know things you guys don't. So, how can you say it's better for her there? It isn't. I do know that, and I know her, and I know her story, too. She's going to get hurt there, and who cares? I...well, I thought we did, you and me. I thought we were doing something important for her." Nate clamped his mouth shut. Why couldn't he bring himself to tell

Grandma the truth about the Woldcott boys and their plans?

She patted his arm. "There's nothing else I can say, except bless your heart, you tried. Best get to bed, now. Go on, it's getting late."

"I've asked Pistol to drive me to the train, you know." he said, standing. "I just don't want to see too much of Grandpa for a while." He turned at the edge of the porch and looked back. "I'm sorry, but he said he'd be here."

"We all have some time to make peace, Nate. Let's use it well. Get to bed, now."

Without another word, Nate walked toward the tent.

Maybe he should have said goodnight, but he didn't want to. He should have told her more details about why Lotty ran. At the door to the tent, he turned. The light went off, so she had gone inside. Too late, to start over now.

He couldn't resist walking over to the barn and climbing the stair to Lotty's room. "Nothing here," he whispered, looking around. "Nothing in the closet, either. Grandpa must have made her bring it all. It's awful empty." He sat on the floor and fought the emotions that were trying to escape through his eyes. "Butch," he said, then left the barn for the tent.

Butch welcomed him with a wagging tail and nudged his nose into Nate's chest.

Nate hugged and squeezed him harder than he ever had. Butch tried to wiggle away, but Nate's grip held too much power. "Sorry," he said, relaxing his hold. "Going to miss you, old pal." He lay down on top of the sleeping bag without undressing. Sleep eluded him for many hours.

Chapter Twenty-Five

Lotty hid inside an abandoned van in a wooded area near an unfamiliar small town. She began thinking again about Henry, when they'd sat in his truck and he'd told her not to run. But run, she did, right after he went into the store. That hadn't been a mistake. She was certain. A memory of Nate telling her what his grandpa would do if he ever caught her solidified her resolve. She'd done right in taking no chances.

"How could I trust in Henry?" she whispered to God. "He started out one way, switched, and could've changed back to his first plans at any time, just as fast."

Only silence responded. She let out a breath. Hearing no strange noises nearby, she leaned her back against the metal side and closed her eyes.

"I wonder where Nate is right now," she whispered. "He's probably in the tent with Butch. Lucky, both of them. Wish I was still on the farm. Even hiding in the barn and waiting for him to bring me some supper was better than here."

She stared at the hole where the van's dirty floor had partially rusted through. "I hope no critters can climb in here." She shivered, despite the heat. "We'd both be trapped."

The window in the driver's door still had glass that was rolled up, but the other door had none. Cobwebs filled most of its window, reminding her of the earthen cellar where she'd first waited for Nate. She yawned, longing to sleep, but thoughts of being found in there kept her awake. That and the possibility of curious wild critters coming to visit.

When the sun had completely set, and darkness offered safe avenues to disappear into, Lotty climbed out the back and moved with purpose and care toward a dark tree line a short distance from the edge of the nearby town. Her body cast no shadows in the cloud covered almost moonless dark as she covered the distance to the trees in good time.

Working her way into the forest, she discovered a jutting, high rocky ledge. With determination, she slowly climbed to the top. Looking out over the forest, she relaxed some. This height put her out of sight of any strangers who might wander through the woods. Far off lights from the town helped with a warm feeling. All felt safe.

She wrapped her old blanket around her shoulders, hiding herself further and adding a sense of comfort. After a short prayer for safety, she drifted into the shelter of sleep.

After sunrise, the report of a nearby shotgun jolted Lotty awake in an instant. Keeping her head down and blinking in the glare of sunlight, she strained her ears for any other sounds. Her heart pounded. Someone was moving around down there. Then the hunter, or whoever, moved past her position and continued walking away. Whatever he'd aimed at, he must have missed.

Braving a look over the edge of the rocky bed, she watched the man's backside disappear into a dense tree line. Sighing, she fell back on the blanket, then smiled up at the clear blue sky.

"Better get going," she whispered. If she could get back to Nate, maybe he could help her get far enough away. Marvella, too...maybe. She rubbed her arms. "Just gotta avoid old Henry."

She packed her blanket in her bag and, gaining a sense of the right direction in which to travel, climbed down from her ledge. After leaving the forest, she crossed an empty field, then found a gravel road. The open field and road made her feel exposed to possible danger.

"This way is north, for sure," she said aloud. "Has to be. The sun's on my right side, so straight ahead must be the way."

She walked for an hour before passing a farmhouse. A young girl on the porch spotted her and ran into the house, yelling for her father.

Lotty started running, recalling the posters Nate had said were scattered around with her story on them. Just then, a car came upon her from behind and passed her, then stopped a short distance ahead. Frozen, she stood shaking.

An older negro woman stuck her head out the open passenger window. "Lost, little lady? Can we help?"

"God is good to me," Lotty whispered, walking fast up to the car.

She climbed into the back, and the husband drove off. She started to fidget as no one had asked where she was going. They must be waiting for her to say. Good they were still heading north.

"Hartsville," Lotty said at last. "That's where I need to be. Are we anywhere near there?"

The man pulled over and looked on a map. "Yes siree," he said. "Real close. Mebbe one, two more miles or so. We gotta turn off here, now, but you're so close you can shamble on over there in no time."

"Old man, you give the little lady some courtesy, now," the woman said. "You is gonna keep a-drivin', and don't be sech a stingy piker."

'Now listen up, here," he said, "you know I cain't be goin' there. Did you fergit?" He turned toward Lotty and said, "Deary, this is far as we go. You hop out here, and all the best to you. Get a movin' on, now, girlie."

Lotty opened the door, stopped, then said to the wife, "It's okay. Y'all got me a long ways, and with a titch more luck, I'll soon be home. Uh, well...I mean, I'll be just fine. And thank you both. No telling what you saved me from today. I mean it, many thanks."

As she climbed out, the corner of a sheet of paper sitting on the front seat caught her eye, and she stifled a gasp. Her name was printed across it. She closed her door fast and tapped twice on the roof of the old car, then stepped away.

As they drove off, she whispered, "Well, here I am again, walkin'' into Hartsville."

Chapter Twenty-Six

This was it...Nate's last night at the farm. He sat in his quiet tent with Butch, still awake and thinking back over the summer. He and Grandpa had said little to each other all day, making the whole place feel awkward, but they'd chosen to leave it that way. Maybe like Nate, Grandpa didn't want to say anything he couldn't take back.

"He's so stubborn," Nate muttered.

The one thing Grandpa had told him was that Lotty had escaped and he didn't know where she'd gone.

"I wish you'd have talked to me first," Nate had said.

Grandpa had huffed. "You weren't here."

Nothing more had been said.

Early in the evening, Nate had watched the quiet way Grandpa left the dinner table for his living room. He'd sat a bit slumped in his chair and stared out the front window, without turning his television on. Nate had wanted to talk to him, to sit with him, but couldn't.

"No question he's feeling bad," Nate whispered. "Maybe as bad as I do."

Nate just wanted to steal the truck and find Lotty. He

knew where the key was, always in the dash. No problem there. More than that, he wished Pistol would drop over. That would, no doubt, work better, but it wouldn't happen. All he could do was sit in his tent, shaking his head and sometimes clenching his fists.

Grandma had set out good clothes for him to wear on the train the next day and had given him the tickets. He'd tucked them safe into his suitcase. They'd shared a short version of their goodbyes and thank-you wishes, but there would be another round in the morning before Pistol drove him to the depot. Sadly, no reminiscing or storytelling would take place on this night. Especially about shotgun blasts and running through a cornfield. Everyone wished it could. This time would never come again.

"I should have warned Lotty to be more careful around here," he told Butch. "How much is my fault?"

The sun began sinking, and the barn created a wall of shadow between the tent and the sunset. Nate frowned at how dark it was getting for this hour.

"Was a pretty good summer, all in all," he said, scratching behind Butch's ears. "Coulda ended better, though." He lay back on top of his sleeping bag and closed his eyes, even though there was no way sleep would come easy.

Butch sniffed, rose to his feet, and moved his fastest over to the tied-shut door flap. He let out a pitiful, low growl.

"Nate," Lotty's quiet voice said from outside. "Nate, it's me. You in there?"

"What the..." Nate shouted, bolting upright. "That really you?"

"Open up, c'mon," she said. "Yes, it's me. I'm alone, too. Hurry, now, c'mon."

Butch was pushing his nose into the canvas door, trying

to open it. Nate moved him aside and untied the straps. Lotty scooted in before anyone could have asked questions. She hugged Nate around his neck, and Butch worked hard to nuzzle in between them.

"Where you been?" Nate said, keeping his voice as low as possible.

"Your grandpa caught me," she said, letting go. "Tried to take me back to the Waldcotts' place, but I ran."

He nodded and sat on his sleeping bag. "How'd you make it back here?"

"Either pure luck or the good Lord's will," she said, glancing around. "Maybe a bit of both. Anything to eat?"

"Sure, sit still a minute. Wow, good to see you." Nate hugged her again, then opened his suitcase and took out cookies wrapped in wax paper. "Best dinner anywhere... well, not counting Grandma's southern fried chicken. Eat 'em all."

Lottie had the first one down in two bites. She breathed deep, then took more time with the second. "So, now what?" she asked.

He shook his head. "Not a clue. I mean, I'm supposed to catch the train tomorrow morning."

"No!" Lottie shouted, rising onto her knees.

Nate squeezed her shoulder, touching a finger to her lips. He begged her silence with his squinting eyes, then squeezed both shoulders.

"Nate, you can't leave me now," she whispered. "What will I do? I can't just take off again on the run and hope I'll forever be lucky like finding you." She blinked fast, as if warding off tears. "Can't you stay here longer? Please."

He cleared his dry throat. "School starts next week. They're not going to let me stay. Got a dated ticket, too." He looked away. "Besides, I'm not getting along too well with

Grandpa. We need to park you somewhere else. Some-where he doesn't know about. Yup, that's our plan."

"Nate, listen," she said, leaning closer, "I told your grandpa why I ran in the first place. In the truck, it was. He said he understood. Said something about the Waldcotts being awful people. Low-lifes, I think he said. Not sure what that is."

"Low-lifes is right," Nate said in a growl.

"Anyway," Lotty said, waving a hand, "he left me alone in the truck when he went inside to pay for the gas, we were about halfway to the Waldcott place. Told me to stay put, but I got scared and took off. I thought about you telling me he would never understand. But maybe he did. He was really being kind to me after I told him everything, but I was afraid and ran anyway. Getting so close to that place shook me up plenty, and I didn't know if he'd change his mind again after he told me we'd come back here. Maybe I goofed up."

"Okay, I'm seeing it, now," Nate said, the knots in his stomach loosening. "I think Grandpa is feeling bad, too. You should see him. Never said a word at dinner, except wondering when the Waldcotts would show up here looking for you." Nate balled his hand into a fist. "He'd called them, you know, from the drugstore in town. Said he was on the way there to drop you off. I'm just not sure what to do...yet." He forced a smile. "Let me think a while, because who knows what he'd pull now."

They sat in silence and let the chirping crickets and the winds gusting through the leaves bring some calm to their spirits.

Chapter Twenty-Seven

"Wake up, Nate. Time to go," Grandma said, standing next to the tent. "C'mon, now. You awake in there? It's morning already."

"Yup, yup, just getting dressed, is all," Nate said, looking around the tent for anything he might have forgotten. "Be right up there. Don't worry. Almost done." She walked off. He snapped the suitcase closed and ushered Butch outside. Wanting to stay close to Butch as long as possible, he walked at a slower pace. When they reached the house, he knelt, then rubbed and petted his friend, hoping the dog would last long enough to still be here if he ever returned. "Maybe next summer, old friend," he said.

Butch lay down on the cool grass, his breathing shallow, but tail wagging.

"Pistol's here," Grandma called to Nate. "Ask him if he's had breakfast, will you?"

"Forgot something in the tent, Grandma. Be right back." He ran down there and found Lotty crouched just behind the door flap, holding her bag's handle tight in both hands. He crowded in and said, "Okay, coast is clear. They're all in the house. Scamper up the side yard, and then disappear into the cornfield. Be sure to duck low when you pass by their bedroom windows. Tuck in close to the house, drop low, and keep moving."

"Then what?" Lotty said. Eyes wide, she stared at Nate, holding her breath, and never blinking.

"Duck into the field as far as you can. Keep moving, too. Never stop to look around. Just get as far from the house as you can. And really, don't stop. You get me?"

"Uh...sure, keep moving."

"When Pistol pulls his car onto the road," Nate whispered, "I'm going to have him stop in front of the house and give them a goodbye honk, maybe two. When you hear that, you get right to the front edge of the rows, as close to the road as you can but still out of sight. Be ready to jump out and open the back door when we stop. And remember, get as far as you can so they can't see you or the car when we get there. You got all this?"

"Sure do. Okay...move, move, move, stay out of sight, listen for the horn, run to the car."

"Nate!" Grandma yelled. "Time's a-wastin'. C'mon, now."

"Right away, Grandma," Nate yelled back. He left the tent without another word.

Pistol was walking down the hill with a piece of buttered toast in his hand, so Nate sped up to keep him from getting too close to the tent.

"Hey, old pard," Pistol called. "Big day. You all set?"

"I hope so. But we have one more adventure, you and me, but don't ask until we're in the car. Promise?"

Pistol smirked. "Adventure's my middle name, bucko. You should know that by now."

Both laughed, and Nate stood taller. They couldn't miss.

Nate placed his suitcase on the passenger side of the back seat, so Lotty wouldn't have to climb over it, being in a hurry and all. Pistol started the motor as Grandma hugged Nate longer than he'd wanted. She finally let go and handed him a paper bag full of sandwiches when Grandpa walked up. He placed a folded envelope in Nate's shirt pocket.

"What's this. Grandpa?"

"A note. Something to remember your summer by."

Nate took two steps, grabbed Grandpa around the shoulders, and was tempted to kiss his cheek but that might not go over well.

Grandpa squeezed back, let go, and said, "Best be moving along, now. Fast trains and bad weather wait for no man."

Holding down his emotions, Nate got in the car and set the food bag on the floor.

Grandpa and Grandma both entered the house, holding hands and not looking back.

Nate laughed. "People in Minnesota sometimes wave and follow you halfway down the block when you're leaving, but not this place. I guess here, over is over."

"Pretty much," Pistol said. "So, what's this adventure?"

"Tell ya in a bit. Listen, when we get in front of the house, stop, honk the horn a few times, wait a bit, wave, then drive on. Okay?" Nate gripped the edge of his seat. Lotty would hear the horn and move close to the edge of the field, hopefully plenty far down the road.

Pistol did as he'd asked. "Now what?"

"Drive ahead real slow," Nate said, craning his neck. "And when you see her, stop."

"See who?" Pistol asked, passing rows of corn no faster than they could walk.

Nate gave his friend a wide grin. "Who do you think?"

Lotty sprang from the field and almost bumped into the car. Pistol pushed the brake pedal hard, and the car slid a little sideways on the gravel then settled, perfectly placed for Lotty to open the door without moving.

Once she'd climbed in, they drove off, everyone smiling. A few times, Pistol looked in the rearview mirror at Lotty, as if hardly believing his eyes.

"Better duck way down for a while," Pistol said, the Ellis dogs barking as they drove by.

Half a mile farther along, a newer pickup truck sped by, heading in the direction of Nate's grandparents' farm. Even though the truck was enveloped in a cloud of grayish-brown dust, Nate could make out the driver. Otto Waldcott.

Nate and Pistol spent the next few miles insulting Otto nonstop and laughing as they tried to outdo each other with more and more outrageous put-downs.

"Can't we talk about what's next, you two?" Lotty said, still crouched below the seat back. When they didn't stop laughing and talking smart, she let out a sound halfway between a groan and a growl. "Ugh! My mama was right. She'd always say, 'You know how boys are.' Well, now I do." She thumped Nate on the back of his shoulder. "So, c'mon! You guys each have a home. I sure don't, so tell me what's going to happen here?"

Nate squirmed about on the seat, while Pistol drove into a gas station and stopped next to the pump.

Pistol stared into the rearview mirror and said, "Cool it a while, sister. Nate, check the oil for me, will ya? I'll pump some gas."

Both boys got out. As Nate closed his door, Lotty

popped up, dangled her arms over the top of the front seat, and stared at the empty spots they had just vacated, shaking her head.

Nate opened the hood, then inspected the dipstick, grinning at all he'd learned over the summer. "Oil's okay," he said. "Just one whisker low, and plenty clean."

Pistol went inside the station, and Nate walked around the side of the building, looking for a bathroom door. "Gotta take one for the road," he said, quoting Y.T. and smiling.

Nate finished up, then walked back around the corner. He reached the front of the station just as Pistol came out, and Lotty screamed from inside the car.

Inhaling a deep breath, he took off running, Pistol at his side.

Two boys stood on the driver's side, one yanking on the back door's handle. He grew red-faced, and veins stuck out in his neck as he forced the door open. Through the window, Nate caught a glimpse of Lotty lurching forward, still gripping and pulling back on the inside handle.

"Ha!" the boy yelled as the door popped open, but its quick swing pushed him backwards in an arc, away from the car's opening and Lotty.

Nate and Pistol sprinted around the rear of the car just as the boy righted himself and grabbed Lotty's arm. Eyes narrowed and jaw set, Pistol punched him under his chin. The boy lifted off the ground, then landed hard on the pavement, unconscious. Lotty caught the door, just in time to prevent falling through it, and fell back onto her seat.

Nate glanced around for the second boy, who was making an escape for their car. He ran after him, caught up easy, and tackled him. Holding him pinned to the ground, Nate spotted the struggling boy's car keys on the concrete inches from his hand. He snatched them, then bent the guy's arm backwards, pulling his wrist high up his back, all the way to his shoulder, until he screamed.

"What're you doing?" the boy yelled. "This ain't your business."

"Stay down!" Nate shouted, pushing to his feet. He stood over the boy, shaking a clenched fist at him, and pressing one foot down onto his lower back.

The boy, whoever he was, stayed still.

Nate turned toward his friends. Pistol was bending over his victim, who issued low moans as his body convulsed.

"He'll be back around soon," Pistol yelled to Nate. "Know who these two are, do ya?"

Nate yelled back, "Crazy fools, I guess...but...oh yes, I might make a good guess."

"The Waldcott twins," Pistol said, shooting Nate a grin across the parking area. "We got 'em good, and they're wishin' they'd stayed home. It's hilarious these two little girlies were so easy to take down. Maybe we'll give em another chance someday. This weren't even hard."

Nate smiled, raised his arm, and launched the boy's car keys as high and far as he could. They disappeared into a swampy area across the street.

"Nice toss!" Pistol shouted. "They'll be walkin' a long time."

"They *are* the Waldcott brothers," Lotty called through her opened window. "Now get us out of here, will ya?"

Nate's heart sped up at the memory of the twins' grandfather shooting at him. "Pistol, make sure he doesn't have a gun," he yelled, then turned toward the one still on the ground and eyeballed the length of him for any suspicious bulges. "Don't do anything stupid" he said, "and if we let you leave, you keep your hands out of that glove box."

The boy raised his head, stretched his hands, palms up,

near the ground in front of him, and said, "All right. Just don't break my arm, okay?"

Pistol walked to Nate's side, glanced back at the other boy still flat on the pavement, then looked into the second Waldcott boy's eyes. "We're leaving now, so you wait till your brother comes back around, then you two start walking. Wait, make that running...and tough bounce, those keys are long gone."

Thoughts of what Lotty had told him about these two made Nate want to smack the one who was still alert. Instead, he said through gritted teeth, "Don't follow us. You'll wish you hadn't." He pointed to the arm he'd twisted. "You're lucky so far, but that can change quick. We're taking her to Oklahoma City, to a safe place, then to Texas, so forget about your nasty plans, cuz we know all about you two criminals."

Pistol leaned close to Nate's ear and whispered, "I think he's scared enough to believe you."

Nate nodded, then he and Pistol walked with purposeful slowness back to their car and climbed in. Pistol started the engine and drove off, turning to the right rather than left toward the town where the train depot was.

"Ain't givin' them Waldcotts any clue where we're really headed," he said, then made a few zig-zag turns through the town and came out on the north side, the farthest from the gas station. Only then, did he turn west and drive along back roads toward the train depot.

Lotty yelled a long, lingering, "Yes!" through her open window.

Nate twisted in his seat to look back at her, grinning as she punched a fist out into the air. She opened her hand and turned it, the wind helping it dive and rise like a bird in flight.

With a wide smile, she said, "I do have to get outta here. They ever find me now, I'm sunk." Her smile and the twinkle in her eyes remained.

"You're going to Minneapolis, Lotty," Nate said. "Today. Right now."

"What?" Lotty yelled.

"Whoa!" Pistol said. "How's that supposed to work?"

"Just get us to the depot, man," Nate said. "I'll take it from there. She's not staying anywhere around here, and that's a fact. You have any money, Lotty?"

"Not with me," she said. "It's in the barn. You know, my mama's money? I been keeping it all hidden in there."

"Why'd you leave it there?" Nate asked.

"Was afraid someone would see it in the bag. You know, just in case if they caught me. Then, your grandpa moved us along so fast, I didn't have a chance." She paused, as if waiting for Nate to say something, but he just shook his head. "I'd have dug it out this morning, but had no idea what you were doing. You just ordered me to hide in the cornfield. So, I left it." She raised both shoulders and hands high and looked at Nate.

They drove on in silence until Pistol pulled into the parking area of the depot. All three looked around for any signs of trouble before climbing out. Nate and Pistol escorted Lotty into the building, then they walked to the ticket counter.

"Sir, this is a ticket for Minneapolis," Nate said, holding his out to the agent. "This young lady is traveling there today. She's fourteen, too, legal to go."

The agent took the ticket, studied the writing, then handed it to Lotty. "Pay attention to the conductor," he said. "There's only one area you can ride in. Same thing goes when you change trains in Kansas City. There's a special car and waiting area for your people. Pay attention real good, young lady. You understand me?"

Lotty only nodded, as if unable or unwilling to speak.

"Better get out there, then," the agent said, pointing. "She's leaving about now."

Nate led Lotty and Pistol outside to the platform, then turned to her. "I'll be calling Minneapolis after we leave. Either my sister or Margo from the church will meet you. They're both nice, so do what they tell you." He looked into her wide eyes and smiled. "I'll see you up there soon as possible. And hey, that station in Kansas City is huge. You have only a few minutes to change to another train, so find someone fast who can show you where it is. You don't want to miss that one and be stuck in there, all scared and alone."

Lotty wrapped her arms around him, tears escaping down her cheeks and wetting his collar.

"All aboard!" the conductor hollered.

Nate handed Lotty the paper bag of food Grandma had given him. She smiled, then carried it and her tattered old bag up the stairs and into the car. She didn't turn to look back, and he couldn't look away from her. He and Pistol stood on the deck until the train disappeared.

"So...now what?" Pistol asked.

"Wish I knew," Nate said. "You have any ticket money for me? Forgot to ask her exactly where hers is hidden."

Chapter Twenty-Eight

"We'll head over to my sister's place. How's that sound?" Pistol said, driving slow on a quiet side road, Lotty and the train depot now far behind.

"Maybe so, but let me think a while," Nate said. "Not sure what to do. I've stepped into some deep mud this time, and I'm feeling kinda stuck in it. Up to my hips."

Pistol gave his arm a light punch. "Relax. Your grandpa will take this okay. Her, too. But yeah, maybe we just bring you back."

"If I had ticket money, I'd hide out somewhere till the next train, call my parents and..." Nate bolted forward in his seat. "Whoa...wait a minute. Get me to a phone. I need to call home and tell them about Lotty, and that I'm going to be late."

They both laughed, then Pistol shook his head. "We're for sure partners in crime now, buddy. Maybe that's what's so funny. We did get away with this, but still have to end up in the courtroom of your grandpa and grandma."

"You'll probably be okay," Nate said, his teeth clench-ing. "No need to worry too much."

Pistol huffed. "I'm about as guilty as you are, maybe more, and I've still gotta live here. Some would say—like your grandparents, for example—that I could have put the stop to this, and they'd be right. But no sir, I'm not going to just drop you and run. Can't do that."

For a time, they let the road sounds and sights take over. Nate relaxed a little in the security of their friendship. Pistol leaned back in his seat, maybe feeling the same.

After fiddling with the radio's knob and getting nothing but static, Pistol pounded his fist on the speaker grill on top of the dash a few times, but the station still wouldn't come in without crackles. "I guess we'll have to entertain ourselves," he said. "I wouldn't mind running into those nasty boys again. Especially alone on a road like this one."

"I'm lookin' for 'em," Nate said. "But they're walkin' around somewhere else, far from here." He laughed, picturing them walking and scowling.

After a short drive to the closest town, Pistol pulled into a parking lot and said, "Go on in, make your calls, and I'll wait here. You got change?"

"A few bucks is all, but that should do it. I could call collect, too. Maybe I'll do that."

Nate climbed out and walked inside the store, then shut the door to the phonebooth for some privacy. He pressed the receiver to his ear, and the operator instructed him to load the pay phone with a handful of coins. He smiled at the echoing sounds they made in the phone box. When his sister answered, he let out a breath, and told her when to meet the train, how to recognize Lotty, and to tell their parents he'd be on the next train, likely starting out tomorrow.

"New girlfriend?" Maggie asked.

"Knock it off, sis," he said, scowling. "But listen, you'll

like her. You know Margo at church? She's been trying to help me get Lotty up there because she's in danger. If you can see it that way, it's a chance to do something important. So, don't forget, and call Margo right now. She'll know what to do once Lotty gets there. Keep in touch with her, so she knows everything."

"How come you never do anything nice for me?" Maggie said. Before Nate could answer, an operator cut in and asked for money for another three minutes.

"Don't mess this up!" Nate yelled, as if she could hear him in Minnesota even without the phone. The line went dead, and he was tempted to smash the receiver against the phone box bolted to the wall.

"I know she'll do it right," he said, hanging up the phone. Good thing he'd told her to write it down, though. He exited the phone booth and walked to the door, telling himself over and over that Maggie would help. She might be a pain, but she'd always been goodhearted.

Outside, Pistol stood leaning against the fender. "How'd it go?"

"Good...I guess." Nate shrugged. "Talked to my sister. She'll make it all work."

Pistol straightened, winking. "Would I like her? How old?"

"Ha...not a chance," Nate said, opening his door. "She's a cobra dressed in a butterfly suit." He climbed in, and when Pistol joined him, said, "Well, to me, she's that way. She might be friendly toward you, though. She'll think you have that southern charm thing going."

"Just thinking ahead," Pistol said, starting the engine. "One never knows."

They drove toward Nate's grandparents' place, neither

mentioning Pistol's sister when they passed the turn-off to her house.

When they reached the farm, Stony and Sylvie's truck sat in the driveway. Nate sighed. Company might help soften the situation between him and Grandpa. Nate grabbed his suitcase from the back, then followed the sound of voices to the back deck, Pistol close at his side.

Nate set his suitcase on the ground at the same instant his grandma yelled, "What in the world? You two miss that train? Oh, my goodness. What's happened now?"

Nate took a quick step closer, but Butch lurched in front of him and blocked his progress, barking and wagging his tail. "Shush," Nate ordered, then with a gentle hand, pushed the dog away. "I'm fine, Grandma, and no, didn't miss the train. We were there, all right, but—"

"What the dickens happened, then?" she said. "Tell us, now. None of this waiting about."

"I gave away my ticket, that's what happened," he said, stepping around Butch. "Had to, no choice. Gave it to Lotty, and she's on her way to Minnesota, so there's no stopping this now." He stretched to his full height. "She...is...gone."

"You did what?" Grandpa snapped. "You gotta have more sense than that. Tell me what you're thinking." He stood and moved closer to the deck railing.

Nate took a short step backwards.

"Let's just take it easy," Grandma said. "Must be some good reason."

Nate glanced back at Pistol. He'd been right about the "court of Grandpa and Grandma." They stood elevated on the deck, while Nate had to tip his head back and raise his eyes toward them as if they were judges on a high court-room bench.

"Same reason there's always been," Nate said. "She's in

danger and afraid, and since no one else was going to help out...I did it." He folded his arms. "And honestly, I'm happy I did. I mean, sorry if you're angry, but I had to."

Nate took a steadying breath. He shouldn't wait any longer to ask for their help with another ticket. In the past, every time he'd had a big enough problem to fix and waited too long for his courage to show up, it became more difficult to ask. Also, he didn't like how time slowed down while waiting. Having it weigh on his mind always became more painful than asking.

"I need ticket money to get home," he blurted out. "Just a loan, okay? That's all. A loan, cuz I gave away my ticket, and that's why I'm here again." He added without a pause, "I'll pay it back, honest. I'll get a job or something and send it here."

Grandpa let out a good, hard laugh, and Nate stared at him, eyes wide. Not the reaction he'd expected.

No one said a word, but all looked toward Grandpa.

Nate lowered his head. Would he ever get home?

"What's that in your shirt pocket, Nate?" Grandpa said, then laughed again.

Nate felt the outside of the pocket, the folded envelope Grandpa had tucked in there crinkling under his fingers. He pulled it out and opened it. A paper note stuck out under the flap. He slid it free and unfolded it, revealing two twenty-dollar bills.

"Oh, my. What's this?" he said, then read the note.

Nate wanted to sit on a chair. Instead, he handed the note to Pistol, who read it fast, then laughed. Nate sat cross-legged on the grass.

"You're a good lad, Nate," Stony said. "Plenty proud of you."

"Thanks," Nate said, the word barely making a sound. He looked toward Grandpa and Grandma, who were nodding.

"We'll keep ya," Sylvie said, "if you'll let us."

"Hold on, dear," Stony said. "He's coming into those expensive years. Eating like a hungry buffalo and wanting to buy the latest fancy up-to-date clothes, too."

The laughter around the deck was contagious, and Nate joined in, maybe louder than necessary.

Pistol patted him on the back and said, "Told ya."

"I'm button-popping proud of you, too, grandson," Grandpa said, and everyone went quiet. "I mean that. You, too, Pistol. Took plenty big courage, and you both have it. And I'll thank you, too, because this whole mess has helped me learn some things. There is right and there is wrong, of course. We all know it, but it's up to us to bend all those rotten crooked things straight."

Nate cleared his throat. "I know what you taught me,

Grandpa. Remember? We talked a lot about boats this summer, and sometimes about a sailboat you once had. You said if the wind was working against you, and maybe you'd even get sunk from it, you said be sure to remember that we can always adjust the sail. So, that's what I did."

Chapter Twenty-Nine

When the train pulled into Minneapolis, Lotty let out a long breath. Finally, she'd be getting out of this crowded car and away from the noisy old ladies who rustled through their food-packed paper bags. Those chatty eaters had no care for the way their lip smacking and loud talking affected others nearby. Minneapolis also meant she was far from the Waldcotts.

As she carried her old bag down the aisle to the exit door, her neck stiffened again. Had anyone come to meet her? If so, who, and would they be nice like Nate? If no one waited for her, where could she go? How would she eat? Where would she sleep tonight?

She slowed her breathing and stepped off the train, scanning the platform, ready to run if she had to, but why should that be a concern?

"Lotty?" a female voice called from a short distance away.

A tall white girl with long, sandy hair was waving to her across the platform. Lotty squeezed between two negro passengers who'd left the train ahead of her and walked over to the girl. "Yes, ma'am, I'm Lotty."

"You made it. Nice to meet you. I'm Maggie," the girl said, grinning. "You know, Nate's big sister. Was your train ride okay?"

Lotty nodded. "Yes, ma'am, but walking feels good." She smiled at the older girl, some of the worries she'd carried on the train melting away, while others remained. Would everyone welcome her with such kindness? Would the adults treat her the same? Maggie's smiles and warm greeting assured Lotty that Nate's sister was like him. Close to her own age, too. Maybe they could become friends. Was that really possible?

"How'd you ever meet Nate?" Maggie asked, waving her to walk along the platform.

"That's a long story, but we met in your grandparents' cornfield."

A noisy blast from a loudspeaker interrupted. Both girls looked up toward it at the same moment.

Lotty was shaking a little inside and hoped it didn't show. "Do you know when he might be getting here?" she asked.

Maggie shrugged. "Who knows. Later today, tomorrow, maybe. We'll ask Mom."

Lotty stole a glance at her as they walked toward the exit. Maggie did the same. Nate's sister was keeping her sentences short. Was that on purpose? Was Maggie as nervous as Lotty? She held a lot of power over Lotty at this moment. After all her experiences with whites, Lotty was careful to be respectful, hoping for good treatment in return. Maggie also didn't seem sure how to act.

"We're in the parking lot over here," Maggie said, pointing.

Lotty followed her in that direction. "Where are we going first?"

"Oh, I'm sorry." Maggie stopped at the entrance to the lot and turned to her. "I'm not sure how to be a very good host to you. Let's do this...there's a café on the other side of the cars." She pointed again. "See it? Let's get acquainted better in there, and you can ask all your questions. I might need to make a phone call, too."

"Okay, yes ma'am," Lotty said, relaxing a little. She should have guessed Nate's sister would be nice. Then, another concern struck her. Who should pay? And what if the café didn't let her in? She'd be taking some new chances around here, and she didn't want to be an embarrassment.

"Lotty," Maggie said as they started walking across the lot, "You don't have to call me *ma'am*. I'm not that much older, ya know." She stopped next to a car and pointed at the trunk. "You want to put your bag in here?"

"No, ma'am...um, I mean, Maggie. Best I keep it close. It's, uh, well...it's everything I have." She gripped it tighter and pulled it closer to her side.

Maggie touched her shoulder. "Whatever makes you happy, and welcome to Minnesota, by the way. I'm glad you're here." She smiled again. "Try not to worry too much. You're among friends."

Tears circled Lotty's eyes. She took in a deep breath, shuddered some, then said, "It's a bit scary, you know. I mean, can you see why I would say that?"

"Sure, I can," Maggie said, then started walking again. "Well, I mean, you're kind of homeless and in a new place you've never even imagined." She glanced sideways at Lotty. "Sound about right?"

"Yes, ma'am, that's a big part of it." Lotty stepped with care on the uneven concrete walkway. "I miss my family, too. My mama, that is. Nate is the closest thing I have to family, these days. No one else left. Well...a sister somewhere, but she ran off long time ago."

"That's sad, Lotty. For sure." Maggie cleared her throat. "Maybe we can be friends, you and me." Without waiting for an answer, she pointed to the building they approached. "Here's the café. Let's sit and visit a while. The minute the adults take over, we won't have time."

Lotty gripped her bag tighter. The adults. Nate's parents? That church lady he'd mentioned? If only she could stick with Maggie longer.

As they entered the café, she held her breath and scanned the room for trouble. She didn't want Maggie to be embarrassed or hassled for having a negro person with her.

Two older negro ladies at a nearby table smiled at them. Lotty returned the grin. Maybe Minnesota could be kind toward her.

Chapter Thirty

After a short and fitful sleep, Nate awoke fully in an instant. He put on his wristwatch for the first time all summer and looked at it twice to make sure he'd read it right, then wound the spring a few times. Six-fifteen? "I'd better get moving. Trains don't wait for kids," he said aloud.

Butch had to look at him, then snuggled back into his cozy position on the blanket.

Nate opened his suitcase and took out his good clothes. The thought of dressing nice for a change made him smile, but two days in a row? That was a bit much. He doublechecked the bottom of the case for his small bag of dried cornsilk and two full packs of Black-Cat firecrackers. He'd been keeping that stuff hidden for days. Pistol's going-away gift.

"Nate, you awake in there?" Grandma called from just outside the tent.

"I am, and almost ready."

"Don't forget anything. Remember, I went through the attic the other day, and nothing is left up there. C'mon up for a quick breakfast. We need to keep moving, mister."

Before he could answer, her footsteps crunched on the tall grass when heading toward the house.

Nate latched the suitcase, then sat next to Butch, rubbing the dog's neck and shoulders. Butch let out a soft, low moan and nuzzled his nose into Nate's side.

"I'll miss you, old friend," Nate said as he left the tent. Did Butch know he was leaving? Seemed like he should sense something. Nate glanced toward Grandma's car. She'd already opened the trunk, so he set his suitcase inside, closed it, and went into the kitchen.

"I see you're wearing your fancy Indian beaded belt again," Grandma said.

"For sure. Looks like a good day to show it off." He grabbed the glass of orange juice she'd poured for him and sat at the table. "Hey, I don't see Grandpa's truck. Where's he?"

"Mr. Anderson came by around five-thirty. Said there's problems with some of the hired men. A fight, is how I heard it, and the bunkhouse was set on fire, too. He asked if Henry could help him, then off he went." She turned off the kitchen lights and slapped away a horsefly. "He left you that note of instructions on how to get around in the Kansas City train depot. You'd left it in the living room, so don't lose it."

"Sounds serious," Nate said. "Let's get over there quick."

"Those men get cantankerous sometimes, Nate. Anderson can handle them, but on occasion needs extra help. Your grandpa went into Hartsville to call the county sheriff, then he's heading over. God bless them all." She stacked Nate's favorite on a plate, her homemade pancakes, and set them on the table. "Get eating, now. It's just you and me, and we're short on time."

"Shouldn't we go help out?" Nate couldn't sit still and eat while thinking about the excitement at their friend's.

"If you're not going to eat, you'll be travelling hungry," she said in her teacher voice, then grinned. "Well...sort of. I've re-packed a bag of sandwiches and cookies for you. Should get you all the way home." She looked out the window. "Hope Lotty liked the first batch."

Nate smiled, then ate fast. When he left the house, he took one last look at the tent, the barn, and the workshop, then they drove off. He watched the little farm grow distant until it was out of sight. He'd wait until he spoke to Lotty before asking Grandma for help recovering her hidden money.

"What else did Grandpa add to the note?" Nate asked, patting the envelope in his pocket, thicker than it had been before.

"Just do what he wants, now," Grandma said, taking the next turn. "Read it on the train. Don't be digging anymore holes for yourself. When you're already at the bottom, it's best to stop." Each smiled.

They both looked straight ahead and remained quiet for a while. Nate fidgeted about in his stiff, never-been-washed blue jeans. They had that good, new smell, but weren't broken in and soft yet. And he had to wear them all day.

When they passed the place where he and Pistol had seen Otto heading for the farm the day before, Nate said, "Those Waldcott boys were going to hurt her, Grandma. Lotty, I mean. Do you get what I'm saying? That's why she ran in the first place. She was afraid, and she knows what they been doing to other girls like her."

Grandma looked at her wristwatch, then pulled the car over and stopped. "I do get it, more than you, I'd say. But you need to understand our side, too. You and Pistol were lucky to not get killed trying to rescue her from that Waldcott place." She shook her head and sighed. "You might as well hear the whole thing, then, so here it is. Your grandpa found her by the barn. He didn't know she'd been here so long or what you were trying to do. He just thought he'd found that runaway everyone was talking about. So, he figured he had to bring her back, and that's what he began to do."

She paused and waited for Nate to speak, but he kept silent.

"Lotty took off when he stopped somewhere, and she got away."

"I know about that, Grandma. She told me."

"Nate, bad time to interrupt, so listen to me. Grandpa had decided not to take her to old Waldcott's. While they were on the way, she told him the same things she told you. He was thinking of what to do. He stopped in Garrison for something and made her promise to stay in the truck, and believed she would because he was, by then, trying to help her. He'd even told her he was bringing her back here. But when he came back, she was gone."

"I know. Sorry."

"He went looking all over, but no luck. He told me he'd figured she might head back this way. Just a guess, though. You better forgive him. He did try and do the right thing."

Nate looked out the window, collecting his thoughts. "I see what you're saying, and really, I am sorry to you both. We each messed up a little, but in the end, it's working out okay, so far anyway."

"Lotty told your grandpa how long you'd kept her hidden," Grandma said, her smile growing big and wide. "That was the funny part. When he told me, he really didn't know whether to laugh or spank you. Deep down, he is proud, no kidding. You showed him what you're made of. I suppose he's a little angry in some ways, but proud more than anything. He's no fan of Faubus or any of that hatred crowd in the Little Rock schools, either."

"So, what's going to happen now?" Nate rested his hand on her shoulder, waiting for her reply.

She looked at the dashboard clock, then started the car. "No more time. We need to get there. Do lots of praying, Nate. I sure have."

They rode in silence the rest of the way to the depot.

As they pulled up, Nate stared at the long, silvery train waiting along the outside deck. The Kansas City Southern stood silent, awaiting her passengers. Looking shiny and new, her silver wheels still gleamed, not yet crusty from miles and wear.

"Grandma, last week I was excited to be here," he said. "Today, I'm not. Well, kind of I am, but I'll really miss you and Grandpa. Everyone else, too. Tell Stony and Y.T., too, please."

"It was wonderful to have you, Nate." She reached across the seat and hugged him with one arm. "You've brought us joy. I'd like you to know that, and to understand you can't fix the whole world, but you can sure try to in your own little neighborhood. That much is always possible, so never quit trying when you see an opportunity."

He pulled away and straightened his shirt. "Why do you say that? The whole world, I mean? I just want to change one simple thing for one person. Maybe if everyone did that much, imagine—"

"Time to go in," she said in a serious voice. "Train will leave the dep-oh soon."

As he climbed out of the car, Nate smirked, resisting the urge to correct her pronunciation. He thought about how she said *mun-ah-sip-ul* rather than *municipal* and almost laughed. "Sometimes folks do talk funny down here," he said, pulling his suitcase from the trunk, then closed it.

"Folks like who, mister?" she asked, shutting her door. "Anyone I know?" Her eyes sparkled.

"Never mind, just folks, and only sometimes."

They both laughed, then entered the building and went straight to the man at the counter. Grandma handed him a paper, and Nate gave him his cash.

The agent produced a ticket. "She departs in six minutes. Best be getting out there. Say...weren't you here yesterday?"

"Sure was," Nate said, waving as he walked away, "and I hope I'm here again sometime."

They walked to the exit and stopped on the platform. Nate's heart pounded, and he grinned, to be standing so close to a train again. The words "Kansas City Southern" stood out in big, bright-painted letters on each car. "She's beautiful," he whispered to himself, then shot Grandma a sideways glance, glad there was no time for a long, sad goodbye.

"Remember what your Grandpa said about the dep-oh in Kansas City," she said. "It is a big place, and you'll have only twenty minutes to catch your connection. Don't fool around. The instructions are in his note. Keep that safe in your pocket."

"I will, Grandma. Thanks for everything, I'll miss you."

A conductor walked by and yelled, "All aboard!" even though it was just the two of them on the platform.

Grandma hugged Nate and kissed his cheek. "It's not over when you think you've lost. It's over when you quit. So, you keep doing good things, and I'll keep working on your grandpa. He is a great man, and you'll lose him someday.

When that happens, well...when every old man dies, it's like a beautiful, giant library just burned to the ground."

"I'll remember, Grandma, but can we not talk about that kind of stuff right now?"

"Remember this, too," she said, letting him go. "You have many special gifts."

He glanced at the train, then back to her. "What's that mean?"

"Never mind. You'll just know whenever the time comes that you need them."

Nate hugged her harder than ever, turned, and stepped onto the train.

Chapter Thirty-One

Entering the train car, Nate remembered what Grandma told him about sitting on the left side, and to find a seat facing forward with a window to look out of. She'd said the sun wouldn't bother him all day if he sat on that side.

He chose a plush, maroon and blue seat, soft and nice like someone's rich, fancy furniture. He slid his suitcase under the seat and turned to see if he could spot Grandma on the platform. She was there, standing alone, looking sad. A strange gloominess washed over him, and he wanted to see her smile.

A slight sense of motion commanded his attention. The people on the platform and the building behind them looked to be shifting backwards, but he wasn't sure if they were moving or the train. Unlike a car, it advanced steady and soundless. Perfectly smooth.

Turning around and looking backwards, he tried to find Grandma again, but she had disappeared. "Bye," he whispered, then straightened to face forward.

The buildings and homes of the town become fewer

and farther apart. He was already back in the country. "I'm moving now. This is it," he whispered again. Looking through the window, he thought of Lotty. This was what she must have seen yesterday.

A group of noisy men filed in through the connecting door between the cars and took over at least half the seats.

Nate gathered, after listening to their talk, that they were bridge builders on their way to a new job. He grinned and relaxed into his seat. These loud, boisterous, and good-natured men reminded him of people Grandpa had introduced him to on the farms, at feed stores, and in lumber yards around Hartsville. Similar to a few his dad knew, as well. He was happy he didn't feel out of place. They were familiar, and being among them made him comfortable.

"Hey, kid," one said from a seat across the aisle. "You running away from home?"

Two others smiled, looking straight at him, each as suntanned and clear-eyed as their friend.

"Who, me?" Nate shook his head. "No way. I'm going home, back to Minnesota."

"Minnesota? You don't look like an Eskimo." The man raised an eyebrow. "You live there in the winter?"

Nate grinned. "Sure do, always have. We like it."

"Been there once, and you can have it," the man said. "I prefer Florida or Arizona in the winter. Nice and warm. We work outside and get plenty enough weather."

"Are you going to Minnesota, too?" Nate asked.

"Nope, Kansas City. We have plenty work there for another highway bridge. Be there till winter, then we rest." The man turned away and began listening to another next to him.

Nate wanted to read Grandpa's letter and was happy the man didn't seem to mind their conversation ending.

Maybe he'd visit with them more a little later. Opening the letter, he hoped this would be like his birthday cards. As he always did with those, the first thing he looked for was folding money dropping out, but this envelope held none.

That reminded him of the change from his tickets that was in the ticket folder. He glanced around to make sure no one was looking, then folded the bills and tucked them deep into his shirt pocket and gave it a pat. Pistol had taught him never to flash his money around in public. Sighing, he lifted his note and read.

Dear Nate,

We enjoyed you being here all summer. Thanks for all your hard work on the boat. Hope you learned some things. I'll send you a photo when Bill comes by to pick it up.

Grandma and I both wanted to buy this second round of train tickets, too, but we believe it's best at any age that a person pays for their own choices. That lesson, alone, is worth more than a train ride.

Give your mom our best—dad, too—and study hard in school. Anytime you want to come again, you're welcome. Be a good boy. We are proud of what you've done.

Grandpa.

P.S. We hope Lotty does well. She had wanted to travel north, along with you. She told me so.

Nate smiled. So, Grandpa really had changed his position on Lotty. Looking out the big rectangular window, Nate admired the tall green hills of the Ozarks, hoping Lotty had enjoyed these same new sights as much as he did.

Several times, something Grandpa had said yesterday came to mind, and here it was in his note, too. "She wanted to go north with you. She told me so."

Nate bit his lip, wishing she was with him right then. She had to be okay, and not too afraid. He gritted his teeth. Maggie better be a friend to her.

The men across the aisle started laughing again, distracting him from his serious thoughts. He glanced at them, then stared back out the window.

Maybe he'd see her tomorrow. At least she wouldn't ever have to run again. He squeezed his fists tight. He would hurt anyone who tried to do her harm. "I hate these kinds of thoughts." He huffed.

"Hey kid, you look ticked off or something," one of the men said. "What's wrong? Miss your girlfriend?"

"Girlfriend?" Nate said. "Nope, just miss my grandparents...and their dog."

"Too young for a girlfriend?" The man shook his head. "I don't think so, especially around here. Some folks your age be married off already."

A few others laughed.

Nate grinned. People always said he looked older. Taller than most his age, too.

The oldest-looking of the group said, "Hey, kid, do you know what the jockey said to his horse?" The man paused only a short moment. "Give up? Okay then, he asked the horse, 'So, why the long face?'"

Nate didn't get it, but the others laughed.

"I'll be fourteen in two months," Nate said. "That's not

old enough to get married. Besides, I have to finish school and don't have a girlfriend, anyway."

The joke-telling man said, "Well, don't wait too long. The best ones get accounted for real fast. Otherwise, you might get stuck with one who's too high maintenance."

Again, Nate laughed along with the others, but didn't understand why. A few minutes later, he laughed out loud. He'd suddenly understood the horse joke.

Nate had heard the word *rowdy* before and now had faces to match its meaning. The men laughed and told jokes and spit the loose tobacco fibers from their Camel straights and Pall Mall cigarettes anywhere they wanted, with a *pft*... *pft*...each time they launched those tobacco pieces past their lips. They were coarse men who impressed Nate with their red, sunburned necks, colorful tattoos, and good-natured humor.

"Hey, kid, you're the only youngster in the coach," one of them said. "How come you ain't afraid of us? Why're you still sittin' here, huh? Shunt you be in a car with some old ladies?"

"Afraid? I don't know." Nate shrugged. "You seem okay to me. You remind me of my Grandpa and his friends. My Dad's, too." He smiled. "You could win in a fight over me, but only if you could catch me, which you couldn't, so why be afraid?"

A few laughed, others nodded, and a new kind of pride washed over Nate for being strong enough, and brave enough, to become accepted. Showing no fear had given him entrance into their club.

"Minnesota's okay, kid," the first man who'd spoken to him said. "Was just kidding about that. But the girlfriend thing is nothing to fool around with. Get you the right one whenever she comes along, that's all. Plenty trouble if you choose wrong, and maybe half of us here know exactly what I'm talking about."

"Maybe someday," Nate said. "No hurry, though. I'm going to college first."

"College?" The man snorted. "You come to work with us, youngster. You'll likely make more money, and get to travel, too, and have a girlfriend in half a dozen cities." He chuckled. "When you get more height and size to you, that is. What's your name, anyway?"

"Nate."

"I'm Wayne, and glad to meet you."

As they reached across the aisle and shook hands, Nate resisted the urge to widen his eyes. How long did it take someone to get hands strong as that man's?

"And listen, son," Wayne said, leaning back in his seat. "There's only two ways to live, and here they are. Some men shower before work in the morning, and the rest of us, we shower after. Now, that's the only way to go. Shower after. You get me?"

"Uh...sure. So, you're clean for going to bed, I suppose."

"Close enough, boy. You'll figure it out later."

"Think I'll try a nap," Nate said.

"Go ahead, get your beauty rest." Wayne grinned. "Someday, you'll be too busy for naps."

Nate smiled, leaned into the soft chair back, and closed his eyes. Where was Lotty right now? That was his last thought before sleep found him.

"Kansas City, Missouri. Now arriving... Kansas City...next stop." The conductor's loud voice called, waking Nate as he walked by.

Somewhat sleepy and confused, he patted his shirt pocket to make sure all his money was there.

"Well, good morning, young man, "Wayne said. "Have a good rest?"

Shaking his head, Nate glanced around, not awake enough to be sure what was going on.

"You getting off here?" Wayne asked.

"Oh...Kansas City?" Nate said, blinking. "Whoa. We here now?"

"Better believe it," Wayne said. "We're going on through a bit farther, over to the Kansas side, but if you're going north, I'll bet you need to get off, cuz this train be heading west."

"Thanks, Wayne. I gotta get in there. Going north, that's me."

"You be safe," Wayne said, "and keep that cash hidden good in your shirt pocket. I been keeping an eye on it for ya."

"What? You saw that?" Nate quick touched the pocket.

"You had the right idea, son, but not the best technique. Don't hold it up so high when you're countin' and fixin' to hide it." He held a hand, palm down, near his leg. "Keep it down, out of sight, and you better watch the pickpockets in this place, too. They'll cop it and have it spent before you ever know it's gone."

"Okay, thanks," Nate said. "See you later." He doublechecked his pocket again, crinkling the bulge inside. Real pickpockets?

"We say 'see you down the road,'" Wayne said. "So, look for us again next summer."

Nate smiled and nodded, his mind more on where to be next and getting to his train.

After lifting his suitcase from under the seat, he moved

to the door. Turning around, he straightened and grinned. The men were all looking his way, most either waving or giving him the thumbs-up sign. He waved his free hand in return, then stepped out onto the platform.

"This has been one amazing summer." He sighed.

Chapter Thirty-Two

Nate carried his suitcase into the station, then stopped firm only a few feet onto the concourse. "Incredible," he said.

Grandpa hadn't been kidding. This place was gigantic. Where was he supposed to go? He could only stare at the great spaces and streams of people moving about in every direction. The ceiling had to be high as a water tower, travelers' hard shoes echoed off the shiny stone floors, and loud voices bounced off the colorful granite walls. He swiveled his head side to side, trying to make sense of it all and guess where he needed to be.

A mom pushing a baby in a buggy walked by at a fast and determined pace.

She seemed to know where she was going. Should he follow her? Having second thoughts, he remained frozen in place, letting his arms hang straight down. Lowering his head, he sighed.

Many passengers pushed by him. When one bumped into his suitcase, he jerked his head up. Standing in the middle of the entry was neither smart nor thoughtful, and wouldn't get him closer to his connection.

"Oh, yeah, Grandpa's instructions!" he said. After walking to a corner where he could be alone, and no one could get too close, he fished out his grandpa's paper. He relaxed a little. No one could pick his money as long as he stood secluded. He read the paper and frowned. He had no idea which direction was east or west. "Couldn't Grandpa just say *left* or *right*?"

Glancing around again, he spotted an information station nearby. Walking toward it, he kept one hand tight over his shirt pocket. That might look suspicious, though, so he lowered it. He'd just keep a good distance from everyone. He could always put his hand back if need be.

Reaching the information window, he said to the elderly agent, "Mister, hello, I'm lost."

The old man moved too slow to settle Nate's nerves, but he did finally get to the window. "What is it, son?"

"I'm supposed to find a Rock Island train going to Minneapolis but have no idea which way to look," he talked over the noise and bustle of the place. "Plus, it's leaving real soon." He didn't wish to be insulting, but he needed to make sure the old man heard him. Even he had to lean in toward the old teller to hear any reply.

"Let's settle down a bit," the agent said. "Let me see your ticket, please."

Nate handed it over. "Don't drop it, please," Nate said. Would take him all day to get it back, but he kept that thought to himself.

"Okay, wait right there," the agent said. "Don't be running off. You understand?"

"No sir," Nate said, then wrinkled his nose. "I mean... yes sir, I do understand, and...no sir, I won't run off. Can I get there on time?"

"Only if I escort you. You're late, and she's about to

leave. Stay put so I can close up." The old man closed and locked the two glass panels and left through a door in the back.

Nate glanced around. "Where did he go?"

Someone tapped his shoulder from behind.

Nate gasped, then hit his shirt pocket with his free hand and spun around. He let out a breath and smiled at the old man. "Whew, great. Thanks."

"Follow me, young man. No time to waste, either. Just try to keep up."

Nate laughed to himself at the idea of this man being able to outpace him. Together, they did find a somewhat quicker strut than he'd imagined possible. Careful to not let his suitcase bash into the man's right leg, he switched hands on the run, moving the case far enough away to no longer be a danger.

After a few long hallways and open doorways came and went, he said to his helper, "I'd have never known all this."

"All right, young fella, wait up a second." The old man shuffled over to a long wooden bench and sat a bit slumped. As he pulled in air, his chest rose and fell with each silent breath. With his head hanging down, he pointed to a sign a little farther along on the right, his finger bouncing up and down as if to keep Nate's attention.

The sign read, "Platform Twelve."

"That's her, right there," the man said between breaths. "Number twelve. Take your suitcase and run, boy, like a hungry wolf."

"Sir, can I help you any?"

"No time. Be just fine if I sit here and catch my wind. Now, you git, or you'll be waiting till morning for the next one. Your papa and mama be plenty angry up there in

Minneapolis, waiting all night for a no-show slacker like you. Now, git."

Nate wished he had more to offer than a few kind words. "Thank you, sir. I mean it, and—"

"I mean it, too, boy. Run!" He thrust his arm toward the gate and held it there.

His ticket in one hand and the suitcase in the other, Nate ran at top speed through the wide entryway, just as the conductor called, "All aboard!"

"Hold up!" Nate yelled. "I'm here now, too." He ran to the agent and showed him the ticket.

"Hop up right there," the agent said, pointing to the opening on the rear of the nearest car.

Nate ran up the short stairs and had just stepped onto the car's floor when the train began to move. "All right," he said, laughing and pressing a hand to the nearest metal wall. "I did it, Grandpa. I made it, but only thanks to your note, and well, really, that kind old guy." He for sure would tell Grandpa about the old man, the running, and that his first train had been a little late.

He looked around and spotted a perfect seat on the left, facing forward, then took it. Sitting still, he grinned at the thought of being on the Rock Island Rocket, this famous train, dressed entirely in her front-to-rear, shining, silver skin.

How'd he get this lucky? Riding on a train so famous they wrote songs about her. He leaned into his seat and imagined telling Steve and Tommy about it. There were others, for sure, like that Wabash Cannonball, the 20th Century Limited, and the Great Northern. From sea to shining sea, they claimed, but he was here, riding on the Rocket.

Looking around, he compared it to the Kansas City

Southern. This was no luxury coach like his first one, but that didn't matter. Consumed by the aura and the name of this legend, Nate sat back, taking possession of his small part of the train and smiling.

After moving through the large yard at a slow pace, the Rocket began picking up speed, the clickity clack of the wheels growing louder.

Nate stared back at the disappearing yard through his window. That place had more tracks and trains than he'd imagined possible. As he swiveled to sit forward again, his next thought made his smile disappear. *She wanted to go north with you.* He repeated Grandpa's words two more times, then offered a prayer. "Where is she, Lord? Please keep her safe. She's been all alone, and she's only a scared child. She should be here with me."

A conductor stopped by Nate's chair and said, "There's a dining car two ahead, and if you get bored, there's a young lady with children in the next car. She could use some company and help with the kids. She's been riding most of the night and hasn't slept."

Nate hoped the man didn't mean what he thought he did. "Um...okay, I guess. I mean, am I supposed to do something?"

"Only if you want to. She's tired and could use help watching her kids. That's all. Don't worry too much about it. Just follow your heart."

Nate shrugged. "Well, okay, maybe. Let's see, then."

The conductor walked away and entered the car ahead.

Nate frowned. This was not what he'd expected on this train. Maybe some bank robbers would be aboard, or cowboys heading to their next rodeo, but not babysitting. He hadn't imagined this. Still, he reached down to retrieve his suitcase, checked his pocket treasure, and walked slow into the next car.

He found the woman sitting on the right side with two children who looked about seven or eight, and an infant in her arms. He stopped far enough behind them to not be noticed, waited a moment while looking the situation over, then stepped forward and asked, "Could you use some help here? I mean, the conductor told me about—"

"He did?" she said. "He just now said he thought you'd show up. Thank you, thank you. I haven't slept all night. I'm afraid I'll just fall asleep, too, with no one to keep an eye on them. Thank you so much."

He shuffled his feet. "I'm Nate. Going to Minneapolis."

"Caroline, Caroline Wagner, Des Moines," she said. "Going there, I mean. You know, Des Moines is not my last name." They both laughed, then she said, "Angelina, move over here by me and give this man your seat. He's going to visit with us."

Without hesitation, the girl took the window seat, then Nate sat on the aisle seat facing them, next to the other young girl.

"Nate, this is Angelina, and you're sitting next to Whit-tney," Caroline said. "Sleeping beauty here is Eric. We've been visiting my parents in Little Rock. Are you hungry? Here it is. In this bag, I mean. Sandwiches, apples, and a little candy. Hold off on the candy, though, unless you want some."

"I'm okay," he said. "If you sleep, and the baby wakes up, what should I do?"

"He won't. He just fell asleep, and I'll bet he's good for most all the way. He likes the clickity-clack of the wheels. But if he does, wake me. You're a dear. Bet your mama's proud."

"Ha! Maybe sometimes, not so much on others."

Caroline closed her eyes and pulled the baby in tighter.

Looking at the others, Nate asked, "Did you two sleep any?"

"We both did," Angelina said. "Wanna play games?"

"Sure, I guess so. Like what?"

"Like who can see a bird first," she said. "Out the window, not in here, of course. That would be silly."

Nate smiled, then turned toward the window. "I bet you're good at this game, Angelina. How about Whittney?"

"She's the best," Angelina said. "She's a year younger than me, but plays good. Her eyes are newer. We played spot the dogs, and she won, then find the cows, and she won that one, too. I'm hoping I can win this time."

"How about we play spot the blue sky?" Nate said.

"Not funny. Let's just stick to birds for a while. Okay?"

They smiled at each other.

The trio played for over an hour. Angelina did win, four to three. Nate only had one, but he usually waited for one of them to call out any birds he'd already seen. He made sure to find at least one, so they'd believe he was trying.

They shared a lunch from Caroline's bag, and after, both girls nodded off from the rhythms and soothing, repetitious clacking sounds of the steel wheels meeting the narrow spaces between the sections of track.

Nate leaned his head back. They were good kids. Again, his next thoughts brought back sadness. *She wanted to go north...she wanted to...Aw, just listen to the wheels,* he told himself.

Another quiet hour went by before Caroline awoke. "Oh, good. Still here" she said. "Wonderful. The girls are sleeping, too, I see. You're a gift. Where are we? Did you eat? The girls behave okay?"

Nate grinned. She was a little like his mom. Questions connected to questions, never waiting for answers. Would she look at him like he was stupid for not answering every one in order? "We did," he said. "We ate, I mean. Thanks, too. We played find-the-birds, and Angelina won. Great kids you have. I slid my suitcase under the seat, and I'd like to walk around some, stretch my legs a little."

"Do that," she said, yawning. "I'll watch it for you, and I'll stay awake now. I feel good, actually. Amazing what a little sleep can do." She yawned again, making Nate do the same.

He walked into the next car and noticed all the passengers were negroes. They occupied all the seats from the middle of the car to the back. Just past the middle, a partition wall with a doorway blocked off the rest of the car. Nate's shoulders slumped with the weight of all their eyes watching him as he walked through. In the car's other side, only white people sat.

Oh, right. That's what the ticket man had told him and Pistol. Lotty wouldn't have been allowed to ride in the same car as he would anyway. He clenched his jaw and kept walking. She was a beautiful person, so why couldn't they see it? What were they so afraid of?

The next door led to the dining car. Nate took a table and ordered a root beer. Lotty wouldn't be able to eat there with him either. One of his hands started shaking, so he clenched both. He watched the scenery go by until they passed a roadside sign that read, "Des Moines." Almost there. Better get back to that family.

Once he'd returned to Caroline's car, he stood next to her seat and said, "Caroline, did you see it? The Des Moines sign?"

"I did," she said. "Time to get organized. Wish you

could stay with us longer. Come home for a visit, too, meet my husband, and let us take care of you for a while."

He smiled. "Really sounds nice, but gotta get back and ready for school to start. I should thank you. Otherwise, I'd just be sitting back there by my lonesome and not having much fun."

The conductor entered the car and announced, "Entering Des Moines yards. Des Moines, next stop."

The brakes screeched, and the train slowed. On each side, long stationery trains stood—some passenger trains, and others pulling boxcars. The Rocket slid tight between them while moving slow through the yard. Soon, they stopped at the depot.

Everyone stood. Nate took his suitcase from under the seat, then Whittney startled him with a warm, strong hug. Bending low, he hugged her back as she kissed his cheek.

He wanted to say, "Have a nice life," but only tousled her hair, patted her back with his free hand, and said, "You're a good kid. So glad I met you."

After the family left the car, he sighed. He was tired of too many goodbyes.

Chapter Thirty-Three

The bright sunrise warmed Nate's face as he stared out the train window. The blue sky and familiar scenery told him he was back in Minnesota. The colors, the look of the farms, and the lakes scattered about all shouted of home. He'd watched for the "Welcome to Minnesota" sign but must have missed it. Grinning, he thought, *That's okay. Each state has its own special appearance, and this is mine. It's that simple. It just looks like mine.*

Oh, if his friends could see him riding on the Rocket! "Eat your hearts out, guys." He huffed, then pictured the cornsilk he'd stashed in his suitcase, and his smile widened. They wouldn't believe this. He'd get them to go down to the creek, and they'd smoke it. Maybe light off some Black Cats there, too. He'd have to sneak some matches, though.

Plenty to be excited about, but what should he tell them about Lotty? Maybe they already know about her. "I hope she's not so afraid anymore."

Nate squinted at the buildings in the distance. Would they be stopping at the Great Northern Depot? He wanted to compare it to the impressive Kansas City station. He might only be thirteen, but he already had a healthy dose of what his dad called *civic pride*. He'd heard their station was an impressive place, but could anything compare with the giant Crossroads of America building Kansas City had created?

The train pulled into an outdoor stop along a busy downtown street. Decorative black wrought iron walls bordered the terminal on the sides. The walls were mostly open and easy to see through. The gabled roof made the structure look like a pavilion where folks would have family picnics in a park, but on a much larger scale.

The woosh of the air brakes and screeching of metal-on-metal made Nate's heart pound harder. Then, all motion stopped for the first time in hours, though his body hummed with the lingering sensation of moving. All was quiet until the bustle of the passengers began.

"It's over. I'm back," he whispered, a little uncomfortable after the constant sounds and motions.

Passengers started standing and moving toward the doors. He needed to stand, too, and take his suitcase, but he wanted to linger in the quiet a bit longer and get used to the idea that his adventure had just ended. Visions from the summer wandered through his mind until a noisy passenger bumped into his knee with a hard-edged suitcase.

Glancing around, he whispered, "I'm on the wrong side." The platform and doors were all on the right. He'd always stayed on the left as Grandma had advised. Bending to look through the windows and infrequent spaces opening between the tight-packed passengers, he saw a crowd waiting on the platform. Where were his parents? Surely, they didn't forget him.

He grabbed his suitcase in one hand and clamped the other over his shirt pocket, then squeezed into the line of passengers heading for the door. Some moved side-to-side, grabbing onto the edges of seats as if they didn't have their legs under them yet. There couldn't be any pickpockets here. This was home, but he kept his hand ready to protect his treasure.

The two older ladies sandwiching him kept complaining about the crowd until one said, "Let's just sit back down. We'll wait and be the last ones off."

Nate let out a breath as they moved aside. That might help. However, the crowd instantly filled their vacated spots, and he was again trapped between two others.

Looking out the car's windows, he spotted his sister on the platform. "What the...?" he mumbled. "Did they send her to get me?"

She waved at him and smiled.

At least she was glad to see him. Was Lotty with her? His parents stepped up beside Maggie. Mom was wiping her wet eyes with a hanky, and Dad was talking to a stranger, as usual.

When Nate finally reached the door and stepped onto the platform, his mom rushed over and hugged him hard. "So glad you're back," she said. "You okay? Tell us about your summer. You hungry?"

"Hi, Mom. Hi, Dad, and Maggie, you too," he said, pulling away. "Glad to be back. I'll tell you all about it in the car. Is that okay?"

His mom hugged him again, while Dad patted his shoulder and took his suitcase.

"You look older. Taller, maybe," his mom said.

"They feed you all right, son?" his dad asked, then started leading the way to the exit.

"Real good," Nate said, hurrying to keep up. "Tried some new things, too. Like catfish. Not quite a walleye but good. For some reason, they always say, 'Ya really have to know how to cook them.' Hearing that makes them a little scary at first. Grandpa likes them plenty."

"Any new girlfriends?" Maggie asked.

"Oh...sure," he said, grinning. "Too many. They never met anyone like me before. All those hillbillies are kinda backwards, and they—"

"Yeah, right." She laughed. "I bet you didn't even dare talk to one. Well, except Lotty, that is." They all kept walking as they talked.

"Says you, big sis," he snapped, his voice rising. "Tell me about Lotty, I mean—"

"That's enough, you two," Mom said. "Can't we even be friendly for half an hour? You hungry, Nate?"

"Hungry for my own bed," he said, yawning. "Maybe a real hamburger, too. They don't eat those much, except at the Andersons' Wednesday night yard parties. Good grilled ones, you get there. Hey, Maggie, c'mon, you mentioned Lotty. Where is she?"

"Well, she went off with Margo. Isn't that right, Mom?"

"We'll barbecue you up a few burgers tonight," his dad said. "Make new friends down there?"

"Hold on," Nate said, stopping and turning to them. "I'd thought you'd have Lotty here, so tell me where she is. Did Margo set her up okay?"

"We're waiting to find out what they did," Maggie said.

"C'mon, you guys, don't do this today," Nate said, lifting his hands above his shoulders.

"Let me tell him." his mom said. "They went to the Stevensons' to see if things might work out. No one knew how it might go, so they took her to their cabin for a few days to get acquainted. Just them. We'll all know what's to happen when they get back.'

"When's that?" Nate barked.

"Not sure," his dad said, "but the Stevensons have a room for her and can enroll her in school. Should go okay, I'd think." He walked ahead of the others and quickened the pace a bit.

"You mean the Stevensons from church? Them?" Nate asked, trying to catch up to his dad.

"That's right," Mom said. "They're the same as her, and glad to be doing this. If they decide she's a good fit, they'll take care of her, I'm told, and for as long as she needs them."

"Really? Great news," Nate said. "Nice, nice. This is more than I'd imagined. I'd like to see her."

"You will, soon enough," Mom said. "Tomorrow, we're having a welcome home party for you. She's out of town right now, though. They have other kids, too. Their older girl is the same age as Lotty. Plus, they've been fostering another Negro girl for a few years. So, let's all hope this works out between them."

After reaching the car, they all picked their seats and settled in.

"I'm betting it'll work out okay," Maggie said. "She's nice, too. So, tell us who you met in Arkansas. Any new pals or exciting news to share?"

Nate wanted to hear more about Lotty, but they all seemed determined to feed him bits and pieces as they went along. For now, since she was safe, he could relax. "Pistol is one friend I made. We drove around a lot. He has a car."

"A car?" Maggie shouted. "Aren't you a little young for cruising in cars?"

"Not only cruising but driving them, too," he said, beaming. "I mean, driving the tractor and Grandpa's truck. I could pass my license test today if they'd let me."

"Easy does it, now," Mom said. "So, what else happened down there?"

Nate stared out the window at some familiar downtown sights, wishing the questions would slow down. "Uh...okay, so me and Grandpa built a speedboat for his friend. Actually, that was cool. Um...helped Grandma on the last day of summer school, too, and had plenty to do on a farm, for sure. Oh...Butch, the dog, he's my best pal. Miss him already." He stopped himself before mentioning the attempted rescue and the shotgun blasts.

The rest of the ride home went fast. Nate smiled as they passed a friend's house. A few trees had started changing colors, and the air held a slight crispness. He wouldn't miss the Arkansas heat.

"Your pals been coming around, asking when you're back," Maggie said.

Nate smiled.

When they arrived at home, Sam, their dog, sniffed Nate nonstop. The odor of Butch must still be clinging to his clothes. Nate wished he had a tent to sleep in instead of his hot, knotty pine-clad attic.

"I'll take your suitcase, Nate," his mom said, as Dad closed the front door behind them.

Nate gripped the handle tight. "Not yet, Mom. Let me unpack first. Only a few clothes need laundry, anyway. I'm organized. You'll see. Well, thanks to Grandma. I'll just do that."

"He's hiding something," Maggie said.

"Shut up, Maggie. Am not. Maybe I have some presents in there. Ever think of that?"

"All right, tomorrow's soon enough," his mom said. 'You two don't be starting up where you left off. Last week, she told me she missed you, Nate."

"Mom!" Maggie yelled.

Everyone laughed, and Nate hoped it was true...and that they'd forget about his presents boast, because there weren't any. Lotty would be disappointed in him. Still telling tales, but getting better at keeping things honest.

He rushed up to his room, then waited until he was certain no one would barge in. After opening the suitcase on his bed, he removed his treasures. Firecrackers, cornsilk, and the corn cob pipe he'd bought in Hartsville. The word *Ozarks* had been printed on the cardboard the small pipe was attached to, along with a cartoon of a hillbilly in overalls smoking one just like it.

"For the tourists," Y.T. had told him.

He'd told Y.T. another lie about bringing it to his dad, but really wanted to use it for the cornsilk. Had he really fooled Y.T. any?

Thoughts of Y.T. reminded him they had a telephone. He considered calling a few friends, but his bed looked too comfortable. He'd take a nap first. After telling his mom he'd be sleeping a while, he lay down and nodded off into a deep peaceful rest, the kind only your own bed in your own room can provide.

In a dream, he sat and talked with Lotty on the ridge overlooking the valley near Grandpa's farm.

"Feels a bit like I'm still on the train," he said. "I won't see you for a while, so I'll get caught up around here."

A cold wet nose hit his arm and roused him a bit.

"Sammy," he murmured, "c'mon, stay up here with me tonight."

Chapter Thirty-Four

Nate's first thoughts when he woke his first morning home were concerns for Lotty. He turned over in bed, unable to banish the questions that had kept him fitful for days. Would she be accepted here, and how much could they see each other, and what if the Waldcotts could find her somehow?

When the rising sun's heat came through the window and warmed his face, he decided to give up lounging in bed. The fiery intruder wouldn't allow it. He sat up and rubbed his eyes. Maybe he'd just pull the shade down. Instead, he got out of bed and dressed, ready to face whatever would come next.

He wandered downstairs, ate a quick breakfast, then went outside to sit on the front steps and play fetch with Sam. At the sound of voices approaching, Nate looked up and grinned, waving at two of his buddies who were walking across his front yard toward him.

"Must have heard I'm back," he yelled.

"Thought you'd moved in for good down there," Tommy said. "How was it?"

Nate patted Sam's head and stood. "Great, really fun."

"Like how?" Steve asked.

"Well, like driving the truck, and the tractor, and blowing stuff up with firecrackers. That's how. Oh... shooting cans with a twenty-two rifle, too." Nate suppressed a grin. Now, these were things that would make them jealous. He looked up the street, petting and paying attention to Sam, as if he didn't need to notice them. His short account had quieted them, but he'd only begun his provoking. "Other stuff, too," he said, adding a tone of mystery to his voice. "Really sharp-looking girls and a new friend who has his own car."

"Yeah, right," Tommy said. "Like what, a pedal car?" He spun on his heal, folded his arms across his chest, and turned his back to Nate as if to say, "Two can play this game."

"No...for real," Nate said, turning back to them. "Pistol's his name. He's fourteen, almost fifteen, and they don't care about a driver's license down there. They're hillbillies and do whatever they want. Don't you know nuthin?"

"I heard they smoke when they're like nine and get married and whatever when they're maybe eleven," Steve said. "How 'bout all that stuff?"

"Yeah, pretty much. Not so many right by where I was, though. Tell you one thing, and no kidding, there's no phones. No one has them. Just the one at the drugstore in the little town by the highway, and that was two miles from us."

"No phones?" Tommy yelled as he turned back around.

He and Steve looked at Nate like he had said they rode in golden rocket ships pulled by flying turtles.

"That's what I said. No phones. Some don't have indoor

bathrooms, either. But T.V., now that's pretty much every-where. Go figure."

"Are your grandparents hillbillies?" Steve said, backing away a little.

"No way." Nate shook his head, scowling. "They're originally from up here, dummy. They moved there a long time ago but never turned. They're just like us. Grandma now has a bit of a southern accent, though. Grandpa teases her about that. Says she's weak."

Both boys stopped their questioning and stared at Nate.

"You guys want to go down to the creek?" Nate asked.

They both nodded.

"Wait here, I've got something to show you." Nate hurried inside, then ran up to his room and grabbed the small canvass bag he'd filled the night before. The moment he rejoined his friends outside, he said, "Let's go before I get any questions." Nate was sure each boy understood exactly what he meant.

At a faster pace than normal, they scurried across the street to the hill behind the neighbors' houses, sticking together in a precision formation. After walking with care down the steep hillside, they reached the creek and stopped for a short time to look around and make sure they had the place to themselves.

"Creek's low," Nate said. "C'mon."

Without needing to speak of their destination, they took their well-worn trail, hiking along the water's edge to their hidden fort.

Nate examined every inch of their hand-made construc-tion with his eyes, from the part they'd dug out of the hill-side to the broken tree branches with clinging, dried leaves that made the whole thing almost invisible. "Looks exactly the same," he said.

"Why wouldn't it?" Tommy asked.

Nate only shrugged.

"What're you keeping secret in the bag?" Steve asked.

"Just some dynamite...and...*voila*! A book of matches," Nate said, pulling the matches and firecrackers out with a flourish.

"Whoa! Not for me," Tommy said, backing away. "I'm outta here."

Nate and Steve laughed, pointing at Tommy.

"Big chicken," Steve said.

"It's just firecrackers," Nate said. "Black-Cats, you know, the real deal. They can blow fishes' heads right off their necks, and could launch a rock straight up to the tree-tops. Loud, too. Want to try some?"

"I do," Steve said, holding out a hand.

"They can kill ya," Tommy said in a whisper, leaning closer to get a better look. "I mean, you guys heard about that kid over on Fifty-seventh. Lost three fingers off his right hand. Maybe it was four. Coulda been his thumb, too. Let's just wait on this, okay, you guys?"

"You stay here, little boy," Steve said. "Me and Nate are going down the creek a ways and show you how it's done."

Tommy took a few steps back.

Nate and Steve walked several yards away, while Tommy waited. They set two firecrackers on an old cracked and weathered tree stump. After twisting their fuses together, Nate lit a match and touched it to them.

Both firecrackers blew up at the same time. A few birds took off from their perches, and Tommy instantly took another half-step back.

Steve twisted three fuses together, then said, "Tommy, come over and light the match."

Tommy opened and flattened his hands, palms-down,

and moved them back and forth like a referee signaling, "No way."

Steve lit the joined fuses. After the explosion, he shouted, "Be-ee-utiful!" He turned to Nate. "Hey, where'd you get so many matches?"

Nate shrugged. "Snuck 'em from my mom's cigarette drawer. Was easy this time. She has a whole big box in there now. She'll never notice one missing." He spun around, squinting toward Tommy. "Hey...I've got an idea. C'mon, Steve, back to the fort. Wait up, Tommy, don't go running off. We're done with those for a while. We gotta save 'em for special occasions. Got something else you can try. Huh?"

After arriving at their fort, all three sat cross-legged on the soft, dry ground inside.

Nate fished out the cornsilk and pipe, then said, "When corn has grown just tall enough, and the silk tassels on tops of the ears reach a certain nice golden color, like this here, if you pick 'em and dry 'em in the sun, they're really good for smoking."

"Not me," Tommy said, raising his voice. "No sir, that stuff will stunt your growth, and it smells on ya, and our moms will know it, too. No thanks, man."

"Sheesh!" Steve said, slapping Tommy's arm. "You're afraid of your own little sister. Why don't you go play with her dolls or something? Us real men have grownup things to do."

"He's okay, Steve," Nate said. "You can hang around here, Tommy. Okay?" He gave Tommy a light punch on the arm. "You don't have to do anything you'd rather not. Just don't be blabbing this around, though. Maybe next year for you, but me and Stevie are gonna smoke till we choke." He waited for Tommy to show a sign of agreement. None came.

"But if you do leave, I'm never going to tell you about Lotty."

"Lotty what?" Tommy asked.

"She was a...wait up, before I tell you any of that part, you need to pinky swear you'll keep all this quiet." Nate stared into his face. "You gonna swear it?"

Tommy looked outside, as if making sure no one could see or hear him. Nate and Steve kept quiet, giving him a polite space to decide.

Tommy held his little finger up and bent it toward his palm, then crossed his chest with that hand. "Okay, I agree. I mean, I pinky swear never to tell, honest. So, who was she?"

"There is no 'was she,'" Nate said, stuffing cornsilk into the pipe bowl. "There's only 'who *is* she,' and she's here, and right now, too."

Steve and Tommy looked at each other hoping the other would ask first for more information.

Nate decided not to make them squirm too much. "She's a runaway negro girl I found hiding in our cornfield," he said, tamping the cornsilk down. "I hid her in our barn for weeks, and got her food and such, and had planned to sneak her up here for safekeeping. Almost got killed for it a couple times, too. Really close, and I'm not kidding."

"Killed. Oh, c'mon man, you're making this up," Tommy said. "Whatcha mean killed?"

"Shut up, you little wuss," Steve said. "He's not kidding. Can't you tell?" Steve turned to Nate, "So, she is here now. I heard about it, too. That news is all over the block."

"What?" Nate said, almost dropping the pipe. "Who let that out?"

"Your sister told my brother," Steve said, "who told his girlfriend, who bought an ad in the paper." He snorted.

"Just kidding, but the news is out, for sure." He shifted to lean against the hillside that served as a rear wall. "What I don't get is why you would mess with her in the first place. I mean, she is what she is. Did we hear that right? Coulda just left her there where she belongs. Something wrong with you?"

Nate stood, glaring down at Steve. "You have two choices. Either apologize and take all that back, or get outa here but quick, cuz I'm going to straighten you out."

"Hold on, man," Steve said, lifting a hand. "I'm just saying what others are saying. I mean, nobody gets why you did this. Don't be mad at me. Everyone feels the same way, even my dad."

"Then, *everyone* needs to wise up," Nate said, clenching his fists. "She's a good person, better'n you are, Steve. She's an orphan, and the rotten family she had to stay with down there was planning to hurt her. So, I did what I did, and if you don't like it..." Nate couldn't say anything more, so he stared at both his friends, putting enough iron and fire into his eyes that they'd know he was ready to end his talking and start the fighting.

"Good for you," Tommy said. "My mom says you did a great thing."

Nate lowered his fists and looked away. Steve held out a hand to shake.

Nate glanced, then shook it. "Okay then, but remember this, she is my friend, so best be careful."

Steve and Tommy nodded, expressions solemn.

"We better get back to business," Nate said. "Steve, you better pinky swear on all this, too. Let's see ya."

Steve bent his little finger, performed the ritual, swore his allegiance forever, then said, "So...okay, tell us more about their way to pinky swear down there."

Happy to change the subject, Nate said, "Just like us, but if you break it, they chop off your finger and feed it to their hogs." He bent a little finger over far enough to touch his palm, and with the other three sticking straight up, he showed them the back of his hand and raised an eyebrow. "Remember that next time you're eating a hot dog."

They all laughed.

"Not really, you guys," Nate said, "but don't be kiddin' with me. Better take this real serious. I got a sharp knife and a hungry dog. He'll eat anything. He even rolls around on dead fish stuff, too. Guts and all."

All three boys kept their serious expressions while Steve said, "Huh, you're kidding, right?"

Nate winked at him. Tommy and Steve were now true believers, he was certain. Tommy kept staring at him as if wondering how much living with the hillbillies had changed him, which was exactly what Nate had wanted them to think.

He lit the pipe, took the first puff, choked deep, coughed hard, then held his breath so he wouldn't cough too much more. With one hand covering his mouth, he passed the pipe to Steve, who also coughed and hacked until his forehead turned shades of purple red.

"Good stuff," Steve said in a lower, scratchy voice, then pressed his hand over his mouth, tight.

"Best there is," Nate said. "You better believe it."

Chapter Thirty-Five

The next morning, Nate sat in his room, petting Sam and wondering when he might see Lotty. He wanted to believe she was excited to reunite with him as well. Other worries came back to plague him, the ones about imagined troubles ahead for her in a new city. They'd shared some dreams they both hoped for but had only talked a little about what might be waiting for her in Minnesota. He offered a silent prayer for her safety and comfort.

"I bet if those Woldcotts ever come looking for her around the farm," Nate whispered to Sam, "Grandpa and Stony—maybe even Pistol and Y.T., too—they'd be bold enough to set them straight. Humph, I'd like to be there."

Nate spent most of the day alone in his room. His mom had set out new school clothes, so he tried them on, and was surprised her selections were better than just okay. Next, he spent some time thinking about the new school year. His printed itinerary was sitting by the new clothes, so he studied the classes he'd be taking, hoping his friends would be in them, too.

"What about Lotty?" he whispered. "Where will she be going?"

The afternoon went by fast. He hoped the waiting to see her was almost over.

"You better be getting ready," his mom yelled up the stairs. "The Stevensons invited us to dinner you know. Can't be late."

"The Stevenson's...and Lotty?" he called back, hurrying to grab a clean shirt. He grinned at the thought of visiting Lotty at her new home. "Almost ready, Mom. How much longer?"

"None. Time to go," she said.

Nate straightened his shirt, stomped into his shoes, and bounded down the stairs, still grinning. Then, a few strange fears wiped his smile away. Instead of giving in to the fears, he believed seeing Lotty, here and safe, would make him proud. He'd focus on that.

The cool, late summer's evening air helped keep Nate and the Stevensons' other dinner party guests refreshed. They'd invited him, his parents, sister, and Margo to Lotty's new home.

"We'll soon officially become her foster family," Mrs. Stevenson said after greeting them. "It's all worked out, and we want her first nights in this new city to be filled with friendly faces."

Nate glanced around the living room, with its new-looking furniture and family photos placed on every wall. Lotty was upstairs, he'd been told, and would be down soon. The Stevensons, a young negro family, had prospered after moving from the deep South several years ago. Margo had told Nate that Lotty was the second teen to be offered a secure home with them, and that after enduring their own troubled times, they wanted to use their blessings to help a few others. Sure enough, the photos showed another girl Lotty's age beside the couple's own twelve-year-old twin daughters. Nate smiled. Lotty would have opportunities to make friends.

Footsteps descended the hard wood stairs, and Nate turned. Lotty paused halfway down, then ran toward him. Before he could brace for her collision, she grabbed him around his waist and kissed his cheeks, almost tipping him over backwards.

Grasping both his hands, she stepped back until their arms were extended almost straight. "We did it!" she yelled.

"We did," he said, smiling. "Had plenty help, too, but your courage was the main thing. I want to hear all about your train ride and everything."

She hugged him again and wouldn't let go when he squirmed a little.

"Lotty," he said at a high pitch.

His mom and Mrs. Stevenson laughed. Everyone's smiles and bright eyes reflected Nate and Lotty's joyous reunion.

Nate told himself no one noticed his embarrassment from all the hugging and kissing. Lotty wouldn't leave his side.

Everyone filed into the dining room for dinner. Afterward, they all sat on the large outdoor patio, Nate and Lotty seated close together on a pair of side-by-side chairs. The others gave them their space.

"Mrs. Stevenson," Nate's mom said, pointing toward Nate and Lotty, "you're a thoughtful social director."

Both ladies nodded and grinned.

"He's done so much for her," Mrs. Stevenson said, making the tops of Nate's ears burn.

His mom said, smiling, "I think she's done as much or even more for him."

Lotty nudged his arm. "You should see my new room. It's like some kind of dream from a book or something."

"Great, makes me happy to hear it," he said, then lowered his voice. "It's gotta beat some old cornfield or a hot barn loft, and that's a fact."

Lotty gave him a gentle pat on his back, and they both smiled in the way only those with an important shared history can.

"We're close to the lake," Nate said. "Let's go for a walk. I'll show you how nice it is."

She shot a glance toward Mrs. Stevenson and whispered, "Think that'll be okay?"

"I already asked, earlier," he said, "and yes, it is. Let's go. You'll like this place."

They excused themselves, then walked the straight sidewalks toward a local beech, one of many in this town known as The City of Lakes.

"Ooh!" Lotty said, pointing to the branches of giant trees that met high above the wide streets, making a beautiful archway far above their heads.

"They call that a cathedral arch sometimes," Nate said, staring at the patches of clear blue sky peaking between their branches.

Lotty kept looking up at the sight while they walked, tripping a few times on the uneven sidewalk. She smiled the whole time. "This is wonderful," she said. "Never seen such a place. And these houses are castles."

"I guess I'm used to it," Nate said, kicking at a rock, "but sure, it is nice, isn't it? Look-it...here's the lake."

They rounded the next corner and walked toward the calm blue water. The sun was reflected on the still surface, and only a few small gentle ripples found their way toward the shoreline.

He waved toward an empty bench near its edge. "Let's sit by the lake a while." When they sat, he pointed. "See those sailboats out there? Looks like a small regatta. That's a kind of a race. They do those a lot here. Fun to watch, too."

Lotty nodded, and they sat in silence for a short time.

Nate took a slow breath and said, "I'd like to hear everything. You know, about Grandpa catching you and you running away and all that. Right? I mean, I do know that part, mostly, so then what happened?"

Lotty waited in silence, then touched his hand, which he figured was her signal to let her explain in her own way.

After another short pause, she said, "Do you remember when we talked about fate and luck and all that?"

He nodded.

"We talked about the difference," she said, "and if or when there's some unknown power on our lives?" She looked at him, and after he nodded again, she said, "I was so scared, cuz he was taking me back there. Your grandpa, I mean. I found out later—up here, actually, from this lawyer —that old Woldcott had forged my mama's name on some fancy paper."

Nate's eyes widened as he sat straighter and looked at her. "What the—"

"For real," she said. "He did that. He thought he could kind of legally kidnap me back, but I'm getting too far ahead. So, I had a chance to run, and I took it. I know your grandpa was trying to trust me after I told him why I didn't want to go back there. He said he'd bring me back to his place, but I was still so afraid he would change his mind on that. So, having that one and only chance, I ran fast. Didn't know the town, either, or which way to go. I just skedaddled but quick."

Nate shook his head, looking far across the lake, then asked, "Okay, so then what?"

"Okay nuthin'. I was shaking scared. Let me tell it, please." She continued without waiting for a reply. "Well... then, I kind of knew which way was back toward your place. North, I'd say. I kept to the gravel and dirt roads, and guess what? No one bothered me. Can't figure that deal. I mean...fate or luck? It felt like the whole world would know who I was, but somehow, I knew by a peaceful gift that held onto me that I'd be okay. Then, I did get a short ride from some good folks, too. A real blessing."

Nate stood, picked up a stone, and said, "Betcha never seen this before."

"What? don't you want to hear the—"

"Take a look at this stone," Nate said, holding it out to her. "See, it's smooth and flat, about as thick and round as a chocolate chip cookie."

She nodded. "Okay."

Using a practiced and expert skill, he thrust it toward the mirror-smooth lake. It skipped across the water's surface...gently touching only the top, then rising and flying across, touching again and again at least four more times before it slowed and sank.

"Hey, good trick," she said, grinning. "And no, I've not seen that before. No lakes where I'm from." Her smile faded. "So...do you want to hear this...or what?"

Nate bit his tongue to keep from saying, "Or what." Instead, he asked, "Why do you sound so grumpy? We did get you here, and hey, I'll help you send a letter to Grandpa."

She just stared at him, her eyes flinty.

"Sorry," Nate said. "I guess it's just that it was hard for me at that time, you know, not knowing how you were or where you were. Sometime, I'll tell you how we went to old Woldcott's to steal you back and almost got shot. I'm not wanting to live too much of that all over again just now, though. Proud of it for sure. But lets skip it for now, okay?" He shot her a quick glance. "Too happy to see you again. Let's wait on both our stories."

"Deal." Lotty smiled, then looked across the lake.

Nate stood and found another smooth, round stone. "C'mon, stand over here and try this."

She stood, and he placed it in her hand. Then, she curled her fingers around it and lifted her arm back as if to throw it.

"No, no, not like that," he said, catching her elbow. "Hold it flat, tucked into the curve between your thumb and first finger. Here, this way."

He demonstrated the technique to her, then gave her back the stone. She held it the way he'd shown.

"Okay," he said, "you got it. Now, stand sideways to the lake, bring your arm way back like this, straight out, and don't throw it down, but kinda straight out...flat and toward the water. Easy does it, too, then let your hand snap it loose. Make it skip across, far as you can, but don't drown it. Go ahead, try. I know you can do this."

Her throw was perfect.

Acknowledgments

With Thanks To:

The members of the Write Now writers' group of Minnesota.

MaKayla "Max" Erickson: For good ideas, important insights, and an encouraging spirit.

Living Word Christian Center, Brooklyn Park, Minnesota: A place where writers can meet and thrive.

Dunn Brothers Coffee Shop, Hopkins, Minnesota: Where coffee and words just flow.

And Bridgett Powers of B Squared Writer Coaching: For putting up with us all as we've grown.

About the Author

C.J. Wellumson loves a good story. Perhaps that's why he has created dozens of short stories and a few magazine articles, many of which appear in two anthologies: *Fun And Games With A Touch Of Reality* and *Tell Me A Story*.

A long-time co-leader and writing coach for the Write Now writers' group in Minnesota, he is grateful for the joy it is to be surrounded by emerging talent, both young and old.

C.J. loves to hear from his readers, so don't hesitate to contact him at cwellumson8@comcast.com.